FOUR FOR A QUARTER

Other FC2 Books by Michael Martone:

Michael Martone
The Blue Guide to Indiana

4 FOR A QUARTER

FICTIONS

MICHAEL MARTONE

FC2

TUSCALOOSA

Published by FC2, an imprint of The University of Alabama Press,
with support provided by the Publishing Program at the University of
Houston–Victoria.

Address all editorial inquiries to: Fiction Collective Two, University of
Houston–Victoria, School of Arts and Sciences, Victoria, TX 77901-
5731

Cover and book design: Lou Robinson
Typefaces: Janson and Nobel
Produced and printed in the United States of America

The paper on which this book is printed meets the minimum
requirements of American National Standard for Information Sciences—
Permanence of Paper for Printed Library Materials, ANSI Z39.48–1984

Library of Congress Cataloging-in-Publication Data

Martone, Michael.
  Four for a quarter : fictions / Michael Martone.
    p. cm.
  ISBN 978-1-57366-163-8 (pbk. : alk. paper) —ISBN 978-1-57366-827-9
(electronic)
  I. Title.
  PS3563.A7414F68 2011
  813'.54—dc22

                                        2010053816

For

Contents

1

Four for a Quarter   3

Diagnostic Drift   5

Four Fifth Beatles   9

4H   17

Leap Years   25

Four Alabama Seasons   33

Ruminant   37

Four Postcards from Indiana   47

The I States   57

The Sex Life of the Fantastic Four   61

Four Brief Lives   69

2

Dutch Boy   73

Four in Hand   83

Antebellum   87

Four Found Postcard Captions   89

Quadratic   91

Four Men in Uniform   95

Board Games   107

The First Four Deaths of My High School Class   115

Four Foursquare Houses   117

To Hell and Back: Four Takes   119

4 GS-14s   131

3

Tessera   135
Four Corners   147
The Blind: A Blues   151
Four Ironies   157
Harmonic Postcards   163
The Production of the First Xeroxgraphic Copy   165
RPM   171
The Third Day of Trials   183
Deaths of Modern Philosophers   197
Four Susans   203

4

Four Dead in Ohio   215
Four Sides of a Triangle: Proof   223
FAQs   227
Four Eyes   233
Mount Rushmore   241
Four Fourths   247
Chili 4-Way   257
Four Signs   265
Thought Balloons   273
Four Places   275
Four Calling Birds   277
Author's Note   293

"Hit the one!"
—James Brown

Four for a Quarter

Rehoboth

The photo booth is just inside off the boardwalk, away from the crowds. The backs of the white benches swing over the seats. You can sit facing the ocean or sit facing the storefronts. Out on the white cluttered beach, two Amish couples wade in the sheeting waves. Their shoes and socks chest high. Skirts tucked between bare legs. Their blue brilliant against the white sand and sky. Four of them. Two men and two women. They have come a long way. Everyone else pretends, I pretend, we are not looking. They toss bread to the cloud of gulls.

The Children's Museum

It is educational. The photo booth is made of clear glass panels so that the lenses and the machinery that develops the photographic strips can be seen. I twirl the piano stool inside to the right height. I imagine that they have replaced the camera too with one that takes X-rays, and my souvenir will record a transparent me. My heart will be an opaque dollop in the airy cage of my ribs. I watch the coin I drop travel through the machine, and the ghostly parts begin to ratchet and twitch. Outside a small crowd has gathered to watch.

PENN STATION

More than the confession, I remember learning about confession. Behind the heavy curtains of the booths, on a little table next to the priest's chair were paper and pencil. I thought they were there to help the priest remember. Yes, he will note the cardinal sins and the venial ones, add up the penance in long columns of numbers. I saw my sins would be written in a ribbony hand, hauled into the air by fluttering cardinals. The words, unknotting as they flew up, trailed from the beaks of the birds, leaving me as white and clean as new paper.

WOOLWORTH'S

I part the curtains of the photo booth, get out, and wait. Women clerks in pastel smocks (one aqua, one pink, one mint, one yellow) point up. The store's parakeets and canaries are loose. The birds flit between perches of sale banners hanging from the stained ceiling tile. I am the same person now as when I went into the booth. I am the same in each of the four black-and-white pictures of me. I blow on the wet strip. I try to count the birds now roosting on the suspended fluorescent light fixtures at the very back of the store.

Diagnostic Drift

1.

You flowed and flowed. You stood in the bathtub, the blood sheeting your legs. I called the doctor, who said to bring you in and who later said there were probably always this many miscarriages. He was speaking of the general population, not you. Back then, he said, they were mistaken for menstrual bleeding. These days new tests let us know sooner. We call this diagnostic drift, he said, a condition always present but unseen. Until now. Now we know what we are seeing sooner. Now we know sooner what we are seeing. You had held your dress up away from the blood, and I had daubed at your bleeding with a wet washcloth. You hadn't known you were pregnant until you weren't. A classic case, the doctor said. Should we worry? I asked. Should this have happened? It is diagnostic drift, the doctor said. A few years ago you wouldn't even know what happened happened. This happens all the time. We won't even need to notice until the third time it happens, if it even happens again at all.

2.

There, there, another doctor said. It happens all the time. This time, you had known earlier you were pregnant and had been pregnant longer. You'd seen a sign, you said, the day it happened. An English sparrow chick dead on the sidewalk you walked on the way home. This time, in the bathtub, the blood was thicker and there was tissue in the pile of the washcloth. The doctor asked us to bring it with us to the emergency room. There, there, she said. It is difficult, the doctor said. She held your hand. This happens all the time. There is no way of knowing. We know more now, she said, but we don't know everything. We'll keep an eye on it, she said, riffling through the sheets of paper. You looked off into the distance. At a distance, I looked at you, your hair fanned out on the white paper sheet.

3.

It is more common than you might think, this doctor said to me. You were getting dressed behind the curtain. You had started bleeding during a prenatal visit. Things had been going well this time. Your doctor called me at work. He wanted me to drive you to the hospital, didn't want you to drive yourself. She's lost some blood, he said. She's a bit light-headed, he said to me on the phone. I drove through the streets of a new city. We had just moved. All the streets looked the same— three-flats and Cyclone-fenced front yards. It was the doctor at the hospital who said that this was more common than you'd think. While you were there, I walked around the blocks of hospital buildings. I walked around three times. I told the doctor about the other times, about the doctor who had told us of diagnostic drift and that now we should be paying attention. Let's just wait and see, she said. These things happen. I asked her how long we should wait before we tried again, and she thought, for some reason, I meant exercise instead of sex. As soon as possible, she said. The sooner the better. But then when she understood what I meant she said, oh that. I watched your shadow move on the white cloth screen. Give it a few days, weeks, a month or so, maybe. Talk with your doctor.

4.

There is no blood. There's nothing to be done. There is your heartbeat but the other one is gone. The doctor has his nurse make the arrangements at a clinic for the D&C. We know the city better now. The main roads empty into rotaries I must circle, working my way around to the new road I need to take. I drop you off at the clinic. There is no place to park, so I idle at the front gate. You're escorted in through the picket of a few silent protesters. I drive around the city, lazily circling the rotaries a few times, and then cruise along the highway next to the widening river where eights and fours skate back and forth on the smooth surface, disappearing in the shadows beneath the old bridges. I know we know more now than we did, but it is hard to say. I know right now you are being questioned. An aide is asking questions and writing your answers onto forms she keeps in a file. Your history is being worked up. This happened and this happened and this happened and then this.

Four Fifth Beatles

HAIBUN BY YOKO ONO

STUART SUTCLIFFE

a cicada shell
it sang itself
utterly away
—Basho

Stuart's fingers blistered during the long rehearsals. He never played long enough for his fingers to callus. The group often used his flat to rehearse.

❹

Pete's mum owned The Casbah Coffee Club. One night, John and McCartney persuaded Stuart to buy, on time, a Höfner bass guitar. Bad skin and pimples, McCartney said of him much later. Stuart had the skin of an art student.

❹

In Germany, he wears dark Ray-Ban clip-on flip-up sunglasses like baseball players wear. He sings "Love Me Tender." Stuart's hair was the first hair hair. He asked Astrid to cut his hair to look like Klaus's. She cut his greased-back, teddy-boy hair into a mop. And, after that, everyone's hair was cut that way.

❹

December, George is sent back to England, underage. McCartney and Pete attempt arson at the Bambi Kino, are also deported. John takes a train, ferries home. Stuart stays in Hamburg. He has a cold. He meets Astrid, and eight months later he leaves The Beatles. He wants to paint. He wants something else.

McCartney borrowed Stuart's bass until he could earn enough to buy a smaller left-handed Höfner of his own. I can hear Stuart ask McCartney not to change the strings around. And I can see McCartney play it upside down.

Before all this, before the time in Hamburg, Stuart joined John, McCartney, and George. They were The Silver Beetles then. In the Renshaw Hall Bar, Stuart helped John change the name. They liked Buddy Holly. They liked his band, The Crickets, and came up with The Beatals. John later changed the name to The Beatles. It sounded French, he thought, and he got to Beatles through "Le Beat" and "Beat-less."

Later, in Germany, Stuart collapsed in an art class in Hamburg. His condition grew worse. April. Stuart died before the ambulance reached the hospital. Three days later Astrid told The Beatles at the Hamburg airport. His brain exploded. His father did not know for three weeks. He was sailing to South America. A priest told him when he docked in Buenos Aires.

There Stuart is on the *Lonely Hearts Club* album cover. There, among the dead, next to the flat picture of Aubrey Beardsley. "He's the artist around here," John said of Stuart.

sudden ice storm storms
brick hearth the hearth cricket sings
in spite of this this

Brian Epstein

clinging to the bell
he dozes so peacefully
this new butterfly
—Buson

Throughout his life Brian was kind. When John married Cynthia, Brian was the best man and afterwards bought their lunch. During Cynthia's pregnancy, Brian arranged for a private room in a hospital and offered them use of his flat. They needed somewhere to live. He was Julian's godfather.

Brian loved men, though no one knew until years after his death. It had been an open secret among his friends. In the army, he had a tailor make an officer's uniform he wore when cruising the bars of London. He was arrested for impersonating an officer at the Army and Navy Club on Piccadilly. He was never charged, agreeing to see an army psychiatrist instead. They discharged him ten months later. The medical grounds were "emotionally and mentally unfit."

Brian studied acting. He was arrested for "persistent importuning." He was blackmailed. Throughout the later court case against the blackmailer, Brian was "Mr. X." Anonymity was allowed then. John often made jokes about it to friends and to Brian. No one outside said a word.

The night Dylan turned them on to pot in New York, McCartney remembers Brian staring into a mirror, pointing at himself saying "Jew! Jew! Jew!" over and over. McCartney thinks of this as hilarious and finds it "very liberating."

John and Brian went on a four-day holiday together to Barcelona. The Spanish holiday was made into a movie, *The Hours and Times*. There were other books and interviews.

❹

John wrote "You've Got to Hide Your Love Away."

❹

Epstein was overlooked when John, McCartney, George, and Ringo received the MBE. George said that the MBE stood for "Mister Brian Epstein."

❹

Brian's autobiography is *A Cellarful of Noise*.

❹

McCartney said, "If anyone was the Fifth Beatle, it was Brian."

❹

John said that Brian's death was the beginning of the end.

❹

August. Brian dies. A hot summer. An overdose. The Beatles, in India, meet with Maharishi Mahesh Yogi. Jimi Hendrix cancels his concert at the Saville Theatre the same day. Out of respect, he says.

❹

Brian had for years taken pills to sleep. Sleep caught up to sleep. Mr. X.

❹

In a meeting at the music store, Brian had proposed to the boys the idea of managing them. John, George, and Pete arrived late for the meeting—they had been drinking. McCartney was not with them. They told Brian he was taking a bath. He *was* taking a bath. John invited a friend to the meeting so the friend could later give his opinion of Brian. John introduced him to Brian saying, "This is me dad."

> spring grass going green
> there where the scarab buried
> last year's pill of dung

Billy Preston

Even with cicada—
Some can sing
Some can't
—Issa

Billy's kidney deteriorated in his later years, his hypertension. In 2002, a kidney transplanted. Four years later, he died in June, in the desert, in the West. He died of complications and other complications.

❹

A year before he died, he had entered a rehabilitation in Malibu. Drugs. Respiratory failure there left him comatose. For the year he slept, sleeping into sleep.

❹

In 1962, as part of Little Richard's touring band, Billy met the Beatles when Brian promoted a Liverpool show. They'd hook up again later.

❹

The band always already about to break up was recording "Let It Be." George, closest to Billy, had quit the studio, had gone to see Ray Charles in concert in London. There, Billy was playing organ. George brought him back to Abbey Road, a kind of gift, a kind of glue.

❹

He joined the band on the roof, the final public appearance. "Get Back" was credited this way: "The Beatles with Billy Preston." His electric piano is prominent throughout the song. He plays an extended solo.

❹

In the movie, years later, he plays Sgt. Pepper in *Sgt. Pepper's Lonely Hearts Club Band.*

❹

As a boy of twelve, he appeared in *St. Louis Blues*, played W. C. Handy as a young man. He was a regular on *Shindig!*, a member of the show's house band.

❹

"Will It Go Round in Circles" and "Nothing from Nothing" were his two hits. Billy composed Joe Cocker's "You Are So Beautiful." Turning breath into those Os. All those circles, breathing.

❹

He was the fifth member of the Plastic Ono Band. He never put his hands in the wrong place, Klaus said. Or Ringo said it. Or George. Or John. Or I said it about his hands.

❹

John said then, I was Wind. I was Wind. Billy, Breeze.

❹

Touring, Billy, health failing, learned that George had died. He performed in the Concert for George in London, played a tribute song. Get back, he sang. Get back. Get back to where you once belonged.

copper coin heads up
the yellow flag iris bed
Japanese beetle

sounds of a temple bell
reverberate in a circle
a long night
—Shiki

The Beatles auditioned for George in June at the Abbey Road studios. They recorded four songs. Martin wasn't there and only listened to the tape after the session ended. Their original songs were simply not good enough, George thought. And he asked each Beatle if there was anything they didn't like. George, The Beatle, said to George, "Well, there's your tie, for a start."

❹

In September, they recorded their first recording, "How Do You Do It." George thought it would be a hit. Everyone else hated it. It wasn't a hit. The next song was "Love Me Do." George asked Ringo to play tambourine and maracas, and he did though he was not happy about it. In November, John and McCartney begged George to record another of their original songs, "Please Please Me," and he did, but as an up-tempo song not as a slow ballad. George looked out over the mixing deck at the end of the session and said, "Gentlemen, you have just made your first number one record." He would be right that time.

❹

Much later, after it was all over, George post-produced *The Beatles Anthology* that once was to be called *The Long and Winding Road*. George used an old four-track analog mixer to mix the songs instead of a digital deck. He found the machine somewhere at EMI. He explained this by saying that the old deck created a completely different sound, which a new deck could not recreate.

❹

He also said the whole project seemed strange. He listened to himself chatting in the studio, thirty years before on the tape between the takes. His voice came back to him in this simple way.

❹

George did not produce the two new singles overdubbing two of John's demos. George had lost his hearing. He left the work to others. He had listened for hours, just listening to John's voice with no desire to change or change it.

❹

George said he scored "Eleanor Rigby" after Bernard Herrmann's score for the Alfred Hitchcock thriller *Psycho*. He liked the way the bows cut through the strings.

❹

With "Strawberry Fields Forever," George blended two very different takes into a single master through careful editing.

❹

George is the not dead one of all the ones who are dead now. He played all the instruments, spliced the tape. He wrote the final notes, scored scores.

❹

On "In My Life," he played a sped-up baroque piano solo. Nothing was ever fast enough, and then later, he thought, it had all been too fast.

windrows dry tinder
timothy exhales fireflies
the second cutting

4H

HANDS

I heard a story once about a boy who, with his own hands, felt through the mass of steaming alfalfa in a windrow looking for his father's fingers cut clean off by the baler. His father had walked back to the yard to sit in the metal glider and wait for the helicopter but not until he had the presence of mind to tell the boy to find the fingers somewhere in the hay. "Put them in the cooler with the chemical ice." The boy dumped the lunch on the ground and got down on his hands and knees to sort through the grass at his feet.

I was all alone when my own hands in their gloves slid off like gloves as I monkeyed with the bean header on the gleaner. My father had gone to town. My mother was at church. My hands were gone somewhere in the idling red machine. My lunch was in the cab. The sky was blue. The machinery had crimped the flesh enough to staunch the heavy bleeding for now. I held my arms up away from my body like doctors do after they have washed up, and I turned and walked on up to the house.

At the county fair each year I showed an animal or two, currying the coat of the steer, ratting its tail into a cloud, raking back the white lick on the forehead 100 times. The judge slaps the rump of the winner and leaves his handprint in the smooth fur. The animals give a kick or two. And later, the auction is a field of waving hands. That night in the show ring us kids chased the pigs, tried to tackle them in the mud. We clawed at them as they ran between us and through our legs. I had one in my hands, all slime and scum, and then it tore away from me.

That boy found most of the fingers, placed them one by one in the palm of his hand, then plopped them, one by one, down on the bottom of the plastic cooler, on the frozen plastic packs of chemical ice. The fingers were like bait, or more like what you've caught for bait, fingerlings. He closed the cooler and turned and walked up to his house, hung on to the door handle and listened for whump whump whump of the chopper blades coming from the city.

HEAD

The screen door was open, and I backed into the kitchen, a bit light-headed now. It was dawning on me now—I no longer had my hands—and, now that I think of it, now that it is over, I paused to consider using words like *grasp* and *handle* to tell myself what had happened to myself and found it so funny that we think of thinking as something like a hand. Get a hold of yourself, I remember remembering.

We are still on a party line even now way out here in the middle of nowhere. Talking on the phone you can hear the voltage bleed out of the wire, draining as another phone is picked up along the line, and the person you are talking to retreats into all that distance, the voice getting smaller and smaller, the message reeling out into a whisper while you silently nod so as not to say what you are thinking and hope the shaking of your head or the lines on your face get picked up and transmitted on their own past the neighbors tapping in. I need to find a pen or pencil, something, I thought, to dial for help. And the phone in the kitchen must still be dialed dialed. It's not a touch-tone, the adding machine pad of numbers that people still say they dial.

I nosed the pencil across the tablet where my father had that morning played with some puts or calls, doodling the numbers on the blotter. We were getting deeper into futures, to hedge our risk, and placed orders over the phone in code to confuse whoever that moment was listening. We went to Chicago to meet our broker and watched the pits at work. It was all hands flocking above a pastel herd of men.

The pencil. I remember smelling the paper and the crumbs of rubber from the eraser and the tinny smell of the crimped tin sleeve connecting the eraser to the wood part of the pencil and the rusty metal smell of greasy lead, but that might have been the drying blood. The pencil fell on the floor and rolled a bit beneath the table. I was off balance and had to, of course, fall to my knees because there was nothing left to catch my fall but my knees. I was bobbing for pencils there for a second until I worked the pencil—it was painted red—into my mouth with my tongue, licking the point like you lick the point before making a mark. And then I had to climb back up, all leg, an armless lift—snatch, a clean and jerk. I was hefting the pencil, and it weighed a ton.

HEART

My mother has a thing for hands and hearts. Sometimes just hearts or hands that hold a heart, a heart in a palm of a hand. It is Irish, I think, or Amish. The hex sign she hung on the pole shed, the circle of heart-shaped petals, the petals like palms, hearts held in each palm. She majored in such stuff at State, where she met my dad, spending time in laboratories of fabric and model kitchens of the future. As a kid, I'd watch her quilt, the extra snub-nosed thimbles capping each one of my fingers and thumbs, armored touching. I'd press the pebbled tips into my skin and pull them off, leaving a cluster of vaccine scars, a constellation of little moons all pockmarked. She shows the finished goods at the fair along with all the embroidery she's done while watching the home shows the satellite dish sucks in. Those shows are always the same. They start with a mess and then, by knowing how, end in some revelation of order. Look, they always say, and the shot isn't of the thing but of the people looking at the thing.

I looked at where my hands had been, weeping—my wrists not me. The carpet was new and still out-gassing that smell of new carpet.

My mother won a ribbon once on the simple strength of folding cloth, crimping napkins into the shapes of birds or pineapples or a kind of cotton geyser spouting from a glass. I'd watch her hands fold the flat fabric into a life. It seemed such a shame to watch my own hands undo all that work, leave the used-up napkin a balled-up fist on the plate, the wad expanding as we watched, another kind of life. It was etiquette, she'd always say. The right and proper thing to do, to use up the art, to put the art to use.

Still, she has her taste is all I'm saying, and she keeps house.

Rescue found me in the sunken bathtub sunk in, my handless hands, my arms up above my head, my head light-headed and turning lighter. There was new carpet. I'll be in the tub, I told 911. Spinning overhead was a border of hearts near the crown molding she had trimmed with the small pointed brush. The hearts like fruit on vines, entwined with them, pulsed and looked like pulses on those machines on doctor shows. The wallpaper was a readout, spikes and valleys, and as I followed the track around and around, the lub dub I could hear in my own ear I could see pictured on the graphed paper papering the wall. I followed my heart around the room, a cartoon caroming from corner to corner to corner to corner.

They found me, they said, in the bathtub in a bath of my own blood, fit inside the ceramic shell, all pith, a kernel's germ, a soaked organ in a cracked-open chest. And the carpet spotless, as good as new.

HEALTH

The sign says that I should wash my hands for health. The doctors put them back together, my hands, as best they could. They even used some toes. The skin is a patchwork jumble of patches of my skin from all the other parts of my body, like my mother's quilts, the crazy kind. Who knew I was made up of such shades in color, grades of grit, like sandpaper, the differences in each tuft of hair?

I have to look at my hands now to know what they are doing. They are attached but not connected, the wiring all frayed and shorted out so that when they move they don't send to me, to my brain, a signal that they are moving. I have to watch them. I have to say to myself—well, not to myself but to the hands—"Look," I am watching. Do this, do that. "Look," they are moving.

It is hard this way to squeeze and slip the bar of soap around and around in my hands, working up a lather, bubbles. It had been so effortless, a simple task. I never thought about it before, how the fingers work together, one after the other, to get the cake of soap to spin on its own thin layer of melting. Now, I drop it a lot.

I am in the bathtub where they found me. I put my hands in the water to search for the soap. The surface of the water cuts my hands off at the wrist and they drift beneath the surface, twitching wreckage, a sore coral reef. It is not like they can feel anymore either, that sense all whacked and warped. I feel both the losses of my hands—the phantom limbs, as if I had lost them altogether, and the overloaded feedback of having these trumped-up hands after all. So, maybe, I am feeling too much. Feeling and feeling that feeling of how it used to feel, all that memory of what feeling felt like before. Before. It doesn't stop.

I can drive the combine. My new cobbled hands perch on the wheel of the big machine. It power steers. I think of them, these hands, as machines now too—all gears and guy wires, cables and sprockets. The machine I am driving takes apart the corn I am picking. The various operations of separating the grain from the cob, each kernel—cut clean and polished—collected in the bin. It happens all around me, the shutter of the massive sieves and augers, screens and belts. The combine is painted red. It's a dumb machine, but it knows what it is doing and it does what it does effortlessly.

When I pray, and I still pray, I crash my hands together in a mangled ball. Where did that come from? Who thought that up? Palm to palm, like that, that says you are praying. When I pray, I thank the Lord for the miracle of microsurgery and the mechanism of the whirlybird and the chemistry of soap made up of ash and fat, the leftover parts put back together to make us clean and new and better.

Leap Years

ELEVEN DAYS

She always said that she just wanted their one night together. One night, that's all I want. She wrote this in notes to him. She said it once or twice each time they talked on the phone. She wrote it on a postcard. We will have our one night together. They had been together in the way they were together for many years now. Both spent nights in different cities, with other people. There had been times they had been together but not one whole night. Rooms that lasted an afternoon, or a morning or an evening. A day rate, the hotels called the arrangement. Someone else would have the night in the room. The house-keeper arriving, shooing them out as they were leaving. There had been the lunches and breakfasts, the brunches, the buffets and dinners, the drinks at bars, with other people and alone. The conversations on couches in lobbies, airport lounges, train station waiting rooms. On sidewalks. In hallways passing each other. In his car or hers, driving or stopped or parked. Or outside of cars, in the shadows of parking decks, the expanse of parking lots, the moon off in the distance struggling to rise. Waiting for a bus, standing in the subway, riding in cabs, the cab that one night. There were rides in empty elevators, empty but for them, a few seconds between floors to embrace, their hearts racing as the car stalled to let on someone else. They had been together, but not one whole night. She added up all this time together—the seconds, the minutes, the hours or two she remembered being together—and figured it accumulated into a semblance of a few patchworked days—a spotty night or two, perhaps, cobbled together a week of such fractured moments made up of hours, minutes, seconds. Catch as catch can. She was good with numbers. But none of the moments were sustained long enough, false continuity, into one whole night, a night long enough not to simply sleep with one another but to really sleep with each other, together, to fall asleep, to waste the time together in that luxurious unconscious proximity. No, that had never happened. She wanted that, that one night together. But on all those other nights when she stayed up thinking about this dilemma, stayed up alone, her husband asleep beside her, wanting that one night together with this other man, late those nights she let herself wonder if even that would be enough or if that one night would be too much. In the night, in the dark, she thought of all the nights divvied up to her, the nights she had already spent and the finite number of nights not known to her yet that she would have to spend on this or that, another night without being together. It added up. Awake she thought about the falling asleep with him, and then falling asleep she thought about the waking up with him there. That would be some kind of leap, that one night of being together so that they could be apart, to have, finally, the time, some time they could skip over together—they would be there and not, suspended out of time. Out of time, at last, and out of time, outside of it. It made no sense late at night. The time distorted her sense of time. She remembered that the world still ran on two calendars, an old and new one. She thought of the time when the new calendar began to replace the old, of the eleven days the world gave up to switch from the old calendar to the new one. Everyone went to bed one night and woke up eleven days later, a chunk of an October missing. And history would record nothing happened on those days, that those days never happened. It didn't matter if one used one calendar or the other—both erased those days, lost them. She imagined how it felt, this artificial eclipse, the world both standing still and, still, jumping forward. This happened years before movies, before time-lapse film that sped very fast to record in very slow motion the explosion of a flower or a bullet flowing through an apple. A fortnight of still pictures gave the illusion of movement. In the theater, they sat in the dark to see the light. They watched a movie together, holding hands in the dark, another part of a night. It flickered and skipped, the interrupted image. In this dark, with him next to her, trying to put together the images, she imagined a night eleven days long, eleven days of night to be together.

A Leap Second

He opened the box of extra seconds, letting them warm to room temperature. The seconds, packed in like eggs, hummed in the carton. He turned to the window to pass the time. Later, he would select one second and add it to the official time, but for now he thought about what had happened. Outside, it was snowing. It seemed to always snow at this time, at times like this. The snow was a kind of static in the window. Not long ago, she had said it was over. This this was over. A moment before they had been a they and then, then. One day, way before that moment they would no longer be a they, there had been that other moment, a moment when they had become a they. Time passed as he thought of these two distinct points in time. Outside, it snowed regularly. The earth was slowing down. One day it would stop all together. But that wouldn't be for a very long time. Meanwhile, time needed to be corrected. Brought up to date. Another extra second needed to be added in order for time to synchronize with the decaying speed of the world, the planet stalling. He will spend the rest of his life doing this, what he is doing now, turning to the box, his hand hovering over the thrumming seconds as if to select a chocolate from a sampler. The rest of his life will be an accumulation of these second seconds. Suddenly, he thinks.

Fall.

Fall, in the middle of the night, she was riding the Century Limited west from New York to Chicago when, suddenly, the train came to a creaking halt in the middle of an Ohio cornfield.

Such delays are not all that unusual for a passenger train that runs its routes over private, freight company rails.

Passenger trains are often shunted off onto a siding, letting the proprietor freight have the right-of-way.

But this pause was different.

Time was falling back.

Time zone after time zone, time was turning back time.

This wrecked the train's schedule.

If the train didn't stop, it would actually arrive early at the next station.

The train's schedule had to catch up to the train.

Pass it.

She stood looking out the open top of the Dutch door in the vestibule between cars.

No lights, but cornfields everywhere, she knew, or bean fields that next year would be cornfields and bean fields that next year would be corn again in the rotation.

All over the country, trains, passenger and freight, were slowing down, coming to a halt where they were.

Trains waited, panting, stopped in their tracks.

Out of time, she waited for the time to overtake her, time to catch up everywhere.

Time would, she thought, slam by shaking the whole car like when another train on the paralleling track slammed by this train, rattling the windows, drawing the air out of the coaches.

Time expedited, a true "Limited."

Tracks cleared, the light green, time highballing west.

Then, the brakes would sneeze, and the travel in the coupling would groan and take hold and the tug would stutter through the cars, one after the other, and she would be moving again.

Trying to catch up now.

He would know to wait.

He would have remembered to turn back all the clocks, say to her, when they met again at the station, that they had lost the hour.

Stalled, she watched the moon move west over the cornfields, the bean fields, out ahead of the train, extending its lead.

He watched the moon rise over the lake, bearing down, gaining on the train somewhere out there behind it. The moon's a clock face, handless, or its hands a blur, a faceless clock, unstoppable.

It seemed he had now this extra hour to live through again, this time to kill, but it didn't really count.

She would arrive an hour late.

They all lied when they said they hadn't really lost the hour, that they weren't really late.

Everyone was instructed to set their clocks back before they went to sleep.

He stayed up and waited for the time, for the time that time officially drifted.

Looking up at the stars, he remembered he was looking back into time.

The light landing on earth this second was ancient.

And in the spring, when they might see each other again, he flying there or taking a train or driving, he would have to give the hour back again in any case.

Time was distance, distance time.

He was here and she was there.

Seconds opened and, then, closed.

Leap Day

They broke up then on leap day over e-mail, sending ever-shorter messages back and forth by hitting the reply button until the final word *stop* was the final word.

They left the subject field blank except for the abbreviation for regarding, re:, which multiplied with each reply to one another so, at last, the space read: re:re:re:re: etc.

Each of them, miles apart, paused a moment to read again what each had written on the screen, the fingers poised about to send the other this next leap.

Four years later, all the reasons for doing what they did are lost to them, the e-mail program purged, but this extra day returns to both a surplus sadness.

Four Alabama Seasons

Even when the fans are not running under power, they feather in the breeze. Turning over, the blades mill wind. Flatbeds stacked with chicken cages piled two stories high pull in behind the wall of fans, parked for their turn unloading at the loading dock. White chickens stuff the black wire cages. The fans start up, turn, blur. The air pushes through the cages, and feathers spit out the other side. Everywhere on the ground are loose white feathers. The feathers blow across the street, cars stirring up the feathers, catch in the breeze that has not been manufactured. Breeze that is breeze. The feathers form a drift of down next to the red cedar slat fence of the city's junkyard. Balls of feathers, hefty as chickens and as plump, tumble into the ditch. Up north, a fence like that would be strung along a highway to knock the snow out of a blizzard. Loose feathers swirl around wrecked police black-and-whites in the lot, begin to tar the cars, coat the surface of muddy puddles left by the rain.

SPRING

Spring and all is new green grass drowned by new white, white sand of the golf course groundskeeping. The rain puts a crust on the traps that must be raked until they shimmer, a sawing corduroy seen from a distance, a breeze chopping up the surface of a scummy pond. Pollen, the gist of the season, tarnishes every surface, takes away its shine, a mat of grainy finish. But today, see? Spilled sparkle of sand curved through the black-topped intersection out front, traced a dump truck's too-tight turn. Already, house sparrows bathe in the fresh dune, intermittent puffs of dust along the drift, a moon's crescent in shadow. There, the white sand turns black. A mockingbird on the strung cable mimics the neighborhood's air conditioners. All emit this compressed chatter as the sun clears the stand of oak soaked with wisteria. It will rain later and the sand will melt, forget itself. That dawn's gesture's just grist.

SUMMER

Sundays, a white city pickup truck steams slowly through the side street spraying for mosquitoes. The fog machine's engine, an insect, drowns out the sound of the truck's engine, a steady gearless whine. The fog itself leaps from a funnel off the bed, appears to propel the truck along, a jet of clouds under pressure. The white spray dissipates, gets grayer as it spreads, and, heavier than air, it trails the truck, a wake that spreads and skirts the curbs of the street. It spills down the hill, fills the hollow, evaporates like that afternoon's rain turning the concrete to vapor. Later, the truck crisscrosses the grid in the neighborhood, the sound muted and amplified by the spaces between houses, the trees, the yards, and the residue settles into the bunkers of the golf course, a ground blizzard sweeping over the greens, a fluid tarp. Above, the moon breaks up, fogged in the fog as it sets through it. The summer air twice thickened.

FALL

White pine. The new needles replace needles that fall as straw, rake into springy piles in the gutter. The hardwoods stay bare limbed, leaves exhausted. Clouds of mistletoe are caught in the branches, twig mist. The spindly azalea understory. Too far north for Spanish moss, the trees trap trashed plastic bags. But in the crevices and corners and on the stripped branches, lint from the cotton fields gathers. On the scored red brick and the dull mortar in between, woolly cotton patches of the stuff stuffs the joints, points the grout, a seeping spun sugar. The lint escapes the screened-in trailer trucks of the raw harvest or gets kicked up by the gleaning in the fields and threads itself into the wind, winds up coating anything with a burr enough to stick. It snows, little squalls of it accumulated in the niches, the pockets fall has turned out. It is snow that is not snow, a white reminder, until it dyes itself with all the other detritus, becomes the glue of bark and twigs and leaves, leaving nothing but filth, tilth, a kind of felt.

Ruminant

Visible Cow

I think of him thinking about his cows. I never even knew he
was a dairyman. At the Starbucks in the Student Union where
I worked he'd ask me about the steamed milk—real milk,
right?—in the latte. I think of that now. He'd nurse the drink
all day, staring off into space, the space so thick I could almost
see that electromagnetic soup of digital bleats bawling from
the laptops, the cell phones, the other students all around him
nudging and pawing, grazing through their e-mail, their texts.
I drifted over to him, started talking. He bought me a mac-
chiato stained with milk and never let on he left a dairy farm to
come to school. Though once early on, now that I think about
it, he told me one could major in ice cream if one wanted to. I
majored in numbers. Made ends meet. Thinking about it now,
there were infinite silences between us like the silences between
the bits of the binary alphabets herding around us in the ether.
He didn't say much at all, but that is the nature of farm boys,
I guessed, or at least the ones I met back then, weaned in the
vacuums of all those empty acres out there. All that absence to
fill with work or with the internal working of the brain. I guess
you get used to it, can hear, in those silences, yourself think. It
was only later, when we were breaking up, that he showed me
the snapshots of his cows posed on some hillock somewhere
out there. They had names of course. The names began with *A*

or *B*, Apple or Bossie, Alice or Betty, the initials trading places through the generations, a to b to a to b like some equation or formula or the rhyme scheme of a sonnet's endless couplets. I could tell a lot by the way he tiled the photographs like the descending cataract of a table full of solitaire. He had shuffled through the lot of them again and again. He recited the names. I think now this must have been what he was thinking of when I watched him thinking. The album of pictures. The list of names. They all looked alike to me, the cows, all of them, white on black slabs of clouds, stayed by the four little guy-wire pegged legs pegged to the ground. All of them caught in the act of chewing. He liked to take me then to the dairy barns on the edge of campus, to the herds of milling cows, mewing calves, the blocky steers rubbing their coats on the white wooden fences. There he found the one sad beast with a flap in her side, a fistula the bovine scientists covered over with a plastic window. The cow, content in her stanchion, snuffed up the grain in neat piles at her feet. I watched him consider the animal, all lost in thought. Through the porthole I could see the churning stomach percolate the fermenting feed back and forth. It was complicated like mixing a drink back at the coffee bar, all agitation and vapor and the chemistry of layers breaking down, so busy, all of these goings-on, going on on the inside while we, stock still on the outside, stood, lost in thought, struck dumb.

BUTTER COW

Driving to the State Fair, I think of him thinking. I am along for the ride. Driving through this state, you don't have to think about driving. The car has its own head, trails straight on, knows its own mind. Mindless. In this state, the grid of the section roads is interrupted by only one diagonal highway. You just drive. You can't get lost in this space, only lost in thought. The cornfields switch to soybean fields on the right side of the car, and on the left, they switch, the soybeans and the corn, the other way around every half mile, then back again to the other—corn, soybeans, corn, soybeans. And every mile another road intersects the one you're on at the squarest of right angles. In that part of the state, the fences are gone, have all been torn out. The crop rows shoulder up to the shoulder of the road. I am thinking, he is thinking which fields of corn, fields of soybeans, were once pastures, once hayfields with windrows or scattered herds of drying bales. He sees again the fences, contemplates the gates, how they open and shut, the mazes of lost fenced lanes and vanished grass alleys between the fields, and the cattle and the hogs and even some sheep turned into a field of stubble to stumble around, snuffling in the furrows to glean. The cows drifting, staggered and staggering, find the highest part of any acre finally to arrange themselves randomly like humans in an elevator, meditating without thinking about it, a moseyed contemplation, as the sky lowers and the shadows the sun throws grow longer and the cow shadows jostle with the cows, as the cows and cow shadows rearrange themselves again—constant minute adjustments, diplomatic dances, specific gravities attracting and repelling, a grinding inclination, the cows pulling the heavy thoughts of themselves through the grass by their teeth.

And at the fair people there walk and eat, lap up against each other, wave the paper napkins stained with four kinds of grease across their moony faces, work their way around fried solids stuck on sticks as they circle each other and circle the animals parading in the show rings and pacing in the paddocks and pens. Stunned by the sun, he trudges forward, and I follow after. We can't stop eating, continue eating clouds of cotton candy even as we find ourselves in the cloud showers set up on the Grand Concourse, the spun sugar turning to syrup in our hands that we then lick clean, licking without a second thought. We escape into the cool Varied Industry pavilion, wander up to join the crowd surrounding the glassed-in refrigerated room where a woman constructs this year's cow sculpted in butter, Brown Swiss this time, the breeds taking turns through the years—Jersey, Guernsey, Holstein. She layers the spans of butter onto a cantilevered skeleton of bent wood and sprung metal. Through the glass before me I see through the glass on the other side of the room the rows of patient people there lined up, staring, chewing something as they watch her fold the butter into the lips of the dewlap and saggy melted skin above the brisket. The slabs of butter she is working onto the articulated flanks look like slabs of meat, all marble. The butter's edges are curried into each other over the hook and pin bones, worked then into the valley of the thurl. The crowd around us forgets they are chewing and chews, forgets to swallow, lost in the whorl of butter spread like fur over the jacket of fat. I think I know what he is thinking as he watches. How the assembly line of slaughter takes an animal apart, down to tabletop cuts, now unrecognizable pucks of flesh. He is thinking inside about the whole exposed anatomy in butter. Each organ inside—the heart and lungs, the liver and kidneys, the tongue and brain—made of different breeds of soft cheese. The milky blood all milk. The butter udder. He is thinking of all the slathered transformations. How the four-chambered butter stomach would transform butter grass into buttermilk and the butter grass buttermilk turns into buttermilk butter cream and the butter cream into creamy butter butter. How the butter of the butter cow would look like this butter butter. How even the nails and washers and fencing scrap and baling wire cropped up by the grazing butter cow, finding its way to the butter hardware stomach, would also be sculpted in butter. The butter metal would lodge in the butter reticulum—indigestible, inorganic—its rust made up of a rust made up of butter.

I am thinking about these cows, thinking about what is going on inside them. They are first calf heifers, all pregnant, two dozen or so strolling my way across the loafing shed, chewing cuds, all their big black eyes rheumy already, rolling to a stare, staring at the scoop shovel of feed I've got balanced against my flexed knee. I am thinking about what is mixed up on purpose in the feed mix, the chemical, PBB, that is killing them slowly without them even knowing, and the calves inside them curling up tighter, frying, drying up, the stem cells splintering, splitting up all wrong, sputtering, the threads of DNA all fraying inside the cells, twisted, busted, losing their train of thought, forgetting to remember the remembering of parts, the blueprint turning blue. It is Christmas, and the experiment the heifers are part of knows no holiday, the dosing to continue through the long winter break.

Outside the barn, it is snowing, of course, the snow a kind of fabric, a white drifting silence we can all drift through. The snow accumulates in the shadow of the fencing, floats on the frozen surface of the ice in the corrugated troughs. Hearing the shovel hiss through the grain in the bin the herd turned toward me, began to drift itself, the sound all the stimulus it needed now, all those stomachs thinking, thinking of food. As they move, the knocked-up cattle are lowing. The cattle are lowing. No babies wake. No sounds but the shuffling sawdust, the snuffling and sneezing as they move. The chemical attacks the big cathedral lungs, the naves drowning in fluid, forgetting how to bail. I've filled mangers. The mangers are filled with hay. She is in the adjacent barn feeding the control group of identical cattle, mucking out their stalls. Later, I will hear her fire up the Deere, use the power-take-off to run the chain rake through the gutters, fork the spoiled straw into the spreader. Leaning on the Dutch-door, I'll watch her, later still, make a pass or two through the fuzzy air, hauling the manure over the field, the green tractor's lights blazing, the shit illuminated, flying through the steaming steam, flung by the blades of the red spreader. We've given up our holiday to help out, knew if we were back home we wouldn't be able to stop thinking of these cows dying in measured increments. Out in the world away from the campus, the chemical had gotten into the feed supply, a fire retardant mixed into the silage, a co-op's goof, the poison churned to milk inside the cows, the tainted milk poured out on the ground, cattle everywhere put down. I think of the farmer, what was he thinking, as he walked the string of cattle tethered on the lip of a pit he'd just dug, drilling a bullet in the big brain of each cow as he passed. And I think of the scientists here whose experiment this is, who are at home, right now, in front of a fire each of them poke, thinking of the ways the chemical works through the guts of the animals, how it gets swallowed and coughed up, combines and divides in the grinding up of the ground-up feed, how it gets absorbed, how it does its slow soluble work in the limpid pockets of the ruminant body. The cows nuzzle me from behind looking for more, their tongues scraping the folds of the hard Carhart jacket, wanting a taste, a taste of the dust. The barn is cold. The heifers blow clouds of steam from their wet muzzles that hover like bubbles of thought. What are they thinking? I think of the balls of calves caved up inside them, dying hearths, turning to ash, and the destroyed cattle at the bottom of those pits, the storm of lime snowing down on them. And later after all the chores, all the domestic husbandry, we will go back to her place, make love in the dark, the stink of the barn on us both, the sweet smell of the shit, the general spoil fermenting, turning off all the thinking, going to that thoughtless place within us, then, and then her hot slick blood on me, the time of the month, after I've pulled myself out of her, her blood drying and turning cold on my shrinking shrinking skin in the dark.

I think of him thinking inside the cow. He is inside the cow thinking. He is supposed to be handing out the coupons he holds in his hoof. Instead, he stands off to the side at the entrance of the food court, near the dozen trash bins lined up in their stalls. Inside the cow, he regards the worker, the big fiberglass head listing to the right, as the worker extracts the stuffed sacks of spent paper napkins, slimed pressed-board plates, sweating cups, plastic cutlery from the bins buried behind the wagging tongues imprinted with "Thank You." "Thank You" after "Thank You" repeated down the whole row. The sacks sag, the melted ice from the drinks, the dregs of sauces, sopping salads, as the bags are lifted from one bin and dumped into a bigger bin on wheels. The cow, a Holstein, black and white, reared up on its two rear legs, its front hoofs clutching fans of coupons, regards the man in the jumpsuit, snapping open a new plastic sack to replace the plastic sack he has just emptied from the bin. He lines the empty bin again, stores it away behind the swinging "Thank You" sign.

Inside the cow, he is thinking of insides and outsides, I think. The tables in the food court are filled with hundreds of people eating, moving the mounds of food off the paper plates with plastic forks, spoons, lifting the food to hundreds of mouths. Looking out from inside the cow, he actually sees through an incision in the cow's throat, a slit covered over with a screen of gauzy black-and-white fur. The head of the cow is more like a hat perched on top of his head inside the cow's head, looking out the slit cut into the cow's throat. The spot, he will tell me later, where one would insert a knife right after slaughter to drain the animal's blood before the butchering.

He is working for a fast-food franchise that serves only chicken. The chain's advertising adopted animated cattle as spokesmen, employs three-dimensional life-sized cows vandalizing billboards with the misspelled command to eat mor chikin, the graffiti awkwardly applied by hoof.

Inside the cow, he is to direct the milling people mulling over the growls of their stomachs, thinking about the illuminated menus of the food court, to eat mor chikin. The sandwich board he wears is printed with that child-like hand, the cow-like hoof. Later, he will tell me that he thinks it's funny that inside the cow, the cow is sandwiched inside slices of sandwich board, the sandwich sign urging the reader to eat more sandwiches. He thinks that he becomes, inside the cow, another sign, a menu that the people in the food court consider, attempt to decipher, as they decode the messages emanating from their stomachs. In what way are we hungry? he thinks they are asking as he asks himself the question again and again inside the cow.

In the neck of the cow, there is the slit so he can see, but there is no opening for him to eat. The cow's mouth is not a real mouth. The tongue extending out of it is fabric stuffed with batting. Later he will tell me how during the long hours inside the suit, drifting through the corridors of the mall, children pulling the cow's tail or rubbing the rubber udder on his stomach as if to make the cow let down, he imagined himself a manifestation of all the different insides of the animal, its skeleton, its mass of arteries and veins, its trunks and branches of nerves, its nodes of lymph, its backwaters and oxbows of guts and guts and guts and guts.

When it is time to eat, he can't remove his head, the cow's head, in public. I see him inside the cow in the distance. The cow's black-and-white head extends above most of the shimmering car roofs in the mall's parking lot. Inside the cow he must turn the whole body left and right as he turns back and forth to look for me inside my car in the parking lot. The head above the shimmering roofs and hoods of the parked car does not pivot on its neck. The whole cow cranes this way and that. I have parked over by the war memorial with its display of mottled hulking tanks. Inside the cow, he sees me, waves his now empty hoof. He slowly makes his way through the maze of cars to mine. He leans over the hood of my car once he arrives, catching his breath. He is thinking, looking deep into the pool of polished metal, his reflection, the cow's reflection reflecting back to him through the slit in the throat. Before he gets in the car, he removes the head, twisting it off like a deep-sea diver's helmet. He stores the head in the backseat and gets in the front to eat the lunch I've brought him, hamburgers with the works, waffle fries, and black cow shake from a competitor's place.

He eats. He eats, I think, without thinking, mouth open, exhausted. He sweats inside the cow and, inside the car, the car fills up with the sweet sweat smells and the smell of the sweated onions, the rancid grease, the reeking suit. It is close inside the car, and it is getting closer still. He eats without talking. He eats in silence, a silence only punctuated by the sound of his chewing, chewing. He eats. The empty head in the backseat, I catch its look in the rearview mirror, the big soulful eyes staring back at me into space.

Four Postcards from Indiana

On the way to Story, Indiana, 315 T'ed into an unnamed road, and, at the junction, the side of a yolk yellow farmhouse stared back at me with four identical windows on the fading façade, each window divided into four picture panes of glass. The green information sign indicated that Story was five miles thataway with an arrow pointing to the right. A white picket fence separated the sign and the road from the house, and, dead ahead, fenced in its own little precinct of half-sized pickets, some kind of monument caught the light already filtered by the gobo clusters of leaves in the copse of tulip poplars in the yard. I parked the car.

Crossing the road, I saw the plinth of stone transform as I got closer, watched as it sprouted shoulders, then grew a head, busting out into a rustic bust, its face pancaked, its contours— the lips, eyes, and eyebrows—charred black. A black widow– peaked helmet of hair. Matte muttonchop shadows burned each cheek. A coy naive sphinx. The stone head's etched left eyebrow arched, waiting for the question already answered. Tattooed on its roughed-out apron of a chest, a hand pointed left to Columbus and another hand right to Fairfax, a town no longer on the map. Take your pick.

"What's your story?" I asked it.

The cicada brood bloomed and buzzed in the trees. Cardinals chewed out each other, flitted overhead. There, below

47

the folded hands, not much of a clue—a year, 1851, and a diminutive signature of *H Cross*, its second "s" washed out as the sandstone melted into the seam at the base. At that angle, the stone head turned into the Hoosier Mona Lisa, the crisscrossed hands, the unselfconscious conscious smile, the eyes half-lidded, backlit by a painted landscape more animated than the foiled subject.

I looked back at the car. I'd left its hazard lamps blinking, the indicator lights signaling that both ways were a possibility simultaneously or that each canceled the other out.

In the end, I turned away from Story, bore the other route toward Columbus—the town filled with autographed churches and fire stations, those modern slabs of steel and glass that just so happened to find themselves planted in what had been an Indiana cornfield. And where I found, in an ordinary gas station, a postcard picturing the corner I left behind—the yellow house, the picket fence, the knob of stone with its unreadable and unreachable directions, and the sign pointing to Story that I sent to you asking one last time: Who should we tell? What should we do? Where should we go? Why?

"A watch means that conditions are right for a tornado." As we drove, I explained the difference between a watch and a warning. This was her first summer in Indiana, and every time she turned on the radio she found herself in another depression, pressure dropping. An imaginary line extending just north of and passing through the counties of La la la and Mmmmm. The Balkan states of the weather map. It would be in effect for a couple of hours.

"Is that us?" she said.

"It's just a watch," I said, and I told her what to look for, though I had never seen one myself. I remembered sightings, hearing of funnels over towns. One Easter. One Palm Sunday. "If you see one, we get in a ditch. Someplace low." I remembered feeling this way every spring and summer—too hot, too still. You can hear better. There was this picture in the grocery store encyclopedia of a drinking straw driven into the trunk of an elm. She had seen violent storms in Baltimore but only the leavings of hurricanes, not this kind of wind—all eye and finger, one that can see and feel.

Of course, it started raining, and the voice on the radio tracked the storms, interrupted by the sizzle of static—soft or loud, close or far away. I'm here now, the static said. Teasing. Moving.

"It's not us," I said.

In the half-light we passed the statue of Santa Claus, melted limestone, in a field surrounded by broken skeletons of farm implements slick with rain and submerged in mud. Horses, startled by the lightning, shied and ran sideways away from the sound. The book said the statue said: For the Children of the World.

Triple A just mentioned the St. Nicholas Inn, the only motel in Santa Claus. It was made up of little bungalows, Munchkin-size, scattered behind a gas station.

"A mite windy," said the woman, letting us into number 4. The baby riding on her hip yelped each time it thundered. "No one stays here. They drive up from Louisville or down from Naplis to see Santa Claus. My baby sees him every day."

We went into our room and found everything half-sized— the TV, the end table, the bed. "Think," she said, "to grow up seeing Santa Claus every day but Christmas." Yes, in the part of the world where flying is easy—lawn deer, flamingoes, silked jockeys.

As we slept did we shrink? Were we that small? Did our feet touch the ground? Did we count each other's sheep as they clouded that tiny room? We heard the baby cry all night through the storm.

The next morning I knew the sky was clear before she pulled the drapes and turned on the morning news. Eyes still closed, I heard that a tornado had touched down in the Baltimore zoo the day before. A woman reported that she survived by being blown into the hippo house. A miracle. The world is full of miracles. Closing my eyes again, I see the woman blown into the hippo house. One puff, a blow to the belly, arms and legs trailing, millions of shrimp swimming backwards into the hippo house. Size has no scale. I am asleep again.

Later we wrote our postcards in the car, parked next to the post office. The doors were open. To keep the post office, the natives changed the name of their town from Santa Fe to Santa Claus. Now, besides the amusement park, the post office is the town's only industry. All the letters come here. All the ones addressed to the North Pole. All the lists. All the directions home. We came here to mail some from the eye of the storm. All the stamps were airmail. It is too hot for Christmas, too still. You could hear the sleigh bells.

"Look. Look," I said, pointing across the evaporating parking lot to the back gate of Santa Claus Land, "Santa Claus." In shirtsleeves and Bermudas, he swung a black lunchbox as he went to work. He was sweating and he wasn't whistling. She didn't look up.

"Where?" she said.

But he was already gone through the gate and hidden behind the scraps of newspaper caught in the Cyclone fence. I pointed with my finger.

"There."

We came into the valley from Santa Claus and skirted the grand hotel fronting the road, a walled city. We crossed the old Monon tracks, the spur where the private cars from Chicago were switched right up to the door of the resort. "Monon," you said. I told you again about Hoosier, who's there. The French in Indiana. We stayed down the road in a motel—half in French Lick, half in West Baden. Alsace-Lorraine. "A lick," I said, "was for the wild game. The seasoning in the ground." I showed you the salt blocks in the supermarket.

"Kiss me, there," you said.

We walked back over to the grand hotel. In the coffee shop you had a tongue sandwich, and the waitress behind the counter said I was the first to order a bagel and cream cheese "since I've worked here. What do I do?" Next to us on the little stools, a couple argued about the food. She complained about her peas in French. He scolded her in English. We came for the waters, you said. But really you only wanted your postcards canceled with French Lick. We played Space Invaders in the arcade, and they kept coming. Then we lingered on the veranda, following the deck chairs to the spring. The spring was in a gazebo, bubbling through a pool of green water. "Kiss me, here," you said, but the sulfur smell was too strong. "If nature can't Pluto will." You read the sign. "This is what they came for?" you said. "This is what they came for, the presidents and gangsters?"

The next morning you wrote your postcards, naked, at the desk. Maids were making up the next room. I watched David Letterman on TV making jokes about Muncie. Turning, you said, "Let's," licking ten cents Justice, "go there next." On my way to the shower, I stopped behind you. You were writing that animals need their licks. The sounds you make, the ones that are not quite language, name nothing.

"Knock, knock," I say in your ear. "Who's there?" you say from another world.

MUNCIE

In Muncie, we are staying at the Hotel Roberts, downtown. And, though the elevator is automatic, a man wearing a Nickel Plate conductor's hat pushes the buttons. We have learned that the third Middletown study is in progress. We are mistaken for sociologists by the old men we sit with in the lobby when we watch TV. Before we can quiet them with the truth, they tell us their church affiliations and bathroom practices.

The first night here, we ordered a pizza by phone from a campus takeout to be delivered to our room. Since then we have gone through the yellow pages for anything that will be delivered. When it arrives, Theresa answers the door wrapped in the hotel bath towel. After awhile we begin to receive all sorts of things we never ordered—pints of macaroni salad, goldfish cartons of fried rice, heads of lettuce. They are delivered by college boys wearing Ball U T-shirts, who then sculpture obscene animals with the warm tinfoil. Everything seems to have the same tomato paste base.

If we leave the Roberts at all, it is to watch the summer basketball leagues play on a court next to one leg of the high school drag. The cars go by honking. The players glisten in the single scoop lamp. The backboard is perforated metal used in temporary runways. The hoop is a red halo with not even a metal chain net dangling from the rim. Or we go to the Ball factory and watch them make mason jars, press the rubber lips to the tin lids. They have shelves of jars the Ball brothers canned seventy-five years ago. The seal holds stewed tomatoes with yellow seeds, embryonic eggplants, black butter chips and sweet gherkins no one will taste, okra, of all things. We have been there several times, and unlike other factory tours, there is nothing to sample unless we care to can and wait a season. We do keep our loose pennies in a Ball jar, and Theresa makes the boys reach in it for their tip, a monkey trap. They can't withdraw their clenched fist through the narrow mouth of the jar without letting go of the money. She leaves them laughing, closing the door against them with the flat of her foot.

But all of this is typical here, or, because we do it in Muncie, it is typical. We have seen the sociologists on the sidewalks, shielding their eyes with their clipboards, trying to cross the street. They take pictures of barbershops and trophy stores. Or they sit and count cars in and out of the parking lot or look for butts beneath their feet. In every room there are questions to be answered with special pencils. "What brings you here?" In each case, love. We write that our dream is to open all the cans one at a time and eat vegetables older than our grandfathers. We want everything delivered to us. Theresa wears nothing but two pasties of pepperoni. I am reading books on pickling. The scientists will figure out what is going on here.

The I States

Idaho

As he plants, he dreams of potatoes. Enough already with the potatoes, he dreams, but continues to dream of potatoes. In the mountains of Peru, farmers grow potatoes above the clouds in terraced fields each no bigger than a backyard in Illinois. Hundreds of varieties are all mixed together. The tubers are the size of marbles, golf balls, gooseberries, gallstones, mothballs. They look like each kind of toe on a farmer's foot. Potatoes that look like carrots. Potatoes that look like radishes. Potatoes that look like potatoes. And the fields are not contoured but planted in rows with the furrows pointing straight down the slope so when it rains all that Peruvian rain it doesn't rain potatoes. The water runs off quickly, spilling like waterfalls over the sides of the mountains onto fields below before it has a chance to erode the crop on the one above. One day, he thinks, he will buy up the abandoned rail bed here and turn it over, planting his potatoes in one long pass, no turning the machinery. One swipe for the planting. One long haul for the hilling up. Another single pass to root out the fruit that will bubble up in his wake and float on the tide of the tilth. In Peru, the potatoes come in all colors. There is the purple potato. There is the red potato like the red potato here in Idaho. There is an orange potato the size of an orange. There is a green potato that isn't poisonous. There are hundreds of different browns. There is the blue potato, the blue potato of Peru. In Idaho, his seed is certified.

ILLINOIS

The way they see it, it's their job to strip-mine this state. They go from one little town to the next looking for the mom-and-pop shops going out of business and buy up all the inventory they've had in the basement or attics or out back since the forties, the fifties, the sixties. Sundresses and alpaca jackets. Indian bead belts and saddle shoes in their original boxes. Leather letter jackets and tartan jumpers with the mint safety pin. Pegged pants and silk Hawaiian shirts. Rooster ties and Arrow collars. Brownie sashes and Cub Scout kerchiefs. Untouched and packaged, the package as valuable as the thing inside. It's all shipped back East or to the West Coast. And they must eat in the diners on the main streets where they have always imagined the women cooking there would turn to them at the counters and display the secret to the homemade mashed potatoes. Look! The implement itself. The worn wood handle. The chrome tang. The oscillating business end of the utensil, still caked with the milk-white paste of potato. But that never happens. The breaded tenderloins are served with french fries in plastic baskets lined with stained waxed paper.

Indiana

Above the sink in the kitchen was a window and, on the sill, an old jelly jar, the color of the cartoon caricatures etched on its glass fading from too many washings, perhaps, or from the constant exposure to the sunlight. There, there was always a chunk of a potato pierced by a trio of cocktail toothpicks, tipped with brilliant spun-cellophane buds, in such a way that they held the potato suspended on the lip of the jar so that its underside just touched the dingy water beneath where already a fur of roots sprouted and reached down. Soon, soon, the eyes above ripened into those pale segmented branches that ended in a stunted leaf or two and, once or twice, an already fading flower. Something to look at as I washed and dried the dishes and regarded the day outside already lengthening or already turning into twilight.

IOWA

There is only one potato farmer in Iowa, five hundred acres near Muscatine, surrounded by melon farms on the sandy soil. The country gets confused sometimes. One "I" state looks the same as any other "I" state. You tell folks you're from Iowa and they say, Iowa, potatoes, right? Well, in this case they would be right because here is a five-hundred acre field of potatoes the locals say looks like the worst stand of beans they have ever seen. It all goes to chips, shipped to the Frito Lay plant in the Quad Cities. At night, the farmer of the only potato farm in Iowa watches a woman on the *Tonight Show* who collects potato chips she has found bearing images of the famous rendered on the canvas of starch during the deep-fat frying. "You can see Nixon," she says. "And this one looks like Gorbachev right down to the stain on his forehead." She is from Indiana, where the country that watches late-night television now believes its potatoes are grown. "Here is Queen Victoria, Mickey Mouse, Kojak, Betty Crocker." She has hundreds she keeps in jewel boxes. She holds them up to the camera, waxy cameos. Working his field of potatoes, he resists thinking that things look like other things. The sun, as it sets, for example, is not like a slice of potato. His face, reflected in the dusty windscreen of his tractor's cab, is not his face.

The Sex Life of the Fantastic Four

INVISIBLE GIRL

Where he touches me, I vanish. The back of his hand stroking my face erases my cheek. Involuntary, the skin initially, then the deeper flesh. The skin first, gone when it feels his fingertips. I feel the surface disappear but still feel feeling there. His touch sinks in. The subdermal layers go. The nested cells he polishes clear, his soft palm hovering. By the time I have stripped off the blue bodysuit, stepping out of the spandex which retains, for a second, the shape of my body as it falls, the body it reveals has already become translucent, the meat turning milky, the bone wiped clear in streaks like a smear of butter melts the white from a paper plate. I become clarified grease beneath him. Entwined, we are tangled up in the skein of my airy sinew, the ropey braids of my circulatory system, its cartoon of primary reds and blues. My blood thins in the extremities but knots at the nodes of erectile tissue, clotting a nipple visible again beneath the sheen he has left from licking what looked, a moment before, like air, now, me, there, concentrated into rubbery ruby light again. It disappears into his mouth. I am down to the broken dashes of the central nervous system, suggesting, still outlining, the outer neural net of my skin, feeding me the synaptic code of dots and dits from the dissipating periphery. His hands, as they caress nothing, reveal me to myself, leave the afterimage of his movement burned upon the transparent wall of my retina, the lightning streak of his skin shaping the borders of my own body. I close my eyes and watch as my eyelids dissolve. My vision passes through skin first, turning then to scrim. And I see, now, through another unoccluded lens. I see through my lids, through myself, see his cock, clearly, moving inside of the vast and now empty empty space which must be me and must be not me.

The Human Torch

I sit at the bar, usually, drinking ouzo neat, a Jordan almond dissolving at the bottom of the shot glass. I have set the liquor on fire swizzling it with my finger. I like to watch the floor show and the show on the floor. The tunnel crowd weirded-out by the drag queens doing stripteases or singing old torch songs "One for my baby and one more for the road," sending up Lady Day or Barbra, that kind of thing. I dump some water into my aperitif, extinguishing the blue flame and turning the drink chalky like a precipitate in a test tube. My current favorite is a Liza interpreter who vamps this obscure number—is it by Mercer?—that plays with the line "You've let yourself go." She sings to her lug of a lover how he has grown fat and dull, how their liaison has suffered the consequences. There follows a litany of complaint. What a schlub, she sings. "You've let yourself go." But it turns in the end. It always turns. "Come on over here," she whispers, "come on over and let yourself go." I tear up, naturally, but it isn't saline staining my cheek. It's a dab of molten lava percolating there in the corner of my eye, my own brand of running mascara. I have to watch myself. Spontaneously, my eyelashes can ignite, throwing sparks up into the tinder of my eyebrows, which can smolder for hours without my knowing. Once, I set the sprinklers off in the Russian Bath House on 10th. I've stopped looking for a boy who can top me. It's too dangerous. The leather bars. Too hot. I was cooking inside the horsehide Eisenhower jacket, cooking the jacket, the seared meat smell an additional turn-on, I suppose. These powers we have acquired seem to fall into that dark space between the involuntary responses wired into us and those we can modulate. Not like the heartbeat on the one hand or walking home on the other, but like blinking and winking, say, or like desire itself. There is only so much one can do to help oneself.

Oh sure I can bellow "Flame On" all I want followed by the stunning transformation from solid buff flesh to superheated gaseous vapor. The controlled burn. Here precision scalding. There the delicate sweating of copper pipes. But in the weaker moments, when I am weak in the knees, a stranger's hand on my hand will steam off skin. I can't watch myself all the time. A human touch sets off the human torch. I am a captive within my sublime hide.

MR. FANTASTIC

To make the edge of the famous samurai swords of antiquity, the smiths beat the iron flat into foil then folded the metal over and hammered it flat again. And then another fold and peening, and still another and then another. Thousands of times. Fold and flatten, fold and flatten. Until, in this primitive way, through brute force and patience, the metal's crystalline structure became saturated with itself. Atoms packed inside the spaces between atoms, at last, both the surface and simultaneously its underside now no more than a molecule deep, the edge of the matrix serrated only by the minute undulation of subatomic matter, a sine wave, spanning a mere handful of angstroms, of the outermost electrons. Sharp, you bet. It is what I find myself doing to my own skin in private moments. I stretch and fold and knead it back together. A wrinkle in the loose hide on my forearm, a flap of fat at my chin. It is the very definition of definition, and I spend hours honing my musculature, ironing in the pleats on my belly, increasing the cant of my cheekbones with the finest shade of a sharpened pencil line. I know what people are thinking. The elasticity of your normal everyday run-of-the-mill uncosmicly irradiated penis is, itself, a goddamn miracle to most. The ways it inflates, its skin thinning to the gauziest of tissue webbed by diaphanous capillary sponge grown thick with the stiffened rebar of packed and interlocking corpuscles. Sure, I've tried it all. Swallowed myself whole, took myself in myself from behind. For awhile she liked to watch it snake toward her across the floor, liked the way it coiled up a leg then threaded the cleft of her rear, whipping around her waist then back up her back, curling over her shoulder and back down between her breasts down her stomach, parting her down down there and then her labia and into her from above, how its tensile strength lifted her in this hardened harness, held her weightless as it expanded within her and all around her. We haven't done that in awhile, and everything, believe me, grows familiar. Recently our lovemaking has tended toward the less baroque. A simple vertical embrace, my member remembering its scale from before the accident. Sue, her legs wrapped around my waist, is saddled on my hips, riding this altogether unfantastic appendage and me supporting her, strapping my silly, pliant arms around her, then around me and then around her again. Stretching, another lap and lapping another lap, another band around us both, belting us to us. My arms still encircling, encasing us from head to toe, this cocoon spinning while we kiss, my elasticity nearing its end, effaced to the point of transparency, my thinning skin becoming, at last, the clear outer covering, at last, of this new creature we create.

THE THING

I don't really need the briefs down below since my thing ain't there no more. It's more for show to let the folks know I was once a guy. A scrap of cloth for the modesty of the citizens craning their necks to take a gander at me. They can't get past the orangey crust of skin. It's something all right. Little do they know I am all hanging out there for anybody to see. My Johnson, or what I take to be my Johnson (Johnsons really—I don't know since there is no other thing like me, as far as I can tell, to let me try out these doohickeys of wadded callous and thingamabobs of oozing mucus) is plopped there in front of their collective noses. Just more eruptions and rashes on the sliding plates of my scaly surface. The Doc explained it to me, showed me the Tinkertoy models of your typical twisted normal gene, and then how mine's been tripled, another worm squirming around that ladder of goofy golf balls. It's simple for everybody but me. Male and female. Male and female down to everybody's bones but me. No bones for me. No in and out. No on and off. A whole other dimension to nookie. What I have become needs a couple other things to reproduce, I guess, not just one other. Sex, as near as I can figure, is like nothing you can dream of since those dirty pictures your brain's pumping out are made up of, you got it, those same twin strands caught wrapped up in each other. Well, I am another other. And I am on the lookout for other others like me. Meantime, when I'm alone (but this could be in the middle of Times-freaking-Square, a public spectacle where the public can't begin to see the me that's me) I make myself have this nameless thing, feel this Thing thing I have no words, no more, for.

Four Brief Lives

Contributor's Note

Michael Martone published his first book, *Big Words*, in graduate school. The children's book could only use thirty age-appropriate words taken from the Dolch Word List. A kind of poetry.

Contributor's Note

Michael Martone grew up in Fort Wayne. Philo T. Farnsworth, inventor of electronic television, was his neighbor. Martone spied on Farnsworth. He watched the inventor watch the local stations sign off.

Contributor's Note

Michael Martone grew up in Fort Wayne. Each August, his mother took him downtown to shop for new underwear (briefs). Always August meant underwear. Later, married, Martone switched to boxers.

Contributor's Note

Michael Martone worked for the Fort Wayne newspapers, where he wrote the obituaries and maintained the morgue. Everyday he would add details to his own obit he kept on file.

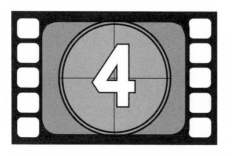

"The hint half guessed, the gift half understood…"
— T.S Eliot, *Four Quartets*

Dutch Boy

32-V

Soap Opera

32-V-1

If you ask him, her husband finds it strange that she paints and repaints so often the living room of their house. If you ask her, and he never does, she would not tell you the real reason she paints and repaints the living room of their house. She paints and repaints the living room when she believes she will, finally, break it off with her lover of long standing, a man she has slept with, off and on, for a dozen years now. Sometimes she paints after she has told him it is over, painting as a distraction, or painting as a reward, or painting as a dramatization that she has moved on, but, by the time she finishes, she has called him or he has called her. Inhaling the heady odor of the drying paint, she weeps into the phone to say she wants to meet again. At other times, she begins to paint to build up momentum to tell him it is over, the painting a kind of mental conditioning, a signal for her to signal her lover that their affair must come to an end. It is perhaps the thick rich smell of the paint, the vapor of its evaporation, that is the trigger—canned inspiration. That perfume's endnote is the endnote of the affair. Or, perhaps, the end is signaled by the visual stimuli of blur, the blur the paint-mixer makes at the paint store as it mixes the cans—the cans vice-locked in place with the thumbscrews, plates, and springs. The electric motor whirs, the slurring glug of the liquid inside the cloud of can, that metallic blubbering blurring. Or there is the folding and the unfolding of the paint-splattered drop cloth with its sloppy archeological record of the past paintings, the drips and smears in stark contrast to the pristine walls whose color never really has time to age or dull or even fade. Sometimes the paint hasn't had time to dry, has barely even dried before she begins to mask out the window sills and doorjambs with the blue, blue masking tape whose sound, that long zipped ripping, also contributes to this ritual of change—the whole elaborate complex of her particular compulsion that the larger project, consciously and unconsciously, conspicuously represents. To mask. It is complicated. It has never been easy for her, the affair, and the energy expended in meeting, the anxiety of discovery, and the persistence of guilt—all of it goes into the walls regularly. Painting draws this thing to a close, and painting promises a new beginning. Clean slate. Eggshell finish, of course. And painting, the sheer act of painting, is a soothing contemplative repetitive exercise, an applied yoga of application, that allows her to meditate on the course of the affair, its ups and downs, her marriage, its lefts and rights. As she paints she eyes the various shades of aching grief, the tint of ecstatic pleasure. She paints with brush and roller. She stirs and stirs, watches the paint slide down the stick, drip, like paint, into the soup of this occasion's color. The drips drip, disturb the surface tension on the surface of the paint in the can. She knows, now, these four walls intimately. Here the slight buckle of the load-bearing, there a water stain that she never quite seals or covers. She's spackled again, patched the holes made by the picture hanging. The wall opposite the window warms differently than the wall with the window. Painting the four walls again brings her face to face with memories of painting these four walls before. In that corner she thought this, or along the floorboard, there, she thought that, and when she gets to those places again with this new paint she will remember what she was thinking two or three coats ago and remember remembering, just a coat before, what she was thinking and remembering about her thinking now all mapped on the wall, a location that coordinates with the wiring in the gray matter of her brain. Here around this outlet she thought of her thinking, thinking about her gray brain. She loads the brush—always a new brush—to begin again to paint the living room. The furniture pushed to the center of the room covered by the dappled drop cloths that form a kind of scale model of an idealized mountain range, its glacial folds falling to the floor covered by the new unspoiled ice-blue tarp.

MARBLEHEAD

32-V-2

It will be a gray this time, another gray. She is thinking this, this gray, even while her lover is finishing behind her. Her hands are flat against the wall, pushing the wall to push back against him as he pushes into her. She has already come. The wall in front of her is a gray. She can't be sure. There's a trick of the light in the room as the late afternoon shadows break across the surface before her eyes. She senses an unevenness, what seems to be another kind of shadow, a shadow of the drywall in the space between her spread arms, flexing, springing back against him. No amount of paint can disguise it, a sloppy application of the mud, that lack of sanding. Tomorrow she will look through the paint chips for the right gray. There are hundreds of chips, each tweaked to register the slight variation of brightness, intensity, saturation. After she has been with him, she likes to paint the living room of her house. She has lost count of the number of times she has painted the living room. She has been seeing him a dozen years. There must be a dozen dozens of layers of paint, a gross of layers. How many layers will it take to contract the volume of the room, to build up, to fill in the in of the room? She likes to stay with the neutral colors, the whites and all the off-whites, the grays, and the other grays. Other colors bleed through the new paint, taking too long to cover, needing too many extra coats to cover. The paint's been rolled on here in this room or maybe sprayed. He is moving faster and his hands have left her breasts and moved to her hips. And in the mix, she thinks she sees, some sparkle, a mica fleck. At least it isn't paper with its patterns and seams. Her husband never asks why she paints the living room over and over. He compliments her on the room once it is done as she washes the brushes in the sink, asks her if he can move back the furniture.

Her lover likes to make love to her after she has made love to her husband. She doesn't ask him why. The color of come, she thinks, is the color of this wall, the wall she is looking at as her lover finishes behind her, inside her. It lacks the pearlescence of semen though, cloudy nacreous mix of light and its reflection, the wet paint sheen that encapsulates the flat depthless milt beneath the shiny marble glass skin. She likes to watch it dry. The come. The paint too. She sits for hours in the living room, after she's finished painting it once again, to watch it take on its color, steep and deepen. Sand. Stone. Marble. Mountain. She imagines that a woman somewhere thinks of the names for all the grays, a kind of poetry. Now, he tells her when he is about to, stops, holds still, then does, waits, waits, waits then slides out of her. She lunges away, disconnects, no longer up on her toes, collapses forward, falls onto the wall as if the wall emits its own gravitational pull. She's drawn in, adheres. She presses her whole body along the wall, flattens herself against it, wants to pass right through it into the next room. She turns her head to the side to feel its cool color, feel its pallor, the pigment rub off on her breasts, her belly and thighs, her flushed cheek.

MT. MCKINLEY

32-V-3

v

At the first session of each new Congress the representative from President McKinley's home district in Ohio rises to take the floor and introduces legislation to retain the mountain's appellation, preventing it from being renamed Denali for another two years. The measure is accompanied by additional remarks concerning the mountain to be read into the record.

v

The mountain's gray silhouette indicates two major summits, twin peaks, the southern one the highest, and reveals a massif with a melodramatic ridgeline of lesser ascending and descending slopes out of which flow four major glaciers, variations of the same denouement.

v

On a ridge near the summit of Denali, the Japan Alpine Club has established a meteorological observatory that was donated to The University of Alaska. The weather station is one of only two such installations in the world located above 18,000 feet. Japanese newlyweds consummate their marriages at lodges in the shadow of Denali as the northern lights, the aurora borealis, unfold overhead, in the belief that such conditions are fortuitous for the resulting pregnancies as well as therapeutic for those who have been unable, until now, to conceive.

v

Meanwhile, it is the spring solstice in Alaska. Each succeeding twenty-four-hour period sees an additional five minutes of sunlight added to the day. As the northern hemisphere begins to tip toward the sun in spring, shadows lengthen in the folds found on the distant mountain. The serrated ridge of Denali holds onto the increasing sunlight the longest, an incision of the lengthening shadow etched next to the crest line, rising up to the cloudless sky. The sharply defined horizon tilts south, soon to deny, by summer, the sun's sunset.

THE EDGE OF NIGHT

32-V-4

She changes out of her painting clothes—a plaid flannel shirt and actual white (well, once they were white) cut-off-at-the-knees painter's pants—and catches herself in the mirror, pasted together in broad fields of skin. The parts of her body that were exposed as she painted, her hands and arms, her face and hair, her lower legs, are splotched with gray paint. Dried, the paint has taken on the texture of the pores beneath it, scaled and creased and puckered where it has splashed on her elastic, sliding, scaling skin. Her skin is like the skin old paint generates when left in an old can, a pudding's skin, the color and the medium separating beneath the rubbery suspended crust at the top, a fossil liquid. She rubs off what she can, the fine hair of her forearms snagging in the crumbs of erased paint. In the failing light, her body in the mirror reflects swathes of gray planes, swatches of gray strokes. A sheet of gray on her belly folds under at a jutting hipbone. The tops of her thighs race down her legs, V to the bright dollops of her knees. Her collarbones are cut-out scallops, sloughed epaulets of contracting light. She's contracting too, flattening, an illusion. Over her shoulder, her shoulder blade fans out, ribbed with the weak pattern the window's blind projects. The weakening available light seeps in in the dusk. Paint on her skin picks up what's left of the light, lights up what gloss there is, the speckled constellation along the arm, a milky way of milky paint along the shin. Her forehead is a fresco, a wall, a white-washed wall. Her left cheek has been redrawn, is disconnected from her face, slides down her chin. It is a kind of careless camouflage, this sloppy paint splatter in the dark. She is becoming hard to see. She can't even see herself. She is breaking up, broken up, in bits. She has left her lover again. In the shower, the paint dissolves, peels. It is water-based. She scrubs, likes the feeling, the exfoliation, flaying the same paint that in the living room downstairs is shrinking microns as it dries, to fit a new thin skim on the walls. For a long time she had thought that the Dutch Boy of the paint was the same Dutch boy of legend who patches a dam with his finger, and she wondered what that had to do with paint. But she looked closely at Dutch Boy's Dutch boy on the can. He sits there topped with the hat and bobbed haircut, in the blousy blouse and blousy coveralls, the wooden shoes, holding up a loaded paintbrush like a torch. She supposes it is in a Flemish style, this Dutch Boy, all light and shadow. A brown study. In the shower, she imagines she is the girl on the salt box in the rain, the salt girl running as the paint begins to run. With her finger, she draws through the beads of water adhering to the tiles of the shower stall. As the finger moves, the beads come together, streak and smear, follow the gesture she paints. She pictures a picture of a brushstroke made up of brushstrokes. The swipes of water shatter back into quivering beads. The shower steams. She is made of salt or she is made of the color of salt and she dissolves and is dissolving in the rain, drains down the drain. The Dutch Boy is painting, painting the long wall of the dike that divides the land from the Zuiderzee, the Zuiderzee that disappears in the Dutch distance. And now the thin layer of soap she has applied to her body the color of the color of—but in this light it is hard to tell its color. It begins to peel in sheets as well. It runs. And as it drains, it assumes the spiral habit it has as it disappears in the shadows at her feet. She thinks: it will be that thin layer of paint that holds back that wall of all that water waiting to find its own true straight level.

Four in Hand

I have always tied my father's ties. At the time I started tying my father's ties, wide ones were in style. My father bought big wide ones in woolly fabrics, ones with length. He liked the knobby triangle of the Windsor knot. That's what he had me tie. It was like a fist at his throat. After I tied the tie, I slid the knot down along the narrow end, leaving it knotted, making a loop big enough to slip over my head. I gave the tie to my father. This went on for years. It went on until the day my father died. I learned to tie the ties from following the diagrams printed on a pamphlet I got at the department store where my father bought the ties. "Dad," I said, "this is easy. Just look into the mirror and follow the directions." He directed me to hang the tied ties on a hook in his closet. I'd tie three or four of them at a time. This wasn't good for the ties. It ruined them to leave them knotted like that. The Windsor was in fashion when I started tying my father's ties, a big wad of cloth at his throat. Then that look went out of fashion, and the tie widths and fabric changed. But then ties got wider once more, and my father looked okay again.

Bow

I myself wear a bowtie when I wear a tie at all. Most people think the bowtie is hard to tie, but it's not. It is the same knot everyone knows and uses when tying a shoelace. It's just in a different place. Under your chin. I told my father that. He watched me tie a knot in the mirror. I poked one bow through the loose knot. He had taught me how to tie my shoes. He used his thumb to make the loop. My favorite part of tying a bowtie is holding the loops and the two unlooped ends at the same time, drawing the knot tight in the middle. And I like how easily it falls apart when you untie it simply by pulling one end. I thought I would wear one when we buried my father, but I thought better of it and went with a half Windsor, a neat and subdued knot.

HALF WINDSOR

In the mail, I got boxes of untied ties. Sometimes these were my father's new purchases, but, more often, they were gifts I had given him or ties I had tied years ago for him that had come untied somehow and that he needed retied. Those ties were wrecked with wrinkles, and when I tied them, I could never tie them in such a way that the creases fell and crimped where they had before. After my father died, I undid the lot of these same ties, ironed the ones I could, and gave them to the Salvation Army. Once he called in a panic. He had a new tie he needed to tie. I was a thousand miles away. So I looked in a mirror and tied a tie talking to him while he followed along. My head and shoulder squeezed the phone to my ear, my neck craned. He followed along on the other end of the line. It was hard. I could hear the silk slapping the phone's mouthpiece. I could hear him breathing. I thought a half Windsor would work, depleted as it is of wrapping and tucking. My hands moved by themselves at my throat. I heard my voice and I heard my father's voice repeating what I was saying in the silence between the words I was saying.

FOUR IN HAND

"I can't do it," he said at last. And he never would learn, he said. I told him it was easy, especially the four in hand. Just wrap it around and tuck it back up, under, and through. That is what I tied when I tied the tie he wore in his coffin. The tie was new and polyester. It will last forever, I thought. The department store pamphlet I have with directions for tying the different knots said that the four in hand was popularized by King Edward the VII. Think of that. I watched my father sometimes as he slipped a tied tie over his head. It ruins the ties to keep them tied. He slid the knot up the narrow end. He folded down his collar and flicked his fingers through his hair to fluff it up. He turned to me, and I straightened the knot snug at the collar. For a second, I pressed my hand flat on his starched chest beneath the two ends of the tie and made sure it all looked all right.

Antebellum

The President's Mansion

The story goes that the president's wife, brandishing a broom
on the veranda, shooed away elements of the Iowa Cavalry sent
to burn the college. The event is re-enacted each fall. The dra-
goons slump in their saddles, exhausted by the hard ride and
the day's fighting. They watch a woman race back and forth
on the porch above them like a carved figure wound up inside
a cuckoo clock bursting from its doors on the hour, while their
mounts, nearly blown, shit on the trampled flower beds in the
formal gardens.

Gorgas Hall

They'll tell you that back then this brick building was the college commissary, and it was saved because the Yankees were
hungry and thirsty after burning the rest of the college. Today,
it's used mainly as a venue for fancy weddings where the young
women in the bridal parties wear the antique hoopskirts and
crinolines of the time before the war. Around back, next to the
ongoing archaeological excavation, the wood privy is still in-
tact, or has been reconstructed exactly, and the students working the site watch as a bride fits herself and her organdy train
into the tiny neoclassical house beneath the magnolia.

The Old Observatory

That night, the flames from the college still burning brightly made any star in the sky impossible to see. The guidon bearer, bivouacked there, curried his horse beneath the cracked copper dome where the telescope, long before scrapped and melted for its metal, once stood. Even then, the college kept a little museum of curiosities there. The corporal ended up claiming as contraband a shard of iron like a chunk of grapeshot shrapnel that had, one night before the war, fallen from a very starry sky, striking a house in Pickens County and lodging, finally, in the headboard of the owner's bed while the owner and his wife lay there staring up at the ceiling.

The Little Round House

Legend has it that this Gothic octagon was the only building of any military value at the college. It was built as a guardhouse and lookout and seems, considering the destruction, to have failed miserably in both those roles. The federal troops used it as a surgery where today, still, a hand-lettered sign indicates the bloodstains of a half dozen or so hurried amputations. From the roof, the signal corps tethered one of their new balloons, which floated above the smoldering ground for weeks, its observer gazing over the green horizon for relief or reinforcements which, in both cases, failed to materialize.

Four Found Postcard Captions

THE WADSWORTH-LONGFELLOW HOUSE

Portland, Maine

1.

This most historic house in the State was built in 1785 by Major General Peleg Wadsworth, grandfather of the famous poet Henry Wadsworth Longfellow, who spent much of his life here.

2.

The Boy's Room was occupied by all the Longfellow boys at various times. Here the Poet wrote his first poem. Here also is the old trundle bed and the scarred school desk.

3.

The Rainy Day Room. Its chief interest is in the old desk on which the Poet wrote, in 1841, "The Rainy Day." "It rains, and the wind is never weary."

4.

The Guest Room of the house contains the four-poster bed and rocking chairs of the General's wife, Elizabeth. To this room the Poet brought his bride, and here, later, the Poet's father died.

Quadratic

A

That year, Mr. Clark taught four sections of high school alge-
bra. The classes met the first four periods of the day, finishing
up before we juniors, who took the course, went to lunch in the
basement cafeteria. Pretty early in the semester we noticed
Mr. Clark, who is dead now, had developed a persistent and
pervasive habit of speech.

Some of us were also taking speech and debate. The teacher
there, Mr. Schultz, would have us do what he called a clapping
speech. The clapping speech was meant to illuminate the little
things we all say and do without thinking. Like saying "um" or
"you know" or looking up at the ceiling when you are trying
to think of the next word or licking your lips during the pauses
between words in your prepared text. Mr. Schultz listened to
us give a speech—mine was on "Harvesting the Riches of the
Sea"—and while you were talking, he picked out a particular tic
you were repeating—mine was fiddling with a shirt button, I
think. And then he clapped his hands together, startlingly loud.
You'd jump, but you would have to go on giving your speech,
all the time trying to figure out what it was you were doing.

Mr. Clark said "for it" at the end of his sentences. He did it
so many times that you would be clapping all the time if he was
giving a clapping speech. He didn't seem to notice. The "for
it" was kind of a vestigial phrase. "This is what you would do
for it." It got worse as the semester wore on, to the point where

he would chalk out an equation on the board, turn back to the class, and say simply "for it," pointing at the conclusion, the punctuation of some sentence he was speaking to himself. And then he began saying "for it, for it," sending my classmates, who had begun counting the number of for its, into fits of laughter. "Hey, what's so funny, for it?" he asked. It was something. He retired the next year.

B

All the classes were driven to distraction by this. Everyone was keeping track. We would compare figures at lunch. Mark Maxwell organized the effort and designated an official counter for each class. At lunch each day, he posted the final tally on the cafeteria bulletin board—the aggregate numbers, the total daily accumulation. He kept running charts, the bars of the graphs in different colors, of the trends and averages, the correlation with the days of the week and the weather. There was a special category for the double for it and a place for a triple for it that never did come.

Mr. Clark commented often on our attentiveness. We hung on to his every word. We waited through his long string of explanations and proofs about squares and their roots to get to the periodic moment where he would conclude with a for it. We watched the scorekeeper in our class make another hash mark in his notebook. We looked for patterns at lunch. Did the frequency diminish over time? Increase? Some tried to cook the books, asking questions about the material designed to have Mr. Clark reflect meditatively. This made it all the more likely he would utter the formula.

X

Mr. Clark gave an assignment to create our own quadratic equations. We all used i and t as variables. At the board, Mr. Clark reduced and canceled our redundant integers, our camouflage of multiples. He drew the final = and solved for x. The answer was always the same: $x=4it$. He tapped the chalk on the board a couple of times, dotting the i, and turned to us triumphantly, "The solution is four *eye tee*, for it." We applauded.

c

We didn't learn a thing, of course, about quadratics. It's true what they say about high school math. I never needed it in life after high school. I am writing this, years later, on graph paper I found lying around. I use it to keep the lines of my handwriting more or less level. I thought I would jot down this memory before it got away from me. I like filling in the spaces of the grid, one letter to a square, a word or two or three in each ten-by-ten box of squares. I am doing this early in the morning before my kids wake up. They find pretty much everything I do now hard to understand.

Four Men in Uniform

MEAT

Because I could play baseball, I never went to Korea.

I was standing on the dock in San Francisco with my entire company. We stood at parade rest, wearing helmets, loaded down with winter and summer gear. We were ready to embark. My name was called. I remember saying excuse me to the men in rank as I tried to get by with my equipment. Then I sat on my duffel and watched them file aboard, bumping up the side of the ship, the cables flexing. There was rust in the bilge. I could hear the water below me. Sailors laughed way over my head. It only took a few hours. There were some people there to wave good-bye, though not for the soldiers since our shipping out was something secret.

Nothing was ever said. I was transferred to another unit where all the troops were baseball players. I played second base on the Third Army team. I batted seventh and bunted a lot. We traveled by train from one base to another in Texas, Georgia, and on up into New Jersey for the summer. We had a few cars to ourselves including a parlor with an open platform. The rest of the train was made up of reefers full of frozen meat. The train was aluminum and streamlined. We could stand in the vestibules, or in the open doorway of the baggage car where we kept the bags of bats and balls and the pinstriped uniforms hung on rods, and look out over the pink flat deserts. There wouldn't be a cinder from the engine, the train's wheels a blur.

You would see up ahead on the slow curves the white smoke of the whistle trailing back over the silver boxcars of meat, and then you would hear the whistle. Some cars still needed to be iced, so we'd stop in sad little towns, play catch and pepper while the blocks melted in the sun and the sawdust turned dark and clotty on the platform. We'd hit long fly balls to the local kids who hung around. We left them broken bats to nail and tape.

The meat was our duty. It was what we said we did even though everyone knew we played baseball. The Army wanted us to use frozen meat instead of fresh. We ran the tests in messes to see if the men could tell the difference. We stood by the garbage cans and took the plates to scrape and separate the scraps of meat to weigh for waste. A red plate meant the meat was fresh. The bone, the chewed gristle, the fat. I picked it out of the cold peas and potatoes. Sometimes whole pieces would come back, gray and hard. The gravy had to be wiped off before the meat went on the scale. Those halls were huge, with thousands of men hunched over the long tables eating. We stood by watching, waiting to do our job.

It made no difference, fresh or frozen, to the men. This pleased the Army. Things were changing. Surplus from the war was being given to the UN for the action in Korea. There were new kinds of boots and rifles. Back then every camp still had walk-in lockers. The sides of meat hung on racks. The cold blew through you. Blue inspection stamps bled into the yellow fat of the carcasses. All gone now. That's what I did in the service.

But the baseball didn't change. The ball still found my glove. There were the old rituals at home. I rubbed my hands in the dirt, then wiped them on my pants, took the bat and rapped it on the plate. The pitch that followed always took me by surprise—hard and high, breaking away. The pitcher spun the ball like a dial on a safe. And trains still sound the same when they run through this town. At night, one will shake our house (we live near an overpass) and I can't go back to sleep. I'll count the men who walked up that gangway to the ship. The train wheels squeal and sing. It might as well be hauling the cargo of my dreams.

DISH NIGHT

Every Wednesday was Dish Night at the Wells Theatre. And it worked, because she was there week in and week out. She sat through the movie to get her white bone china. A saucer. A cup. The ushers stood on chairs by the doors and reached into the big wooden crates. There was straw all over the floor of the lobby and balls of newspaper from strange cities. I knew she was the girl for me. I'd walk her home. She'd hug the dish to her chest. The streetlights would be on and the moon behind the trees. She'd talk about collecting enough pieces for our family of eight. "Oh, it's everyday and I know it," she'd say, holding it at arm's length. "They're so modern and simple and something we'll have a long time after we forget about the movies."

I forget just what happened then. She heard about Pearl Harbor at a Sunday matinee. They stopped the movie, and a man came out on stage. The blue stage lights flooded the gold curtain. It was dark in there, but outside it was bright and cold. They didn't finish the show. Business would pick up then, and the Wells Theatre wouldn't need a Dish Night to bring the people in. The one we had gone to the week before was the last one ever, and we hadn't known it. The gravy boat looked like a slipper. I went to the war, to Europe, where she wrote to me on lined school paper and never failed to mention we were a few pieces shy of the full set.

This would be the movie of my life, this walking home under the moon from a movie with a girl holding a dinner plate under her arm like a book. I believed this is what I was fighting for. Everywhere in Europe I saw broken pieces of crockery. In the farmhouses, the cafés. Along the roads were drifts of smashed china. On a beach, in the sand where I was crawling, I found a shard of it the sea washed in, all smooth with blue veins of a pattern.

I came home and washed the dishes every night, and she stacked them away, bowls nesting on bowls as if we were moving the next day.

The green field is covered with tables. The sky is huge and spread with clouds. The pickup trucks and wagons are backed in close to each table so that people can sit on the lowered tailgates. On the tables are thousands of dishes. She walks ahead of me. Picks up a cup, then sets it down again. A plate. She runs her finger around a rim. The green field rises slightly as we walk, all the places set at the tables. She hopes she will find someone else who saw the movies she saw on Dish Night. The theater was filled with people. I was there. We do this every Sunday after church.

WHAT I SEE

I was killing time at the ranger station in West Glacier, twirling the postcard racks by the door. There was an old one of some teenagers around a campfire near Swift Current Lake. They have on dude ranch clothes, indigo jeans with the legs rolled into wide cuffs. The boys have flattops. There is a ukulele. One girl, staring into the fire, wears saddle shoes. The colors are old colors, from the time women all wore red lipstick. Beyond the steel blue lake the white glaciers are smearing down the mountainsides. I saw the glaciers even though it was night in the card. They gave off their own light. No one ever bought this card, not even as a joke. I was looking at this card when a woman walked in with her son. They mounted the stair above the model of the park. The models of the mountains were like piles of green and brown laundry, the glaciers sheets. The lakes were blue plastic. A red ribbon stood for the Going to the Sun Highway. It all looked manageable. The mother pointed. In the corner was the little house. You are here. She said to me then: Is there any place we can go to overlook the grizzlies?

This year the wolves have moved back into the park. And number 23 had mauled a camper, his third this year, but didn't kill her. Children walk through the station with bells on their feet. When the wind is right you can hear the songs drifting in from the higher trails. We were told more people would be here this season because of the way the world has turned. There are too many people here for this place ever to be wild wild.

The cable's come as far as Cutbank. I rent a room in town my days off and watch the old movies they've juiced up with color. But the colors are as pale as an old rug, like they've already faded from old age. Now the blue sky outside looks manufactured, transported here from the other side of the mountain, its own conveyer belt. A bolt of dyed cloth. It drips with color.

And my shorts here are khaki, which is Urdu for the word *dirt*. Sometimes my eyes hurt from seeing the situation so clearly. Every ten minutes or so I hear the ice tumble in the machine out on the breezeway. Then the condenser kicks on. Beyond the hot tableland I can see the five white fingers of the glacier.

All of what I know about the world worms its way to me from Atlanta. The message is to stay put. They have a park in Atlanta. In it is the Cyclorama, a huge picture with no edges. The battle of Atlanta is everywhere. The painting keeps wrapping around me so that even out of the corner of my eyes I see nothing but the smoke and the smoky bodies falling about me. Atlanta is a mustard yellow in the distance. Sherman rides up in front of me. The battle ends and it begins again. I climb out of the painting through a hole in the floor. There is no place to overlook it. In the basement of the building is the famous steam locomotive The General. I see Ted Turner has just painted that movie.

And it strikes me now that I looked like Buster Keaton, my campaign hat tilted like his hat, as I stood next to King on the memorial steps. The monument behind us was white, even its shadows. King's suit had a sheen like feathers or skin. The white shirts glowed. Everyone wore white shirts except for my khaki, because color hadn't been invented yet. The Muslims wore white. Their caps were white. And the crowd spilling down the steps looked like marble in white to stay cool. It was swampy near the river. They showed the speech around his birthday. I am always there, a ghost over his left shoulder. I was so young. I look as if nothing could surprise me. A ranger look. It always surprises me now. Now I know how it all came out, what happened to that man. I look like a statue. King flickers. I kept him in the corner of my eye. I watched the crowd. What I see is me seeing. I don't see what is coming. When they color it they will get the color of my eyes wrong.

In the window of the motel, I watch the day move. I have made a career with Interior. The range is being painted over by a deep blue sky. The glacier grips the mountaintop and then lets go to form a cloud. Then everything just goes.

The Teak Wood Deck of the USS *Indiana*

I stabbed a man in Zulu. It had to do with a woman. I remember it was a pearled penknife I'd got from a garage. I'd used it for whittling, and the letters were wearing off. It broke off in his thigh and nicked the bone. It must have hurt like hell.

I did the time in Michigan City in the metal shop where I would brush on flux and other men would solder. Smoke would be going up all over the room. They made the denim clothes right there in the prison. The pants were as sharp as the sheet metal we were folding into dustpans and flour scoops. It was like I was a paper doll and they'd put the jacket on me by creasing the tabs over my shoulders. And the stuff never seemed to soften up but came back from the laundry shrunk and rumpled and just as stiff, until the one time when all the starch would be gone and your clothes were rags and you got some new.

There was a man in there building a ship. When I first saw it, he had just laid down the keel and the hull looked like a shiny new coffin. This guy was in for life, and he kept busy building a model of a battleship, the USS *Indiana*. He had hammered rejected license plates, flattened the numbers out. He'd fold and hammer. In the corner of the shop he'd pinned up the plans, a blue ship floating on the white paper. He had models made from balsa, the ribs showing through in parts. He had these molds of parts we would use for casting, these jigs and dies. His tools were blades and snips. The antennae in the model were the needles he used to sew the tiny flags. The ship was 1/48th the size of the real thing, as big as a canoe. The men who walked the deck had heads the size of peas. He painted each face differently, applied the ratings on their blue sleeves. He told me stories about each man frozen there on the bridge, here tucking into a turret, here popping out of a hatchway. He showed me letters from the same men. He had sent samples of the paint he had mixed to the men who had actually scraped and painted the real ship, asking if this was anywhere near. He knew the hour, the minute, of the day his ship was sailing, the moment he was modeling.

But this was years later. At first I saw the hull. I saw the pile of rivets he collected from the temples of old eyeglasses. He collected spools for depth charges, straws for gun barrels, window screen for the radar. He collected scraps from the floor of the shop and stockpiled them near the ship. Toothpicks, thimbles, bars of soap, gum wrappers. Lifesavers that were Lifesavers, the candy, caps from tubes for valves and knobs, pins for shell casings. Everything was something else.

Soon after he started building the ship he knew soon enough he'd finish too soon. So he went back and made each part more detailed, the guns and funnels, then stopped again and made even the parts of parts. The pistons in the engines, lightbulbs in the sockets.

Some men do this kind of thing. I whittled, but I took a stick down to nothing. I watched the black knots of the branches under the bark grow smaller with each smooth strip until they finally disappeared. Maybe I'd sharpen the stick, but that got old. Finally I got down to shavings thin like the evening paper at my feet. That was what I was after. Strip things so fine that suddenly nothing is there but the edge of the knife and the first layer of skin over my knuckle.

One of the anchors of the real battleship is on the lawn of the Memorial Coliseum in Fort Wayne. The anchor is gray and as big as a house. I took my then wife to see it. We looked around that state for the other one but only found deck guns on lawns of the VFW, a whole battery at the football stadium near the university. In other towns, scrap had been melted and turned into statues of sailors looking up and tiny ships plowing through lead waves.

The deck of the model was the only real thing. He said the wood was salvaged from the deck of the real ship. A guard brought him a plank of it. He let me plane it, strip the varnish and splinter it into boards. A smell still rose from it of pitch, maybe the sea. And I didn't want to stop. I've seen other pieces of the deck since then, in junior high schools where it's been made into plaques for good citizens. The wood is beautiful. The metal plates engraved with names and dates are bolted on, and near the bottom is another smaller plate that says this wood is from the deck of the battleship. It is like a piece of the True Cross. And that is why I came to the capitol in Indianapolis to see the governor's desk. I heard it was made from the teakwood deck of the USS *Indiana*.

So imagine my surprise when in the rotunda of the building I find the finished model of the ship in a glass case with a little legend about the prisoner in Michigan City. He'd finished it before he died. The porthole windows were cellophane cut from cigarette packs. The signal flags spelled out his name. It was painted that spooky gray, the color between the sea and sky, and from the stern a blue airplane was actually taking off and had already climbed above the gleaming deck where a few seamen waved.

I felt sad for that con. He spent his life building this. He never got it right. It wasn't big enough or something.

I walked right into the governor's office. I'm a taxpayer. And the lady told me he wasn't there, but I told her I was more interested in the desk. So she let me in. "It's beautiful, isn't it?" she said, opening the curtains for the light that skidded across the top cut in the shape of the state. One edge was pretty straight and the other, where the river ran, looked as if it had melted like a piece of butter into toast. I ran my hand along the length of it, felt how smooth it was—the grain runs north and south—when the governor walked in with his state trooper.

"It's something," he said. He's a Republican. The trooper followed and stood behind him. "It has its own light."

The trooper wore a sea blue uniform with sky blue patches

at the shoulders and the cuff. Belts hung all over him. Stripes and creases ran down his legs. Braids and chains. The pants were wool. He watched me. And I looked at him.

Jesus, you've got to love a man in uniform.

I stepped up to the desk and saw my face and the shadow of my body deep inside the swirling wood. I took my finger and pointed to the spot not far from Zulu where I knifed a man and said, "Right there." I pushed hard with my nail. "That's where I was born."

Board Games

He was Grandpa Shaker because he shook, and when he died
he stopped shaking. My great grandpa Shaker lived with his
daughter Mary, my great aunt, until the day he died. I kept him
company.

We played two-handed Rook with two dummy hands on a
card table set up in the driveway during the summer. He had a
glass straw that jangled against the ceramic mug. He breathed
the milky coffee in and out, the straw clanking, while I turned
over the cards. I could never understand the dummy hands and
would have rather been playing four-handed hands with my
friends in the park. In the park then, they let you play Rook
because the four suits were colors—red, blue, green, black—
instead of the hearts, clubs, diamonds, and spades that were for-
bidden because those suits were more real, I guess, and would
promote gambling, poker among the kids. The Park Police actually checked the games, checked the cards.

The parks had pavilions that were staffed, and there on picnic tables, I played pickup games of box hockey, kalah, chess
and checkers, and Rook that got played like poker anyway in
secret.

As a kid, Shaker came north and worked for the Pennsylvania Railroad as a trackwalker. That was before my time and
before he shook. We played euchre too at the table with another pair of ghosts partnering with us. Every hand you shot

the moon. I never won. And we never talked.

When he walked track he walked from the Baker Street station east until he met the trackwalker coming from New Haven, and then he would turn around and walk back downtown, pass the station, out west toward Roanoke, and then turn back again. He did that twice a day every day for years. He looked at the spikes and cleats and ties and rail. He carried a pike and a mallet just in case, and some extra hardware in his pocket—date nails, pliers, joint bolts, and wire for the interlocking circuit. As he walked, he played a game with himself, counted ties, but his stride never matched the distance between the sleepers. There was oil and sand on the ballast and the rotting bodies of killed things with the clouds of flies bisected by the rails.

Monopoly was impossible outside. The wind stripped away the flimsy money, so we played it inside on rainy days and in the winter after school. We never played the rule that said you had to buy the property you landed on. Shaker liked to shake the dice and move around the board, avoiding jail and buying nothing. Doubles let you shake again. We had two dummy hands—the battleship and flat-stamped cannon—that moved from square to square as well. His hand shooed the lead steam engine around the board, from square to square, and during my turn Shaker nudged the glass straw between his lips, rattling like a machine. With his other hand, he tried to tap the accumulating money into neat stacks of color, but he only ended up shuffling denominations all together into one big pastel pile. Sooner or later, my mother came to get me and took me home. I waved good-bye. And he waved back with one hand shaking and the other hand shaking, shaking the dice for another roll, his turn, now, always next, and me, now, just an absent hand.

We rode backwards on the short line from Pirgos to the ruins at Olympia along a stub-end track with no place to turn around. The dumpy station disappeared behind us. All of Pirgos was a ruin, ruined by earthquakes every other year or so. What remained were concrete boxes sprouting rusting rebar on the spoiled roofs. In the waiting room there, we played backgammon in the dust and gloom and ate grilled cheese pies. The stationmaster made clumsy passes at the Swedish students, insisted each should wear his hat while he sang the island songs of Yanni Parios playing too loud on the mistuned radio.

We were going in reverse to Olympia. The cars were blue, of course, and on the curves we could see behind us the black donkey engine pushing us along at a walking pace. Olympia was filled with motor coaches hauling tours that included breakfasts each morning of the trip. So dawn found us at the site before the crowds finished their *portokalada* as the guards, who spend the night onsite, were just waking up and stowing their bedding near the gate.

The place was deserted. Everyone at breakfast. The stones on the ground were where they tumbled, after some other earthquake, into the mudflats the river left behind when it was shaken out of its course. In the middle of what was left of a temple, a tiny Greek church had been plopped down a few centuries ago and was the only thing left standing in the precinct, a token. Falling from the eaves and windowsills, swallows circled above a red tiled roof and then skipped out over the field of debris, the stumps of fallen fluted column drums, the marble just beginning to catch the light.

B&O

I let him play at the piano—my niece's boy, I had no sons—
when I visited my sisters in Garrett. I drank iced tea with my
sisters in the kitchen and told them jokes and shot the breeze to
distract them from thinking about the kid in the parlor, noo-
dling discordant, off-key keys on the out-of-tune upright Kim-
ball. Nobody there plays. Everything in the parlor could break,
the crystal and the porcelain, the glass and the wood. Soon,
when my sisters couldn't sit still any longer, they flew past me
to the parlor and made the boy sit still on the davenport. They
gave him the cigar box filled with the postage stamp–sized re-
ceipts the paperboy left after he collected for the week of whatever. The tiny dates were printed on each—there were a lot of
weeks. They wanted him to sort the bits of paper for them for
no reason.

I got him to come up from Fort Wayne telling him we would
look at the old steam engines. The B&O has a roundhouse in
Garrett, a Division Point shop, and now he winds up here, trying not to move. I wanted company and an excuse to leave after
I had performed my obligation to my sisters—three of them—
who still live in the family place not that far from the main line.

I worked nights in the power plant in Fort Wayne, City
Light and Power. I managed steam mostly, moved it from
one turbine to the next, tapped it from the boilers, vented it
outside, blew the whistle at times of my choosing. The cold
engines of the B&O, black and big as buildings, were being
scrapped, and a couple guys I knew from high school let us
watch them disconnect the giant steel shafts from the driving
wheels, knocking the locking bolts loose with a metal sledge
that drew sparks. They stripped the copper wire clean, disconnected the bells and running lights. I showed the kid the platform on the gap-toothed pilot where the firemen of old would
leap from to throw switches out ahead of the panting, drifting

engines slowly catching up. He jumped up on the step, then on and off for a time, and climbed the catwalk the rest of the way to the cab. The firebox was choked with ashes, and the stuffing from the engineer's seat was leaking desiccated foam rubber sand on the tread plate floor. There were twenty some hulks in the dingy house. The big window wall, gritty with old smoke, filtered the weak light onto the dirt floor sown with cinder.

Driving home, we went under the viaduct labeled with the drumhead logo of the B&O, the capitol dome in the blue circle. I asked him if he could name the thirteen great states the railroad connected to the nation. That took some time, and I was happy when he gave up because I could only count a dozen in my head. To keep him busy we played I Spy and I Went to My Grandmother's House. I showed him the high tension towers and told him those wires there go all the way to the power plant where I work. "It's all connected."

In his pockets were chunks of metal and scrap he salvaged from the roundhouse—rusted rivets and wing nuts, amber glass, a brass toggle, a lump of coal. Later, back home, he arranged the pieces over and over again on the cement squares of the driveway. He was a strange kid. He'd stay busy for hours turning the geared wheel within the geared wheel that turned the grindstone I had bolted to the workbench in the garage. He said he liked to see how they, the teeth he meant, fit together to make it all go.

READING

It opens like a book, made of tin, and all the tiles, each printed with a single letter and its parasitic subscript, are magnets that cling to the grid so that, later, when I get mad about all the words I do not know or could not guess or cannot remember, I can't toss the board over, spilling the tiles and scrambling that game's particular accumulating network of cross-words. It is a travel edition. The train I am traveling in is yawing, and this stretch of old rail still wields unwelded joints. The car skips and shutters. The compartment's above a six-wheeled truck that transmits the stammer through the old heavy metal. One reading light falls on the open game with its sticky scales of letters. The other reading light falls over her shoulder, kicking up dust in the beam, to light on the book she is reading, reading while I take my turn.

I have drawn all vowels, it seems, and most of those are Os. There is a moon outside I can see through the faint reflection of my face in the smeared window, and I can see what look like scattered cattle, black and white, lolling in the gloaming. But here before me, there isn't a tail end of an M on the board to let me couple on an O or two.

I watch her read. Her eyes scan a rhythm that seems to syncopate with the backbeat of the train's. She is reading a travel book. There are no Bs or Ks, no book or look or kook, to hook onto either end. No boo. A travel book about Greece I think—a blue train circling the Peloponnesus, the cog railway gearing up a gorge to Kalavrita.

Then, it happens. The moment when a word like *the* stops being *the*, the the-ness goes out of it. It's all Greek then. I can't make *this* or *that* mean anymore. That *that* will always stop me in my tracks as I read, coming upon this word *this* or this *the* or that *the*, some strange train wreck of letters, everything sprung, Sherman's twisted bowties knotted with the overheated rails.

That's the way this game always feels to me. This impossibility that out of sheer arrangement came sense.

This is the point in the game I would usually hurl the cardboard board across the room, wooden tiles flying, but this particular travel edition has unified its fields of forces—strong, weak, magnetic, gravity—the four black engines of the universe. Things attract, stick, adhere, bond. I'll have to pass. She keeps on reading. She's in a carriage crossing the canal at Corinth, and she is here in some dark territory of Pennsylvania. The train's wheels, those Os, roll over the rail, a dime-sized connection, almost without friction. The whistle yodels an ordinary echo. Echo. Expanding rings of sound waver and warble.

Ordinary is ordinary again. I look at the board of crisscrossing letters, words, sentences, messages. The language chugs. This stands for this, I see. And this stands for this. And this for this. And this.

The First Four Deaths in My High School Class

Steve Huber

died in Randy Neath's swimming pool. He was electrocuted. A short in the wiring of the built-in lights. This happened years before we went to high school, but we think of him as part of the class. At the reunions, he is always listed as one of the dead on the memorial page of the program. Randy graduated. We talked about Steve at the last reunion. He played guard on my PAL basketball team. Randy's hair is still red, and he still lives in his parents' house. In the summers, he swims in the same pool where the accident happened.

Holly Love

died after she was out of high school and married. She might even have had a child by then. She was a high school teacher. Foreign languages. It was something sudden, something in her brain or in her heart, a clot or embolism. She had been in my class in grade school, where she was a lieutenant on the safety patrol. Her job had been to raise and lower the flag every school day. Her best friend growing up was Sheryl Faulkner, a neighbor, who went to Queen of Angels. Holly married Sheryl's brother. Sheryl's husband, Don Krouse, died in a car wreck on a county road. He was our age and would have been in our class, but he went to the Catholic high school instead.

Jerry Kirkpatrick

died with AIDS, but he killed himself before the disease killed him. A gun. We had talked on the phone only a month before he died. This was after college, and he was living, then, in Atlanta. When I called, he was in the middle of refinishing a wooden door. He had just applied the chemical stripper, and he was letting it work while we talked. He said, "I'll let it work." We had met in junior high school. His real name was Ralph, but he went by Jerry. That caused some confusion when "Ralph Kirkpatrick" was listed, in our reunion program, as one of the dead in our high school class.

Fritz Shoemaker

died after killing his wife, Mary, who had been Mary Knight in high school. So, technically, Fritz was the fifth to die in my high school class. He shot himself with the same rifle he used to kill his wife, who I never knew. It was a large high school. There were over six hundred students in our one class. During commencement at the Memorial Coliseum, it took a while for all of our names to be read. We graduated when platform shoes were in style, and everyone in their shiny red gowns walked carefully up the stairs to the stage. Fritz played the accordion, wore glasses, and came to my eighth birthday party when we both were in Mrs. Hanna's third-grade class, where he sat, toward the back, near Debbie Saunders, Greg Street, and Mark Taylor.

Four Foursquare Houses

1730 Spring Street

There is a porch across the full front of the house. The door is in the center. The living room is on the left as you go in with the stairs leading up in the back. The dining room is on the right with the kitchen and a little breakfast nook behind it. Upstairs, the hallway runs down the middle. Two bedrooms on the left and the bathroom with its tiled picture of a flamingo at the top of the stairs. The other bedroom, on the right toward the front, has a linoleum floor I watched my parents install, square by square, the same summer I learned to read there.

1815 Alabama Avenue

There is a porch across the full front of the house. The door is to the right. The living room fills the front half of the ground floor. The dining room is on the left in back. The kitchen is behind the stairs rising from the center, up and to the right, to the landing and then switched back upstairs. There is a big bedroom above the living room and a bedroom behind it with a bathroom across the hall. And in the back, a sunporch, windows on three sides, that looked down on the backyard with clotheslines propped and diapers drying, frozen in the winter, sheets of white chocolate.

519 Northwestern

There is a porch across the full front of the house. The door is to the left. Inside is a sitting room I used as an office. The stairs, halfway back, rise from the center to a landing on the left where there is a door that is locked. The house is a two-flat ordered from Sears and shipped here by rail. The living room is through a doorway on the right. The dining room and kitchen are on the back left, and the single bedroom is on the right behind the living room. There we had a futon on the floor. Plaster dust sifted down from the ceiling when the upstairs neighbors made love.

348 Fellows

There is a porch across the full front of the house. The door is to the right. The living room is the front half of the ground floor. The dining room, to the back on the left. The kitchen in back on the right. The staircases are tucked behind the wall separating the living room from the kitchen. The landing on the right turns back left. Two bedrooms in front with the closets between. A sunporch in the back we used as an office painted pencil yellow and a bathroom in front of that. Across the hall, above the dining room, another bedroom where I fall asleep counting all the rooms in which I have fallen asleep.

To Hell and Back: Four Takes

AUDIE MURPHY AT THE CHINESE THEATER WATCHES THE
MOVIE CALLED *To Hell and Back*[1]

The searchlights out front are surplus WWII, painted silver. The four blue beams of light slid along the underbelly
of the low clouds. It had rained and the streets were still wet,
the marquee lights reflected in the puddles in the gutters. The
acetylene torches hissed in the lamps, pitched above the steady
rumble of the diesel engines that sounded like the diesel engines of Sherman tanks, rotating the lights. Finding nothing
in the sky overhead. The movie is to the part where I call for
friendly artillery to fire on my own position. The battalion
wants to know how close the krauts are. "Just hold the phone
and I'll let you talk to one of the bastards," I say in the movie.
I wrote that in the book. The shells fall from the sky. The sky
is blue. The German tanks are wrong. They are new American

---

[1] *To Hell and Back* (1955) 106m. *** D: Jesse Hibbs. Audie Murphy, Mar-
shall Thompson, Charles Drake, Jack Kelly, Paul Pecerni, Gregg Palmer,
Brett Halsey, David Jansen, Art Aragon, Rand Brooks, Denver Pyle, Susan
Kohner. Murphy (the most decorated soldier of WW2) stars in a very
good war film based on his autobiography, with excellent battle sequences
depicting Murphy's own breathtaking heroic exploits. Cliches in script are
overcome by Murphy and cast's easy-going delivery. CinemaScope. From
Leonard Maltin's 2007 Movie Guide (Plume).

Pattons painted gray. The extras are too old, their uniforms too neat and out of season. They are carrying nothing more than their rifles. And, look there, they have their helmet straps cinched under their chins. The sky is too blue. This isn't southern France but somewhere in Washington State. It is the summer and not the winter. Now here's the part where I hop on up to the rear deck of the burning tank destroyer. The fire looks right. There isn't enough smoke. The machine gun I am firing sounds the same. I sweep it back and forth like the lights outside. And the Germans walking toward me fall effortlessly, hardly acting. They simply fall down like they have run out of gas. Now here's the part where I take some shrapnel in the back. I had to act because I don't remember how I acted when it happened. So this is what I did. The shells falling from the blue sky. No, the shells falling from the sky. No the shells falling. No the shells. Now the real fire is too thin and watery. But I like the way the battle looks. It looks like a battle in a movie because the battle I was in looked like a battle in a movie staged and choreographed the same way. The krauts walking in the rain of shells and the howitzers walking the shells with them and both of them walking, walking toward me over the field. I am watching myself be myself. That seems real. I was watching myself as I killed with the machine gun the walking soldiers walking through the falling shells. I am watching myself watch myself. The camera, me, we all are looking always over my left shoulder as the advance comes on, neither the extras nor the real soldiers knowing what to do, walking until they get their cue to fall down and then fall down.

Audie Murphy Shoots a Scene of the Movie
To Hell and Back[2]

"Just hold the phone and I'll let you talk to one of the bastards."
I hold up the phone and an explosion goes off nearby. The clods
of dirt it kicks up rain down on my helmet. "Just hold the phone
and I'll let you talk to one of the bastards." This time the cam-
eraman is kneeling right in front of me, aiming the camera on
its tripod inches from my face. I can see myself reflected in the
lens, holding out the phone for them to hear how close I am
to the action. "Action," the director says. "Just hold the phone
and I'll let you talk to one of the bastards," I say again. The
crew is a stone's throw away in the line of the advancing enemy.
The director waves and the grip on the ladder drops the bucket
of dirt on my head. They will add the sound later. "Just hold
the phone and I'll let you talk to one of the bastards," I shout

---

[2]Near Holtzwihr, France, 26 January 1945.... Second Lieutenant Murphy
commanded Company B, 15th Regiment, Third Division, which was attacked by six tanks and waves of infantry. He ordered his men to withdraw
while he remained forward at his command post and continued to give fire
directions to the artillery by telephone. Behind him, to his right, one of
our tank destroyers received a direct hit and began to burn.... With the
enemy tanks abreast of his position, Lieutenant Murphy climbed on the
burning tank destroyer, which was in danger of blowing up at any moment, and employed its .50 caliber machine gun against the enemy. He
was alone and exposed to German fire from three sides, but his deadly fire
killed dozens of Germans and caused the attack to waiver. For an hour, the
Germans tried every available weapon to eliminate Lieutenant Murphy,
but he continued to hold his position and wiped out a squad which was
trying to creep up unnoticed on his right flank. Germans reached as close
as ten yards, only to be mowed down by his fire. He received a leg wound,
but ignored it and continued the single-handed fight until his ammunition
was exhausted. He then made his way to his company, refused medical attention, and organized the company in a counterattack which forced the
Germans to withdraw....

into the phone. No one is on the other end. The phone is dead. Dirt from an explosion nearby rains down on me. A stone's throw away I see the advancing enemy. This time I actually see the advancing enemy advancing. Explosions erupt within their ranks. The sound has been added. And several soldiers are launched into the air along with the dirt from the explosion close enough to rain clods of earth down on me. The "Cut!" comes from behind me this time and the shrill whistle to signal everybody to stop, and then everything stops and then everything starts again in reverse as the advancing enemy retreats to their starting places to start over. I understand we are to try each time to get it exactly right and to get it exactly the same as the time before.

At two o'clock in the
afternoon, I see the Germans
lining up for an attack. Six
tanks rumble to the outskirts
of Holtzwihr, split into groups
of threes, and fan out toward
either side of the clearing.
Obviously they intend an
encircling movement, using
the fingers of trees for cover.
I yell to my men to get ready.

I try to tell the ghostwriter that
I just don't have any words for
what happened next. But you
were doing something, he says.
What were you doing? I don't like
to talk about it but I was on the
phone. And still to this day when I
talk on the phone—and I am on the
phone a lot now that I am going to
be an actor—I can't help but think
of talking calmly on the phone
asking the artillery to fire on me.

There you go, says the ghost. The
way we will structure this scene
is with those telephone calls. We
can build to the last call where
you say something dramatic. I am
thinking of something hard-boiled
like right out of the detective
magazines. Bogart, you know. You
read the detective magazines,
Murph?

Then wave after wave of
white dots, barely discernible
against the white snow, start
across the field. They are
enemy infantrymen, wearing
snow capes and advancing
in staggered skirmish
formation.

---

3 "But you've got to understand me. You see, with me—" Murphy paused, as
though deciding whether to go ahead with his thought "—with me, it's been a
fight for a long, long time to keep from being bored to death. *That's what two
years of combat did to me!*"

I grab a map, estimate the enemy's position, and seize the field telephone.

I think to myself, what was this like? Do I even remember? I have read the story about me, about what happened. The after action reports, the medal citations. But I always ask myself, was that me? I know this gets said a lot, how you watch yourself doing something impossible or you watch yourself as something horrible is done to you. You're removed. Things happen in slow motion. It is like you are there and not there. Like you are on the phone talking to yourself far away.

The ghost says, I think we should keep this less abstract, concentrate on the action. You go into a kind of zombie state. I think you shouldn't be thinking. You should be just doing. You become an unthinking professional, a kind of machine even.

"Battalion," cheerfully answers a headquarters lieutenant.

"This is Murphy. We're being attacked. Get me the artillery."

It was like ordering a pizza is today. I first had pizza in Rome on a leave. I couldn't get settled. I couldn't sleep behind the lines. Now that was Hell. A hot bath and hot food. There were women too, lots of them. It's the way they got food.

The ghost says, What about this line? A buddy of yours says just before he gets shot: "C'mon Murph, they can kill us but they can't eat us. That's against the law!" And then he gets shot. Now that's the kind of thing I am talking about. Grace under pressure. That kind of thing.

"Coming up."

"I want a round of smoke at co-ordinates 30.5—60; and tell those joes to shake the lead out."

I was alone. And the smoke was kind of pretty. A tree burst above their heads. They were in snow gear. Did I tell you that? I was always a good judge of distance. The mathematics of this are very old.

How many krauts, the ghost asks, typing.

"How many krauts?"

"Six tanks I can see and maybe a couple hundred foot soldiers supporting."

There were six tanks, I think, maybe a couple hundred infantry supporting.

The ghost asks, How close were they? Jesus, tanks! Why didn't you run?

"Good god! How close?"

"Close enough. Give me the artillery."

They were close enough. Not that I could see the whites of their eyes yet. They were wearing these white camo capes though, drifting like ghosts behind the tanks.

I want to get in a bit of poetry here along with the action. Or action that is a kind of ballet. Was it strangely beautiful, the ghost asks? The snow? The smoke? I think you should be detached. You are an observer, aren't you? You are watching all of this from a great distance as if it isn't real. And it isn't anymore, is it?

Our counterbarrage is on

the nose. A line of enemy

infantrymen disappear in a

cloud of smoke and snow.

The telephone rings.

"How close are they?"

"50 over and keep firing for

effect."

The telephone rings.

"How close are they?"

"50 over and keep it coming."

It took a long time, it seems, after that. It was slow going. The krauts were fighting through the barrage. The shells were walking with them as they walked.

The telephone rings.

"How close are they?"

"50 over and keep blasting.

The company's pulling back."

The telephone rings.

"How close are they?"

"50 over and keep firing for

effect."

Okay, the ghost says, that goes on forever. And then you get on the tank, right? Now this is the amazing thing. It's burning, right? Do you remember how it smelled? What did it sound like? It might be wise to add some details here. We can come back to it.

Dropping the receiver, I grab the carbine and fire until I give out of ammunition. As I turn to run, I notice the burning tank destroyer. On its turret is a perfectly good machine gun.

I change my plans and drag the telephone to the top of the tank destroyer. The telephone rings. "How close are they?"

I do remember the tank commander, a lieutenant, I talked with earlier in the day. What had I said to him? He was sprawled over the edge of the hatch. His throat had been cut. How would you describe that? There was a lot of blood. And I had to move him.

We could say it was a river of blood. Was it like a river? It was more than a trickle? A stream? A small river of blood and it covers the tank, spills down the turret, staining the green. Staining the star. There was a white star wasn't there, Murph? The blood dripping on the white star?

"50 over and keep firing for effect."

"How close are they to your position?"

It is never close enough. After things happen they no longer exist. What is left is a residue. A trail of evidence. Stuff to be pieced back together. The blood was like blood, I guess.

This is what I mean, the ghost says. A real presence of mind. A coolness under fire. I'm not sure that they'll be able to use the word bastard in the movie version. Sure, this is a natural movie. Made for the movies. This was written for the movies.

"Just hold the phone and I'll let you talk to one of the bastards."

Hastily checking the machine gun, I find it has not been damaged. When I press the trigger, the chatter of the gun is like sweet music. Three krauts stagger and crumple to the snow.

We are writing this in the present tense, I just noticed. The gun has thrown the krauts into confusion. They could not conceive of a man using a burning tank for cover. I don't know about that. For the time being my imagination is gone, and my numbed brain is intent only on destroying. I am conscious only that the smoke and the turret afford a good screen, and that, for the first time in three days, my feet are warm.

The telephone rings.

I don't know, the ghost says, this scene could be tighter. Will it be clear, all this telephone business? And is there a way to increase the dramatic tension during the attack? Face it, Murph, there are a lot of phone calls, though calling

"This is sergeant Bowes. Are you still alive, lieutenant?"

down shells on your own position
comes across as not very active.
Perhaps we can get you to that
tank, to the machine gun, sooner,
Murph. What do you think?

"I think so."   I think so.

2ND LT. AUDIE MURPHY NEAR HOLTZWIHR, FRANCE, 26 JANUARY 1945

I must remember to remember everything. The way the snow is falling. The white of the snow. The white of the sky. The white of the map I unfold. I look out at the white field. I look at the white map. There for a second or two I was lost. I was trying not to forget and didn't pay attention to where I was. There is the white snow and the white field and the white map of the field. Hell, I say to myself, hell, and I reach for the telephone.

4 GS-14s

A Clerk Working for the Architect of the Capitol
Flies the Flags That Have Been Flown over the
Capitol of the United States of America

It luffs, sags, as I haul it in, fold, send to a middle school in the
middle of nowhere. There, the invisible's visible, I guess.

The Attaché Explains to His Fiancée the Bolt of
Gingham Cloth in the Corner

Oh, that. The Salamanca Senecas' yearly treaty obligation. I
keep track of all those promises promised—wampum, trinkets—the symbolic stuff. Mine to remember, remember?

The Special Agent Waits on the Platform of the
Metro for the Next Train to Rockville

Last on the tour. I demonstrate. The Thompson. Full auto.
Spent shells. Fly. Kids fight over brass casings. It's a crime. A
waste. My life.

TUESDAY:

BOSTON LIGHT:

BREWSTER ISLAND: 42° 19' 40.85"N, 70° 53' 4.26" W

THE LAST MANNED LIGHTHOUSE IN THE UNITED STATES

The keeper writes when the light, flashing white every ten seconds, shines. *0123hrs. Seas: calm. Pressure: Falling. Skies: Severely. Clear. Stars: Disappearing. 1 X 1*

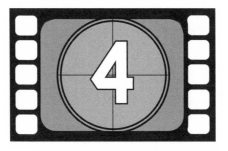

"Why is it that on all other nights we eat all kinds of
vegetables, but on this night we eat bitter herbs?"

Tessera

I couldn't stand the blood. The forty daughters of the king had
lived so long together that the visitation of their monthly bleeding had synchronized before I got to Skyros. Preparing to hide
me there, my mother, as she shaved my body, had rushed to tell
me everything. How the brooches worked and how to comb
and pin my hair, the way to look at a man and how to squat
and pee. She had wheedled from Hephaestus, as she would
later for my armor here, prosthetic hips and breasts made of
gold and ivory, fragrant balsam and elastic willow, the minted
nickel nipples. Whispering all the while, she wove the dyed fur
of the codpiece into the scruff above my cock. The steps for the
dances, the register of the dirge, goddesses I'd never heard of,
all the ointments and unguents and where they go, the way I
should let a man's hand slide over my rump. But she neglected
to tell me how each month, beginning in ones or twos, then in
greater numbers, the girls would leave their father's court and
secret themselves outside the walls of the acropolis in the tents
pitched on unpure ground to bleed. I taught myself to wait and
follow the last clutch of girls from the palace. I imitated them
as they gathered up their kits. We took dried figs and raisins,
olive oil for the lamps, wool to spin, a flute or lyre, and the wad
of cotton rags.

Blood, I've seen. I learned the stitch that knit up your wounds, Danaans, from those girls in exile. The needle, lathered in blood from my sewing, draws its own blood with its work, red pips on the stems of black thread. My spear too does its mending, pulls ropes of gore through my enemies. But men, you don't know what it is like to bleed the way the women do. To sit and seep like that. I watched them, a spot or two always in the folds of each crotch. The stains would slowly spread and soak through until one of the women would stand and unwrap the girdle sopping now on the inside. She'd toss it on the pile to be burned, and her sisters would wash her wound and sponge her dry and hitch a new sheet around her waist and legs. The smell was something. It exhaled each time the dressings were changed. Then the sisters would turn to help another. It didn't seem to stop. And the girls went on about their business, talking mostly like we are doing now.

I have never seen my own blood. Even as my mother's razor scraped the hair from my body, the blade whetted on my hide. Honed, the edge still dully slid over my thick skin, not a nick. I faked my fake menses, smearing jam on the cloth when no one was looking. At night in that stinking tent, I'd dream. Wrapped in sleep, I could not remember who I was. Reaching for myself, my hand burrowing in the rags between my legs, I'd feel the sticky puddle of what I took to be my bleeding. How could I be bleeding? In my mind, the jam had turned into the body's own syrup. I felt the stump of my cock nested in the fur sheath, everything smeared with blood. And I could also feel a cock, not mine, cut off stuffed up inside me. I told you I was dreaming. I forgot what I'd become. I kept bleeding.

Men, we rape. That is what we do. Who hasn't drawn his cock bloody as a sword from some girl no older than the daughters of King Lykomedes? You strip the frothy coating off yourself and then pin her down to let your buddy have his turn.

But for a moment, before you wring it clean, you hold it in your hand, this core of blood. It makes you think.

And there was the moon that night. Of course, there was the moon. I watched it slip out of the sea, red and full, into the black sky saturated with the smoke of smoldering rags. The moon tinged the water with its own diluted hemorrhage. My mother is a Nereid. I've seen her melt into a puddle. She dressed me up as a girl and never wanted me to suffer. I knew I was fooling no one. Though for a while, I wanted to be fooled. Now I know. Men, I am a man, like you.

DRINKING BYRON

"I was never bled in my life—but by leeches....
Perhaps the tape and lancet may be better."
—Lord Byron, in a letter to Hobhouse, 20 April 1824

St. Valentine's Day, 1824. Messolonghi. I fell seriously ill with some manner of convulsive disease. Had it lasted a moment longer it must have extinguished my mortality—if I can judge by sensations. I was speechless with the features much distorted—but not foaming at the mouth—they say—and my struggles so violent that several persons could not hold me—it lasted about ten minutes and came on immediately after drinking a tumbler of cider mixed with cold water in Colonel Stanhope's apartments. Leeches applied to my temples—the aim to break the high fever. Once removed—I bled—profusely, continuously. Doctor Bruno in terror called for Doctor Milligen when he could not staunch the blood.

A week later I was much relieved. Prescribed resinated wine, flavored by the sap leeching from the barrel staves of unseasoned pine, I drank to my health. We all did. Epilepsy—perhaps—we thought then. We sat and waited—for the Turks—whose sappers mined day and night, around this forgotten city, the Evzones retreating before their siege works. It rained and rained. Stanhope and Gamba complained. I no longer write poems. So I wrote, drunk on blood red wine, a Patras claret, this—

> Seek out—less often sought than found
> A Soldier's Grave—for thee the best
> Then look around and choose thy ground
> And take thy Rest

April. The spring come. I have seen a swallow today—and it was time—for we have had but a wet winter hitherto—even in Greece. I rode in the rain with Gamba to the olivewoods. Returned sopping, chilled. The doctors say I labor under a rheumatic fever. They want to bleed me again. I resist at first. The servants already wading in the flooded streets look for leeches. No, not leeches. The tape and the lancet this time.

The blood was wine red. They took twenty ounces. The bowls emptied in the garden, stain the thyme, the sage. Another bloodletting. A third. Later still the leeches once more—to the temples, behind the ears, along the course of the jugular, a kind of jewelry.

The red was wine blood. I compose my last words which will be the ordinary "I want to sleep now." Death will apply pressure to the meanings of sleep, drain sleep of all but its poetic potential. How Romantic!

I will be shipped back to England, bled dry and lung-less—the Greeks kept them, not my heart, steeping in a cask of disappointing port, decanted on deck of a third-rate frigate, riding on the neap tide of the Thames. Some devoted readers who've come to mourn are there to blot up, with the pages of my poems, the spilled preserving spirits to preserve me, the capillary action, the way paper drinks ink.

A Perimenopausal Jacqueline Kennedy, Two Years
after the Assassination, Aboard the M/Y *Christina*
off Eubeoa Bound for the Island of Alonnisos,
Devastated by a Recent Earthquake, Drinks Her
Fourth Bloody Mary with Mrs. Franklin Delano
Roosevelt Jr.

The barstools' seats are covered with the foreskins of whales,
Ari loves to tell his guests, and it was at this bar that Jack first
met Mr. Churchill, but you know that, you've heard that before, as I am in the habit of wading through the historic, an
archipelago of scattered captions, a sign myself, as I allocute,
droning through the landscape of vetted plaque language, ap-
positives and modifiers and subordinate and restrictive clauses,
the constellation of the museum label, your tour guide tape,
who sooner-or-later says the barstools of the *Christina* were
upholstered with the foreskins of whales, baleen, and on them
Jack who would be president sat drinking Bloody Marys, with
the former wartime prime minister of that precious stone set
in a silver sea, that other Eden, that England, two sailors they
fancied themselves, their fannies parked on the tooled foreskins
of whales, cetacean.

❹

The right whale got its name for being the right whale to
kill, and off the Cape we chased them chasing a panicked pod
sounding and sliding down beneath the launch like sleek needles sliding beneath skin. The cows are each as big as an island and sleep like reefs, lolling; the rookery of birds along the
rocky spine started every time a calf breached, leaping up on
a mother's back, slipping off and into the water and breaching
again and tumbling back, again and again, trying to wake her, it
could be days, a wake of waking.

❹

The *Christina* is itself a big white whale making way with its trailing catalog of chase boats, though this flotilla appears thinned, anemic compared to when we cruised off Ithaca after Patrick died, remember? They thought they caught me then, broadsides of telephoto lenses. Now they lag. They stall. Chips off the ship, it seems, they grow smaller in the distance, wreaths or buoys, wallowing in the troughs of waves, our own towed islet chain, a random map.

❹

Cyclades, Dodecanese, Ionian, Sporades—the island chains. Skiros, Skopelos, Alonnisos, Skiathos are the Sporades we are steaming to, we are steaming to the Sporades, sporadic in the northern Aegean. Spores. You should see the charts. Someone has cast the joints of bone like die, not so much a chain these islands but a broken and scattered string of trinkets, and now the dice-like houses on those dice-like islands have tumbled down the dice-like chockablock basalt acropoli, the Hora horribly tossed and tossed into the agitated sea, new peninsulas of chunky ruin, deltas of limey whitewashed dust. Ari says we will all give blood, our blue, blue blood when we get there, and the *Christina's* hold holds vats of water, pallets of blankets, bushel bags of sour trahanas, and egg crates of bottled gas—a dry goods convoy to another powdered and pulverized disaster.

❹

I always heard it said that George Jessel invented the Bloody Mary, half vodka and half tomato juice, the after drinks drink, a sober drink to get you drunk the first thing after the last thing you remember, the transfused eulogy. All the blood in the world could not save Patrick, who died drowning in the liquefied air in which his lungs came packed like a surplus jeep in cosmolene. He was early. It is late. We island hopped too through that mourning. One tragedy after another. The syrup of tomato is just what the doctor ordered, an elixir, a tincture, a kind of plasma. To my blue baby. To the Toastmaster General, our contemporary Pericles who works blue.

To avoid the circling bulls, the she whale rolls over on her back, and it's a sight to see the males attempt to mate that way, climbing, scooting up the beach with all that now not buoyant tonnage, up over her underbelly to the peak of the breach of her and her, just then, rolling over to take a breath before she rolls back over again on her back—a shoal, a hostile jetty, an unnavigable bar. This too goes on for hours, for days, as everything with whales runs in whale time, in whale space.

Whale-shaped Eubeoa hugs the shore of mainland Greece it fractured clear of eons ago in some strike-slip quake that shook the big island free. At Halkida the channel narrows to the narrowest of cuts, and Aristotle himself spent time there on and off through the years observing the tidal flow through the strait first one way, then the opposite, a river reversing itself, assbackward, plum plumbing there. All that motion to no end, an ecstatic static.

But in the veins there are baffles of valves that eddy the spent blood flow upstream, fish ladders, toward the heart. The cells, those dimpled mauve lozenges, lining up like shallow draft coastal tankers en route, convoying oxygen away from the spongy anchorage of the lungs.

Around here somewhere the Greeks becalmed and beached, a thousand island chain of triremes in irons, no way to be made on the way to Troy. It was that headland, or that headland there, where they kited Iphigenia into the sea, a debt owed to some god or other, to wake the breeze, to make it freshen. Troy would be thataway. Telling that story over and over, the tellers want what happened to happen differently like running a length of film back and forth, seesawing the eye, the eye hopping from one moment to the next, island frame to island frame, hoping that this time it will all be different, that other gods will intervene. As one did in Iphigenia's fall, intercepting her midair and turning her flesh insubstantial, her blood into aerosol, and transporting the mist of her beyond the Aegean to some sacred steppes someplace where the history of history one steps into is never, never the same twice.

❹

Oh, let's blame the bloody sun, the bloody, bloody drink. Hell, it's hell, this body in this in-between. The hot, you know, comes at you in waves of layers, molten lava sandwiched between melting glass. The blood, what there is of it, boils and pools, rises to the thinning skin, the blush shedding sheets of heat; I shimmer in my own juices, evaporate, another order of being, state of sacrifice. How did it go, Winnie's witty turn of phrase, the eulogy's eulogy? Not the end. This is not even the beginning of the end. The end of the beginning, then. The end of the beginning.

❹

I never see. I can't look. I won't watch. I'll turn away when they stop up my arm, bend the elbow to tap this other drink. I am so wan, I wane, not enough of any humor in me to fill a flute let alone a liter. I am empty, empty enough. I am all out of going all out. I will clench the rubber ball and focus on the horizon line out the porthole, and, afterward, peel and eat the proffered orange orange. And if they ask, I already know my type. O, I will say, O. Negative. Donor. Universal.

THUCYDIDES AT SYRACUSE

I carry a shield-shaped ostrakon, a fragment of some vessel, with me wherever I go. On the empty side, my name, Thucydides, is scratched into the blank black back of a wine amphora. On the reverse, a red-figured head—all curly curls, laurel leaf–crowned, glazed and unblinking almond eyes—vomits at someone's feet. A symposium, I suppose. A document—evidence of Socrates himself corrupting the flower of Athens's youth. He's dead now. Pericles too. The plague. I survived it somehow. The dying leaking blood from their eyes. Alcibiades, Nicias, Demosthenes, all, the whole lot of them gone. The Athenians gave me a bag of these ballots when they bagged me, sent me packing after my less than stellar performance at Amphipolis's defense. I also have those other shards, the sack of cracked pottery that made me a general. Democracy, a bunch of speeches, then a vote. It keeps the potters in business. I keep the more interesting scraps on my desk as souvenirs.

Lame soldier, I am a writer now, writing what I call History, my own and this endless war's. More often than not, I draw a blank and must make up some great oration or debate or detail, the Persians always just over the horizon, yet another conspiracy or betrayal, and when I'm blocked, I fidget, try to fit the bits of crockery together, imagine I can make all these cracked pieces whole again or patch them up enough to hold water, or no, a cup of disappointing pinot noir, or, better yet, a bitter dram of bile, pushing the memories around on the empty battlefield of parched parchment.

I was in my cups. I am a writer after all. And—here's a good one—banished from Athens, I fled back to goddamn Amphipolis where I first hit bottom to hit it again. My people had some land hereabouts—a rotting olive grove, a spent vineyard, a played-out silver mine. So I have a front row seat to compose

144 michael martone

my own narrative of fucking up. I am in recovery. One day at a time. Sure, I work the program here. I go to meetings down at the Dionysion, a Doric ruin on the south side. My name's Thucydides. Hello, Thucydides.

The shield is the not-so-secret weapon of this war, the most important part of the whole panoply. I hang mine on the wall. The little owl's two big owl-eyes look like shields on the shield. You strap the thing to the forearm instead of holding it in your fist. Heavy with all that hammered bronze, its rim has a curved lip to rest on your shoulder. Big enough, it covered the guy to your left, and the guy to your right covered you. All together, rushing at the enemy's phalanx—the ash spears splintering on the shields. The clatter. Sophocles puts that in all his plays, that thrill. The shock, then, of shield on shield, and then the leaning into it, the othismos, the rank behind you pushing forward with their shields, the aspis cold on your ass, and the rank behind the rank behind you, now, smashing into the back, and the whole massed mess slowly beginning that pivot, a drunken herd stumbling over the litter of popped-off greaves and the mud of men who have stumbled under the scrum, stomped upon, finished off by the lizard killers on the reverse end of the pike. The agon. All of that. And then one line or the other breaks, and the first thing you fling is your thirty-pound hoplon, chuck it at the guy behind you who is unsheathing his sword to run you down now that you are running, no armor on your naked back. With the shield or on it.

So much of what has happened hasn't happened yet in my History. I lag. I rehearse each trauma at the meetings as I draft it—this battle, that skirmish, the siege here, the slaughter there. Fall off the wagon. Invoke the muse. Lubricate my tongue. At night, after I have wrestled with a passage, the massacre at Syracuse, say, I retire to Phoebe's on the plateia, overlooking that wine-dark sea, and toast the German tourists, drinking Jagermeister, with burnished retsina in my super-glued ostrakon. I dance, a regular Zorba, smashing plate after plate on the paving stones beneath the plane trees.

I have been stuck at Syracuse for a long time, the nineteenth year of the war. Last spring I made the trip, a scudding trireme under Hermes's protection. The banks of Assinarus, I stood there. The Athenians there pelted, pressed on all sides for days. Missiles, javelins, harassed by cavalry. They made for this river, thinking they would breathe easier once they crossed, driven on by fear, by exhaustion, by thirst. Thirst. They rushed in here, all order gone, each wanting to be the first to cross, the enemy now on each shore making that impossible. Huddling together, they trampled each other, some killed by arrows, bolts, darts, others tangled in the baggage, drowned. Missiles rained down on them (I can see that), most drinking greedily, heaped together in the hollow of the river. The Peloponnesians followed, butchered the Athenians in the water, now instantly fouled, running red, but they went on drinking just the same, mud and all, bloody as it was, most even fighting each other to have it.

How to write that?

Recovery. They tell you, and you are to repeat, that you are powerless—at the mercy of nature, the universe. The disease metaphor allows one to abandon free will, self-control. There are plenty of higher powers—all the goddamn gods and goddesses, the nymphs and spirits. It's a crock. Impossible to give oneself up, to get over anything. I dip my hand into the cloudy Assinarus, drink and drink and drink. Always, there's never enough, too much.

Back in Amphipolis, still ostracized, old Thucydides (that's me), must suffer random drug tests. He pisses history into a cup.

Four Corners

Utah

So the temple maids had me cornered on that floating platform where you are made to look at the mural of the universe and the white life-sized statue of Christ Almighty at the end of the tour of the temple grounds when I asked them why, in God's name, does everything represented in art here have to be done in this illustrative realistic style when maybe another style a bit more abstract, say, or distorted by emotion, even, could represent the enormity of the things you want to represent, because Christ and all the angels might be real but might not fit best into a realistic frame or might not even be perceived by our puny visual apparatus, you know, might be invisible or perhaps warped in some way, in shadow maybe, and anyway the Impressionists showed us that, hey, yellow haystacks are sometimes purple, like at night or when the sun is behind a cloud, and the temple maids looked at me utterly bewildered, not being able to begin to see what I was driving at and saying to me, again, this is what He looks like, like don't you see, so how, in God's name, can He look any other way than the way he looks.

Colorado

So we turned a corner in downtown Denver and they all stopped me, grabbing my arm and pointing off into the distance beyond one of those glassed-in skywalks crossing the street up ahead, up in the air, and said, look, there, that's where the mountains are and they are just beautiful, you should see them, and I said, where, I don't see anything and I didn't because, once again, it was all hazy, it's always all hazy anytime I'm in Denver, the sky a kind of white sheet backdropped behind all the buildings of Denver, and they said well you should see them and I said again, yeah, I should, but I don't see any mountains and every time I come to Denver people tell me there are mountains here but I never see them even though they point and say there are mountains there so I am beginning to think there aren't any mountains at all, that there never were any mountains, just this funny primed canvas sky waiting for an artist, any artist, to fill in all the details for a picture you all say you can see.

ARIZONA

So out of the corner of my eye, I catch this glimmer of something sparkling off in the distance, out in this painted desert and immediately I think it is some kind of mirage, so I don't look right at it because, I remember from someplace, you are never supposed to look at things square on but kind of off to one side so as to focus the thing better on the curve of your eyeball as if I could even take a look as I am driving like a bat out of hell on this interstate between Phoenix and Tucson, surrounded by a herd of shimmering cars and trucks all going at least a hundred, and I remember that the not-looking bit has to do with stars in the sky, I think, not mirages in the desert, and so I look and it looks like this mirage out in the desert is an airport like the one I just flew into and out of in this rental car like a bat out of hell, but this, that is, this airport, is a kind of mirage, since what it is is one of those graveyards for bombers and fighters and airliners parked out on the dry and preserving desert, so in other words, it isn't an illusion but it is not really what it seems to be either as this airport isn't going anywhere and in a second or two, going like hell, it's out of my range of sight.

NEW MEXICO

So, that night, this Navajo drops me off at a filling station, closed, on the outskirts of Truth or Consequences after giving me a lift from Las Cruces and he gives me a buck for a cup of coffee and points out this diner, catty-cornered, where I go in and I get to telling the guy behind the counter about the trip and the Navajo and the buck for a cup of coffee and the place goes silent and it seems I have stepped into the old story about the ghost driver and the hitchhiker and the guy gives me the coffee and says I can keep the buck since it was given to me by a ghost in a pickup truck who died swerving to miss a stalled school bus or some such and he said it sure must seem to you like a lot of things aren't what they seem around here, like the name of the town which was the name of an old television game show, like the ghosts at White Sands or Roswell, where it seems like every corner of the state is filled up with these squared patches of ground that are off-limits so who really knows what is really happening here, and, by the way, what brought you here, and by that I don't mean an Indian in an old pickup but why did you come here to this or that place in the first place, I bet for no more reason than to verify the truth of some story you'd been told by the talking heads on the TV or some ghost voice that is drifting between the white spaces of some old book you read, you see, you came here to see it with your own eyes.

The Blind: A Blues

LIGHTING ON A BOXCAR

He said, hopping a freight is easy. He said, leaving town is a breeze. He said, you have to wait beyond the yard limit, beyond the sign that says "yard." He said, you watch for the highball. He said, you wait for the hog to pick up steam. He said, you wait for the drag to pick up the slack. He said, you walk in the other direction from the direction the train's going. He said, you walk back. He said, you start watching for the boxcars. He said, you start watching for the rungs on the sides on the boxcars. He said, there are rungs on the head-end and the back. He said, take the rungs on the front. He said, always take the rungs on the head-end. He said, the rung in the front. He said, so when you swing on you won't get hurt. He said, so when you swing on you'll swing into the boxcar's side. He said, so if you swing on and can't get a hold you'll bounce right off. He said, you'll bounce right off and light into the ditch. He said, don't you swing on on the ladder in back. He said, you swing on on the ladder in back, it'll likely take you on over in between the boxcars. He said, you'll just swing on over between the cars. He said, and then where will you be? He said, you'll be lighting on the ground; you'll be lighting on the ground between the wheels. He said, there's no place left to go. He said, that's no place to be.

Empty Reefers

He said, half the time the reefers are empty. He said, half the other time they are full. He said, when the reefers are full they are full of meat. He said, when the reefers are full they are full of dead meat or fruit, fruit or lettuce. He said, the reefers got iceboxes on both ends. He said, when the reefers are filled with meat or fruit or lettuce or what-have-you, the iceboxes are filled with ice. He said, the ice is ice they cut from frozen lakes and rivers. He said, they pack the ice in sawdust in the iceboxes of the reefers. He said, it keeps the reefers cold. He said, but half the time the reefers are empty. He said, half the time the reefers are empty, and the iceboxes on the empty reefers are empty too. He said, now here is a fine ride. He said, here is a fine ride especially in winter. He said, you can get out of the cold and wind, hunkered down in the empty iceboxes. He said, the doors for the iceboxes are on top of the cars. He said, you can get into the iceboxes through the doors on top of the cars. He said, be careful about the latches on the icebox doors. He said, there are latches on the doors of the iceboxes. He said, you have to hold the doors open when you're inside the ice-boxes. He said, no way to open the latches from the inside. He said, you get in those empty iceboxes and the door closes shut, there's no way out. He said, who knows when you get found. He said, the empty icebox on the empty reefer you found won't be empty. He said, you know what you find. He said, meat. He said, just meat.

Something He's Been Told

He said, he's heard everything. He said, he's heard this before. He said, he's heard this a hundred times. He said, do you want to hear it? He said, he's not sure he believes it. He said, the way I hear it, it always starts the same. He said, what they tell goes like this. He said, a conductor or a brakeman is switching cars in the yard. He said, the conductor or the brakeman switching cars in the yard gets caught between two cars. He said, the cars are moving slow in the yard, and the yardman or conductor doesn't get out of the way. He said, the story goes that he gets caught between the cars. He said, the cars couple right through him. He said, the cars couple so quick and so clean right through him, he's still alive. He said, the cars couple so clean, it stops all the blood, stops all the pain in the nerves. He said, the nerves get all crushed. He said, he is alive above the place where the cars have coupled so cleanly through him. He said, he's alive, can you believe it? He said, then everybody gathers around to figure out what to do. He said, he can hear them talking about what they can do with him. He said, sometimes he talks to them about what can be done. He said, sometimes he just listens to them talking about what to do. He said, it always turns out that there is nothing to do. He said, it always turns out that they will uncouple the cars, uncouple the cars that are coupled through him. He said, he will die. He said, he gets that he is being kept alive by the thing that killed him. He said, he gets that he is already dead. He said, then they always say that they go and fetch his wife. He said, when they tell the story, they always tell about the going to get the wife. He said, it could be the wife or it could be a girlfriend. He said, but she is always close enough by. He said, they tell you that they get to talk. He said, they tell you they talk, but nobody heard what was said. He said, they tell you they saw him talking to his wife. He said, whispering really. He said, they tell you about holding her up as she is like to faint at the sight of her husband coupled between the cars. He said, she gets taken away. He said, she gets taken away and you go with her. He said, she's walking away stepping over all the rails in the yard. He said, she is stepping over all the rails in the yard. He said, then you hear the switch engine whistle. He said, the switch engine whistles twice, a warning. He said, the switch engine whistles twice, a warning. He said, that means it's time to move. He said, you hear the whistles, and then the engine moves. He said, the engine moves, and then the whole train moves. He said, then you know what happens then.

THE BLIND

He said, first there is the engine. He said, first there is the engine and then the tender. He said, the tender's where they keep the coal and the water for the engine. He said, the blind's between the tender and the baggage car that comes next. He said, the blind's the doorway on the baggage car. He said, the baggage car door is locked but you can ride in the doorway. He said, riding in the doorway of the baggage car is riding the blind. He said, he liked to ride the blind. He said, a passenger train goes three times as fast. He said, in the summer there is nothing better. He said, in the winter you have to think twice. He said, in the winter you have to think twice because those trains take water on the fly. He said, those flyers take on water on the fly. He said, they don't stop for water. He said, they have to make up time. He said, they don't stop for water, they get it on the fly. He said, what that means is the water is in a trough between the rails. He said, the water is in a trough between the rails and the tender scoops it up without stopping. He said, the tender has a scoop that drops into the water. He said, the engine doesn't stop. He said, the engine doesn't stop when picking up water on the fly. He said, the water flies when they pick up water on the fly. He said, the blind gets soaked by all the water flying. He said, he's been soaked by all that water. He said, you don't want to see the blind in winter. He said, you don't want to see the blind in winter when the train is picking up water on the fly. He said, the whole head-end of the baggage car is covered with ice. He said, ice from the water spilled back from picking up water on the fly. He said, the water freezes when it hits the cold metal of the baggage car. He said, I've seen them hacking at the blue ice with axes. He said, I've seen them melt the blue ice with steam. He said, riding the blind in winter. He said, riding the blind in winter, in the night. He said, riding the blind in winter, in the night, when the flyer takes on water on the fly. He said, I've seen that.

Four Ironies

Not Ironic

You know the scene. A great ocean liner is about to depart on a transatlantic cruise. The ship's orchestra plays "Columbia, the Gem of the Ocean." Passengers lining the many decks dockside wave and wave flags, throw, toward the mass of well-wishers stories below, brightly colored streamers that stream through the flurry of confetti falling through the cold air. Without warning, the ship's horn warns of the impending departure. The vessel trembles, then drifts free of its moorings, begins to slide forward and away from the dock. The band blares over the overdubbing of the plosive hubbub of the throng. Bon Voyage! You regard the illuminated ranks of the passengers as each animated face searches for one last glimpse of a loved one or ones on shore, your own gaze panning the panoply of people packed along the brilliant white railings. Then the crowd parts, and you peer deeper into the ship's graceful superstructure. Revealed there, suspended, it seems, floating even, on the white wall of the bulkhead, a wreath-like orange life buoy, the stenciled name of the ship orbiting the rim: SS *Orizaba*.

SLIGHTLY IRONIC

You know the scene. A great ocean liner is about to depart on a transatlantic cruise. The ship's orchestra plays "Anchors Aweigh." Passengers lining the many decks dockside wave and wave flags, throw, toward the mass of well-wishers stories below, brightly colored streamers that stream through the flurry of confetti falling through the cold air. Without warning, the ship's horn warns of the impending departure. The vessel trembles, then drifts free of its moorings, begins to slide forward and away from the dock. The band blares over the overdubbing of the plosive hubbub of the throng. "From the halls of Montezuma to the shores of Tripoli." Bon Voyage! You regard the illuminated ranks of the passengers as each animated face searches for one last glimpse of a loved one or ones on shore, your own gaze panning the panoply of people packed along the brilliant white railings. Then the crowd parts, and you peer deeper into the ship's complicated superstructure. Revealed there, suspended, it seems, floating even, on the white wall of the bulkhead, a wreath-like orange life buoy, the weathered stenciled name of the departing ship orbiting the rim: SS *United States.*

IRONIC

You know the scene. A great ocean liner is about to depart on a transatlantic cruise. The ship's orchestra plays "Rule, Britannia." Passengers lining the many decks dockside wave and wave flags, throw, toward the mass of well-wishers stories below, brightly colored streamers that stream through the flurry of confetti falling through the cold cold air. Without warning, the ship's steam whistle warns of the impending departure, the ship's big bell tolling. The vessel trembles, heaves forward, then drifts free of its moorings, sliding away from the teeming dock. The band blares over the overdubbing of the plosive hubbub of the throng. "God save the…" Bon Voyage! Bon Voyage! You regard the thick ranks of the passengers as each bright face searches in a slight panic for one last glimpse of a loved one or ones on shore, your own distant gaze panning the panoply of people packed along the delicate white railings. Then the crowd parts, and you peer deeper into the ship's shadowed superstructure. Revealed there, suspended, it seems, floating even, on the ice-white wall of the bulkhead, a small wreath-like orange life buoy, the matte-black stenciled name of this departing ship orbiting the rim: RMS *Titanic*.

Now Strangely Ironic

You know the scene. A great ocean liner is about to depart on a transatlantic cruise. The ship's orchestra plays "Columbia, the Gem of the Ocean." Passengers lining the many decks dockside wave and wave flags, throw, toward the mass of well-wishers stories below, brightly colored streamers that stream through the flurry of confetti falling through the cold air. Without warning, the ship's horn warns of the impending departure. The vessel trembles, then drifts free of its moorings, begins to slide forward and away from the dock. The band blares over the overdubbing of the plosive hubbub of the throng. Bon Voyage! You regard the illuminated ranks of the passengers as each animated face searches for one last glimpse of a loved one or ones on shore, your own gaze panning the panoply of people packed along the brilliant white railings. Then the crowd parts, and you peer deeper into the ship's graceful superstructure. Revealed there, suspended, it seems, floating even, on the white wall of the bulkhead, a wreath-like orange life buoy, the stenciled name of the ship orbiting the rim: SS *Orizaba*.

You wait as this final ship shrinks in the vast distance, sinks over the horizon with a sanguine southern sun (setting or rising, you can't be sure) steaming over its starboard quarter, the ignited sky a kind of stained wake, and this illusion of perspective, the vectored strata of clouds, the lapping waves and the wrinkled ocean beyond, creating in you the sensation that you, you are the one in motion, bobbing, moving further away from the once massive static ship, now mere punctuation, shifting with its cheerful and optimistic manifest of passengers, now a smudge of smoke, a quotation of exhaustion, on the vast yet retreating horizon. You sense that you yourself are sinking, or so it seems. You are shipping water, floundering, adrift even, and cast about for any buoyant jetsam within your reach, its stenciled letters awash, washed out, unreadable, an "S" maybe and another "S" on the water-logged lifesaver, the only "O" the one you mouth, "O", in recognition. Oh, you tell yourself, you get it now, though you can no longer name that ship-shaped vessel that has been launched with such choreographed fanfare or (to tell the truth) tell among the various ways of telling: what is happening, what will happen, what you know will happen, and what (at last) you know you know will happen.

Harmonic Postcard Captions

The USS *Atheneum*. The hermaphrodite-rigged brigantine, the USS *Atheneum*, plied the waters of the Wabash River during the Quasi-War with France. In 1798 the ship ran aground near present-day New Harmony, Ind., where local salvers inhabited the wreck their descendants still occupy to this day. Today, the sun-bleached hulk of the former man-o'-war, its gaffed-rigged mainsail tattered but still visible, decays pristinely at the foot of North Street just yards from the river.

The Restored Eyeglasses of Philip Johnson. The distinct owl-eyed eyewear the American architect Philip Johnson (1906-2005) donned in homage to Le Corbusier is placed in a glass casket reliquary housed in the Philip Johnson–designed Roof-less Church of New Harmony, Ind., by Manolo Blahnik, whose Prada eyewear line underwrote the enshrinement. The congregation attending the ceremony was treated to the premiere of Philip Glass's "Requiem pour Le Monocle de Mon Oncle."

The Lighting of the Tuning Forks. The citizens of New Harmony, Ind., illuminate the Tuning Fork Forest south of the city with strands of electric lights. First planted by the Owenite utopian community in 1825, the forest, in the right breeze, is known to "sing" a sustained haunting note that is also said to produce an amplified sound wave capable of shattering the glass bulbs of the electric lights, throwing showers of sparks in algorithmic patterns that have been known, on occasion, to ignite the sycamores along the Wabash, themselves made famous in song.

Main Street, Old Harmony, Illinois. Founded by distraught European serfs attempting to find property that would own them, Old Harmony's streetscape features the unique asymmetrical traffic light. Out of focus in the middle distance, the water district's ovoid tower oscillates randomly in concert with the prevailing wind and the constant seismic activity generated by the nearby New Madrid tectonic fault.

The Production of the First Xerographic Copy, Recounted by Chester Carlson, Its Inventor

October 22, 1938, was the day. We were turning lead into gold. I hurried to the lab, where Otto already had a freshly prepared sulfur coating on the zinc plate. Otto took up a glass microscope slide and asked what he should write. "Anything," I said. "The day. The place." And he printed on the glass, in India ink, the notation 10.-22.-38 Astoria. We pulled down the shade to make the room as dark as possible, and then he rubbed the sulfur surface vigorously with his red handkerchief to apply the electrostatic charge, laid the slide on the surface of the sulfur-coated zinc plate and placed the combination under a bright incandescent lamp for a few seconds. Oh, it was like eggs rotting in the sun. "Remove the slide," I ordered Otto. "The powder, now the powder," and he sprinkled the lycopodium on the sulfur surface. By gently blowing on the surface I removed all the loose powder. My mouth was dry. And there, there in the light of the bright bulb, there was left on the brilliant golden surface a near-perfect duplicate, in powder, of the notation that had been printed on the glass slide. Astoria. "It's alive!" I said. Otto was crying real tears. Both of us repeated the experiment several times to convince ourselves it was true. We made some permanent copies by transferring the powder images to wax paper and heating the sheets to melt the wax. Then we went out to Spiro's for a lunch of grape leaves, olives, and feta with oil and oregano. To celebrate, we danced, shouting over the music, again and again and again as we got tighter and tighter and tighter, the steps we had taken to make out of the invisible, out of light and static, a copy of a copy of a copy.

October 22, 1938, was historic. Not the golden age of inventors for sure. Not Edison or Ford, but nothing to sneeze at either. We rushed to the lab that morning, where we had a freshly prepared sulfur-coated zinc plate. On the glass microscope slide we took from the drawer, we printed the notation 10.-22.-38 Astoria in a rich India ink that caught the light. The window shade made the room as dark as possible. See, we were the inside, the mechanical workings of the future machine. So then we rubbed the sulfur surface vigorously with a silk shower to apply an electrostatic charge, laid the slide on the surface of the sulfur, and stuck the combination under a bright incandescent lamp for a second or two. We took out the slide, sprinkled lycopodium powder on the sulfur surface. We gently blew on the surface, and all the loose powder shimmered and flew away. And there we saw what was left on the surface: a near-perfect duplicate in powder of the notation, 10.-22.-38 Astoria, which had been printed on the sparkling glass slide. We repeated the experiment several times to convince ourselves it was true. It was as true as it was going to be. Then we made some permanent copies by melting wax paper to imprint the image. And then we went out to lunch, where we toasted ourselves and our little experiment quietly with ouzo, which is distilled from grape stems, I believe, and is clear to begin with but turned a cloudy silver when we mixed it with water before we drank.

The sun just up. October something. Thirty-eight. The sky all
nickeled over. I'm on the way to the lab. Otto had a fresh zinc
plate, sulfur coated. On a glass slide he printed 10.-22.-38 Astoria in India ink. We pulled down the stained shade to darken
the room. He rubbed the sulfur surface with the handkerchief.
That creates the electrostatic charge. He laid the slide on the
surface of the sulfur. He placed the mess under a bright incandescent bulb. A few seconds. It was hot. I didn't get my hopes
up. Nothing comes of nothing. Took the slide out of the light.
Otto sprinkled the lycopodium powder on the sulfur surface.
He gently blew on it. The loose powder blended into the dust
in the air. There, on the surface, a near-perfect duplicate in
powder of Otto's notation, the one he had printed on the glass
slide. Close enough. Enough enough. Only alchemy, at best, I
thought. A cheap trick. We tried it again to convince ourselves it
was true. It was true, more or less. All that glistens is, you know.
We made some permanent copies, burning the powder images
onto wax paper. I've got them around here someplace. Then,
lunch, a Greek place. The neighborhood was lousy with them.
I got drunk on wine, retsina. Tastes like turpentine steeped in
turpentine. Never drank it again. It's the color of piss.

October 22, 1938, was a historic occasion. I went to the lab that day and Otto had a freshly prepared sulfur coating on a zinc plate. Otto took a glass microscope slide and printed on it in India ink the notation 10.-22.-38 Astoria. We pulled down the shade to make the room as dark as possible, and then he rubbed the sulfur surface vigorously with a handkerchief to apply an electrostatic charge, laid the slide on the surface of the sulfur, and placed the combination under a bright incandescent lamp for a few seconds. The slide was then removed and lycopodium powder was sprinkled on the sulfur surface. By gently blowing on the surface he removed all the loose powder, and there was left on the surface a near-perfect duplicate in powder of the notation that had been printed on the glass slide. Both of us repeated the experiment several times to convince ourselves it was true, then we made some permanent copies by transferring the powder images to wax paper and heating the sheets to melt the wax. Then we went out to lunch to celebrate.

RPM

78

I start with the cashews. There're never enough. Watch this—how the waiter steps onto the turntable, off of the dance floor we're circling, a little skip. The DJ's got two turntables. Turntables too. The bar's parked around back behind. We'll come back around. The waiter has to watch it, stepping off of the stationary dance floor onto the moving floor at our feet. It's all relative. We are on a moving floor but when we are on it, it seems solid enough. The waiter negotiates the dimensions, bringing our drinks. We'll start with the Screwdriver. It should take us one revolution. Out there, over there in the shadows is Henry Ford's village. He collected houses, stores, outbuildings, even outhouses, and such from before there were cars. I've been there. Here's the thing about cashews—they're never in the shell. Why is that? Poisonous, I think, the shells. It's better after dark. We'll see the lights come on all over the city below. The sunset's behind us. We'll pick it up again as we head to the west. There's downtown Detroit. The downtown's a ruin. Of course, I felt safe. Nobody's down there downtown. They have this train. It's fully automatic. I was by myself. I rode from stop to stop. It's all automatic. The doors of the train slid open at each stop. The train has a canned voice. "Hotel Cadillac," it said. The place is a ruin. Not enough money to tear it down. Pigeons and other birds flew out the windows. "Step back from the doorway. The doors are closing." The train slides on. Stops at the next ruin. And so on. You want to dance? That floor isn't moving. It's Motown all night. Every night is Motown in Motown. Though that sounds like the Ink Spots filling the room. "Don't Get Around Much Anymore." Victor. His Master's Voice, the spotted dog hypnotized by the twirling disc. Up there's Superior. That's where they grow the famous cherries. You want your orange slice? I eat them by sections. You forget that you're moving. The trees, there, are turning. Here comes the sunset. Orange like the drink. Out there's the rest of Michigan. I bet that's Indiana. I do this a lot. Come to the top of tall buildings. That this top spins is gravy. San Francisco's tall buildings. A Hyatt. One panoramic window is all water. The elevators are glass. The cable cars there below. They turned them around right there. Another turntable. Everyone gets out and pushes. Cashews, don't you think, prove the existence of God? They're that good. Have the last one. You can't even feel it, the moving. But you know you are moving if you just pick a point in the distance and stare. Before you know it your whole head has been turning and you are looking away.

Next come the filberts. There're always only, never more than, a few, and you have to poke around among the peanuts and almonds for them. Hazelnuts, filberts—I think they are the same. Whose idea is this anyway, to have this saloon keep moving? It seems so 70s, so disco, and, look, there's a disco ball there over the dance floor, and it is moving too, or is it rotating the other way, against the way we are going? Or the mirrored ball standing still goes backward as we go forward, not fast enough to throw its sparks. It's as if the lights are being plucked off, square by square, plink, plank, plunk. Silent wind chime. I swear the DJ must be spinning old Platters' platters. "Twilight Time," "Only You," "The Great Pretender," "My Prayer." They have that sound. Mercury, Mercury Records, a red diamond. There was that plastic gizmo you popped into the big hole in the center of a 45 so the record could be played on the long-play spindle. It looked like legs running after legs. The waiter has mastered his sea legs, steps on to the scuffed dance floor after leaving this moving one moving but not moving at our feet. Bringing our drinks. Let's stay with vodka but change the juice, Cape Codders this time around. My urinary tract is fine, thank you very much. The museum down there is meant to look like Independence Hall, but I don't know, twenty times as big, another one of Ford's big ideas. And they have it stuffed with railroad steam engines and everything, steam everythings, and cars of all sorts, of course. And hanging from the ceiling, the Spirit of St. Louis slowly rotates, but not the real one—or it is real, but a real fake, the one used in the movie. In the shadows is Henry Ford's village. Cars are prohibited except for old Tin Lizzies and Model As. There are wagons and buggies and surreys and carriages. And the horse manure is real too. I've been there. Hazelnuts seem oily and European. I think they grow on bushes. They are the same as filberts, but

I'm not sure. You want the last one? It's all dark all the time now. The lights are coming on, and all the cars below are invisible save those pools of light the invisible cars sweep along the street. The streetlights show up the grid of the old townships, big squares that aren't square but seem to merge to triangle angles way off north. The sunset's set. And maybe we'll get lucky with a moonrise tonight. We'll keep an eye out the next time around. There's downtown Detroit. I was there for the riots in '67. I was on a field trip to watch the Tigers, Willie Horton, in my Little League uniform. I remember the endless bus ride out of town. Our bus being passed by trucks of troops and trucks with trailers hauling tanks and APCs. The downtown's a ruin now. Of course, I felt safe going there because no one else was there. They have this train that runs fully automatic in a big broad circle. I was by myself on the train. I rode from stop to stop. The doors of the train slid open at each stop, and this voice came on, a prerecorded voice, announcing the stop. "Hotel Cadillac," it said. The old hulk of that hotel looks like a wedding cake frosted with pigeons, the walls smeared white, and then the frosting flies up, a sheet of birds in one big flapping field. The door tells you it's going to close and then it closes. The train slides on and on. Every stop is a new ruin. The train makes a big loop. You want to dance? That dance floor isn't moving. The dance floor isn't dancing. It's Motown all night. Every night is Motown in Motown. Michigan's shaped like a glove. The dark lake, Huron, I think, outlines the shore all the way to Mackinaw, an island with no cars. I wonder if this cherry dotting the eye of my drink was grown up there. You want yours? I like them. They make every drink they're in seem more like a drink. Maraschino cherries aren't grown in any nature I know. Manufactured fruit. It's a kick to pull them off the stem, that little pop behind the teeth. You forget that you're moving. And you forget, way down below the earth is moving too, twirling and sliding like a dance. You want to?

The fall is falling. The sunset set. You can see just a hint of it in those clouds beyond, the light bending and bouncing over the horizon. Out there's the rest of Michigan, Michigan ready to rest. But maybe that is Indiana or Indiana is over there on the other side of where the horizon used to be, invisible. I like to observe from the observation decks of tall buildings, to go up as far as I can. Baltimore has a restaurant downtown that turns like this one, and, as it turns, you can see the bay, and close by is this old clock tower that looms into view every hour or so and then retreats. Bromo Seltzer advertised around the face of the clock, the hands so big and always moving, it seems, in time with you as you drift by, constantly moving yourself as if you mesh, one gear into another. And then you're back to the panoramic window of water and toy boats and the factory with the sugar sign. The elevators there are glass and slide down the side of the building. And off in the distance is a roundhouse or two owned by the B&O, and the roundhouses are round. That's why they call them roundhouses. And now they are museums too. Filberts or hazelnuts. Hazelnuts or filberts. I'm not sure I know the difference. The last one is yours if you want it. You can't even feel it, the constant turning, the torque, the twist of the restaurant moving. It is pleasant, this journey going nowhere. It's a wonder how they do it, the smoothness of the mechanism, the gears. You hardly notice at all. It is all relative, the motion, depends on your point of view. If we remembered high school calculus it would help. We could plot all the points of all this pointing. X. And Y. And Z. The stars are out. And even time, that fourth dimension, is out. The time it takes for things to change and the square of that, the time it takes time, the time time takes.

33 1/3

The almonds look like arrowheads. Almonds seem to be as abundant as filberts. I like them smoked, but just what is artificial smoke? Imagine, the artificial smoke factory making artificial smoke. Its smokestacks belching the exhaust of artificial smoke or maybe even artificial artificial smoke, artificial smoke the waste product of the process. Still it's good, the taste of almonds. The tooth of almonds. I like their density, the dentistry. They look like teeth, incisors, incisive. And they have ridges like fingernails do. Aren't they a cure for cancer? No, that was apricot stones, peach pits, I think. Whose idea is this anyway, to have this saloon keep moving? Maybe it can't be stopped. They leave it on all night, constantly turning. Vacuuming the carpet would be a snap with the maintenance crew on the stuck-still dance floor letting the floor come to them to be cleaned. Hold still, this won't hurt at all. The janitor then would dance with the buffer, waltzing over and over the wood floor. He turns and turns over the parquet, revolving slowly, riding the gyro of the polisher, the circulation of shine. All the time, the outer rim keeps orbiting, the rings of Saturn, the custodian coiled up in the twisting coil of the electric cord. Checkmate, checkmate, it's the Checkmates now. "Put It in a Magazine." Highrise Records, an L.A. Motown Motown sound. I swear the DJ is seriously esoteric. The waiter is waiting on us. He is coming round the bend. You can take that and that and that, but we are still working on the nuts. The waiter waits with us. He is dangerously close to the joint in this joint. The fault line is slipping by. Let's go back in time this time around and order a White Russian. Enough with the fruit. Bring us the cream. Or, no, make mine black, a Black Russian, the coffee will wake me up. The museum building—here it comes again—is meant to look like Independence Hall but, I don't know, twenty times as big. A model bigger than the thing it models, and inside is every model of every model Ford ever built. The wax models and the models made of clay. Every Edsel too and even models of cars that were never built, just lists of their names. There in the dark is Henry Ford's village. The only light beams out from Edison's factory Henry had hauled in from New Jersey, the generator still generating. And he poached the shop from Dayton where the Wrights warped wings and attached them to the leftover parts of bicycles. And somewhere deeper in out there is the shed where Henry himself pieced together his first runabout. In the village only old Fords are allowed to putter around. And somewhere in there is the chair. Not the electric one, though that might be in the museum, a technology of the twentieth century. Did Edison invent that too? No, Lincoln's chair. The one that would fit him, in the box at Ford's Theater. No relation? I remember it velvet, all stained with blood. Ten after ten, the clocks all say, the moment when the shot rang out. Ten and two—that's the proper grip for the wheel Henry invented. Hand over hand steering, turning. I learned on a simulator in the basement of the high school, that scripted FORD on the hub, a button for the horn. There's the last almond, a raft on a sea of peanuts. Look, out in the dark another circle circling. They've lit up the test tracks. See the moving circles of light circle through the puddle of light, a roulette ball on the banked banks, black braking red black white. Endurance trials probably. In that tight little orbit are all the simulations they need to weather the weather. Let it rain and it rains. An endless stutter of bumps, a washboard scrubbing the rocker panels clean off. No moon as of yet, just the map of one spilled on the ground. There's Detroit reborn. I swear the buildings have grown since the last time we've looked, and all the windows winking on. Hard by there, there, is Greektown, where they are setting fire to cheese and those shanks of pressed meat rotate like we are doing now, tubes of flesh turning, twisting on an upright spit. Hey, I'm getting hungry. You want to dance? Cut a rug? Now there would be a collection for the museum in our wake, on our way. A gallery of cut rugs. The Lindy. The two-step. The fox-trot. The box step. The waltz. Yes, the shag. The shag rug. The dance floor doesn't move. And no one dances. We could lay some carpet. No, tile it in checkerboard squares. Your move. I liked the night. The knight. Up one, over two. Cha cha cha. Over one, down two. Cha cha cha. It's Motown all night. Every night is Motown in Motown. The Checkmates aren't Motown but they should be. Spilling off thataway, that big blank space outlined by lights would be the desert of Lake Erie looking eerie, black on black. I eat the ice. I eat it after I suck all the white out of it, all the black. No fruit with the Russians, but these cubes melt to a kind of fruit, a grape-shaped nougat, don't they? I know it's impolite to spit them back and let them bathe up another coating. The ice another product of Michigan. All that water, turning too to ice, to steam. You forget you're moving. Ontario is over there, and that's the best bar bet there is. Driving due south from Detroit, what is the first foreign country you run into? Folks'll say Mexico, the Yucatan, Cancun, or worse. Colombia. Panama. They are thinking south, mind you. When it was right there all the time. Canada creeping under the chinny chin chin of Michigan. Due south. In New Orleans the ground floor of the Hotel Monteleone has a carousel bar. The room doesn't spin like this one here, the bar a fixed center. There you ride the ring of the bar itself, stools and all canopied with old-fashioned circus gothic awnings, lots of brass poles. I remember calliope music as you ride it round and round, cantering past the big front window facing Royal Street and the circulating revelers of the Quarter short-circuited from Bourbon. Here we are above the water and there you are down below it. The pool is on the roof, and swampy and soaked and floating your turn on the rubber raft, you look out at the vast waterlogged delta on all sides and feel, in your steeped state, you are sinking into, going down this particular drain. Almondine, the slices shaved from almonds look like fish scales. The scales scale the fish. You know, if we went faster we would be thrown through the windows off into space. I feel like I am floating now—an object tends to stay in motion. Just keeps going. But space is curved and this merry-go-round keeps us rounded off, rounding us off. Centrifugal. Gesundheit. Our faces all distorted, all plastic, pulling Gs. Gee, I want to stick my hand out the window moving fast and feel all that is invisible push back.

The rest is peanuts. Henry Ford rebuilt George Washington Carver's slave cabin in the village. The father of the peanut. It's out there somewhere in the darkness coming up. I've been in some bars where you are encouraged to crack open the shells, pop the nuts in your mouth, and then throw the shells on the floor to be trampled into a fine mulch and create studied road-house neglect. These are chain stores, franchised bars pretending they are the honky-tonks they are replacing. Rough and tumble. The slave cabin's dirt floor has dirt flown in from the dirt floor of a slave cabin in Missouri. Says so. Mr. Peanut with the hat and spats, slumming groundnut all up in the canopy of the trees. My mother always said to wash behind my ears. Dirt enough to grow peanuts. No, potatoes. If the bar was stationary we would be buried up to our ears in all the crap we've hatched, but this place keeps moving so nothing settles, little accumulates, even the air is spun dry, squeegeed of smoke and the stale, leftover conversations. And the words all picked out of their shells, nutmeats, cute meets, a current of errors in the circulating air. That's why they do it—set this ship in motion. A slather of blather. A channel of chat debris. Keep the ball rolling. When the only way to go is down, it's nice to have this simulation of perpetual motion, this gyroscopic story, the top story of the building. Shush. Listen. It is Smokey now. The air's gone out of the room. Motown in Motown at last. Tracking tears. The M of the labels could be the silhouettes of tall towers, each with their crow's nests of restaurants and/or bars circling, circling. Do you even remember records? Records with the skips and pops as the needle tracked the tracks through the wax. It wasn't wax but vinyl, and that attracted the dust that caused the skips and pops. There was that old notion that each time you played a song a little bit of sound was lobbed off by the slicing stylus, the groove hollowed out by listening, the emotion of it dredged away, a deep channeled silence to follow. One last drink? One for this endless road? The waiter has a bowl of popcorn, the kernels turned inside out. Look closely, that's what happens. Mix it in with the peanuts and you have a poor man's Cracker Jack without the sugar coating. And since we are being so healthy, how about this round a Bloody Mary? The museum building—here it comes again, there—is meant to look like Independence Hall but, I don't know, twenty times as big. It is a hulk in the night, a wrecked ruin. The night out there is vinyl black, all swallowed up, turned inside out. The museum has galleries of appliances—washtubs and dryers, TVs and radios, vacuum cleaners, vacuum tubes, and all the gramophones and phonographs, stereos and eight tracks, and quadraphonic components hooked up to turntables, tape decks, reel-to-reel. One of the houses in the Village is the Robert Frost House, the poet of walls and roads, and when I was a kid on the tour I needled the guide about its history. Had he written those poems there? The guide had about enough of me, W. C. Fielded me to the side. "Look, kid," he said, "Ford was just collecting houses. He needed an example of Greek Revival and found this house in Ann Arbor." It did look like a little temple. Ford found out later that Frost lived in it for a year when he taught at UM. It is all a black hole of memory. The cheap Cracker Jack peanuts offer no surprises. They seem to be dividing, multiplying. The miracle of loaves and fishes. You can't eat just one. Never enough and never ever over with them. There's Detroit reborn. The lights in the towers are all lit up like crosswords, but the dark squares are winning out. The towers look like they are burned out, like the light has escaped into the night, leaving behind an empty husk. Hey, I'm getting hungry. You wanna dance? The dance floor doesn't move. And no one dances. It's Motown all night. Every night is Motown in Motown. It's a miracle, that music. Made for the night. This town. Pulses of it heading out into outer space, a kind of throbbing beacon in the night, that rhythm records made when the needle made its way to the end, that endless hiss, the needle skating back and forth and around and around that final margin of black ice. Down below, my favorite lake, St. Clair, a dollop. It is a great lake all right. I eat the celery. I can appreciate the utility of it, the celery, consuming the utensil used for consuming. It's good, all sopped, a science experiment where you can trace the gravity-defying osmosis, the juice sluiced up the straw of the stalk, stalking. You forget you're moving. Over there is over there and up there is up there, all space. And I have taken a turn in Seattle, geared inside the Space Needle that looks like a spaceship going nowhere fast. It creates its own gravity, a kind of saucer hovering above the clouds that coat the city below. Those same clouds seem to levitate the whole Cascade Range, off in the distance. They float, all of them, a few hundred feet off the floor of the forest. We seemed to be worming our way through space in that needle, a Phillips-head screw biting into the air, the atmosphere. This is where I get off. I am getting dizzy. Stop the top. As the record winds toward its finish, it has to go faster. Circles inside of circles. Until. Space. Silence. An empty empty place. And you. You, away, way over there, drinking all this, all of it, all in.

The Third Day of Trials

In the back of the motor home, the men played euchre loudly, trumping quickly and tossing in the hand after the first two plays. Phil and Bill Erhman looked like bowers themselves, one full-face, one profile. They were not partners at the table and argued over a loner and the number of points allowed. They were in the asphalt business, entertaining clients today, contractors mostly or state highway inspectors. Whenever the motor home hit a new patch of pavement or a new stretch of concrete on the interstate, they would all start up, and listen.

"Shhh. Shhh. Shhh," Phil would say, concentrating on the pitch of the tires. "Marion. Marion, Indiana." And someone would look out the window, and there we would be, passing Marion, Indiana.

My father, sitting across the tiny galley table from me, was explaining something about football with coins, all heads-up and vibrating from the road.

"The belly series," he said, "depending upon everyone doing the same thing every time, every play. Faking is the same as carrying the ball. Always covering the belly." My father had played football with the Erhmans on the 1952 mythical state champion team of Indiana. Father had been the quarterback of the full-house backfield. The Erhmans were the halfbacks. The fullback, A. C. Russian, was in prison.

"One game I started limping after each play as I carried out my fake," Father said. "Watching the end every play, sooner or later, I lulled him to sleep. He forgot about me. He thought I was really hurt. And on the next play I kept the ball, put it on my hip, and rolled right around him." He scooted the dime toward me with his index finger.

We traveled down the interstate from Fort Wayne to Indianapolis. We hit a bad bit of road and a hollow ringing bridge. "Muncie," Phil shouted from the back, and there was Armick's Truck Stop. Its lights were gravy-colored through the tinted window. Many trucks squeezed together in the lot, lights out, exhausts idling. It was still early.

This was the second weekend of time trials, the third day of the Indianapolis 500. Father took this trip every year with his friends. They started with a party the night before and left early in the morning. They continued to drink, tell stories, and do business. The Erhmans like to sell asphalt at night, when the patching and puckering of the road was invisible. We had to stand up in the motor home every time we passed over a section of the road they had paved so that we could feel it through our feet. "Take your shoes off. Walk around." After last year's major accidents at the track, they hoped to place a bid with the management to resurface the whole course. Father had nothing to do with the business but went along for the ride. To see the trials.

"On the third day of trials someone is on the bubble," he said. "That's why I like the third day, because of the bubble. That means, usually, the whole field is filled up and the bumping starts. The slowest qualifying time from the first weekend is on the bubble. If someone goes faster, his bubble bursts. He gets bumped out of place just like that. You want a beer?"

It was barely light by the time we reached Indianapolis. We took the sweeping banked curve with the John Deere dealership nestled behind it. The green and yellow tractors became visible. The ground around showed black, recently disked—a demonstration. The one banked curve on the straight highway anticipated the city.

"A two-stroke engine has a baffle. Have you ever heard an unmuffled engine?" my father asked. "Really?"

I had lived in Indianapolis for a while. In those moments when the whole city became quiet in the late afternoon, when the various oscillations of noise matched their pulses of hills and valleys, in the small depressions of silence I could hear the yawn of an engine coming from the track and the tatter of a loudspeaker voice drifting after it. That would be the tire tests. Spring.

"I taught you your left and right in a car. The left hand was where the steering wheel was. The oncoming traffic messed you up again. All the daddys were on the wrong side. Fooled you."

The motor home eased on to an exit ramp, kept left and looped over the top of the highway. It then descended upon and merged with 465, belted around the whole city. Going east. The wrong way. The long way. The track was on the west side of town. This was done every year, too, a trip taken every year all the way around the city. A parade lap. The motor home wallowed back and forth between the four lanes, jockeying for no reason, responding slowly as things came up. The Erhmans lapsed into a spiel on slurry and expansion coefficients. We swayed by the first Steak 'n Shake drive-in, black and white, a shadow in the bell of a trumpet exchange. The striped awnings of the restaurant were already down in the new light, and a boy in white was on a ladder changing lightbulbs in the sign that read dimly, In Sight It Must Be Right.

"When you were little I took you to every one of Don Hall's drive-ins," my father whispered. "Each time he had a son, Don Hall put up another drive-in. He gave them all names. His sons and his restaurants. Both the same names. Trying to get both of them right. The Hollywood next to the Roller Dome. The Stockyard. The Old Gas House. The Factory. The Prime Rib.

Imagine, Prime Rib Hall. The Lantern. You had one of those car seats with the little plastic wheel. It had a little mousey horn. The parking lots were flocked with pigeons pecking crumbs."

We panned around the sun and slingshot to the south, snapped north again. The sun was on the other side of the motor home. When I lived here, I walked in Crown Hill Cemetery, the third largest cemetery in the country. John Dillinger is buried there. Most of the land is still unused, bounded by the old canal on one side and brick walls that disappear on the other extremes. James Whitcomb Riley has his tomb on a hill, the highest point in Marion County. From there I could see most of the cemetery, the plots and tokens. At times I could catch sight of the few deer that had been walled-in long ago and continued to reproduce, living in the wooded areas. A few other people would trudge up the hill, some stopping occasionally to read the legends on the stone, pulling on the sleeve of a companion and pointing. The ends of the cemetery blended into the neighboring houses. Deep in the city someone tended the flame on the War Memorial. In a plaza, the flagpoles that raised and lowered state flags automatically using an electric eye did so every time the light changed. When a cloud closed off the sun. Clouds streamed from the east over vaults and tombs and pillars, giving the impression that the day was being manufactured just over the horizon and distributed above the city and, then, dismantled behind my back. Behind my back, I could hear the engines.

"Do you want something to eat?" my father asked. Memory interrupting memory. "Once you get inside, it will cost you an arm and a leg."

Seen through the binoculars, the sunlight streamed up from the grill and bumpers, strapping itself across the hood like wet paper. The guardrail blurred. Unmagnified, the car drifted into the banked curve, leaking light, a bearing in a roulette wheel. Trimming itself as the curve unwound, the car wedged into the shallow pool, splayed out wings of water, emerged, hit the brakes, slid until the drums dried out, then locked and skidded parenthetically 180 degrees, shifted into reverse, y-ed around, took off again through the pylons and stuttered over the railroad ties, geared down, ground and took the hill. Father and I watched International Harvester test a new model Scout. We alternated, passing the binoculars back and forth while eating French fries from a cardboard box. From where we sat among the wild carrots, we could see most of the track, the factory, and the lots packed with Transtars and army-green two-and-a-halves.

"That's right out of your future," my father said, handing me the glasses, "by at least two model years." I watched the old guard stumble up the hill toward us, one hand on his gun and the other pulling against the long grass for balance. He had come back to chase us away again.

My father was limping. Half-circled around him the freshman team he coached looked on. Central Catholic had been his high school, too. The practice field was behind St. Vincent's Children's Home. I watched him limp. I sat up on the shoulder of a giant statue of Mary that capped an outside altar. Beyond the field and the cinder track, the old New York Central tracks wound into Levin and Sons Junk Yard. In the yard, bodies and frames of wrecked cars fit inside one another. Flattened. The usual fires burned. The trucks moved in and out of the yard, over the scales by the gate. Coming in full. Going out empty.

"Hey, kid," someone yelled from below, "come on down here." He was with a group of orphans from the home. They were about my age. I climbed down. They wanted me to do them a favor. I was to go beg for a football from the team's manager. The orphans already had two or three helmets, kicking tees, and whistles. "Tell them you're an orphan," one of them insisted. "If you do that they'll give you anything you want." Chin straps dangled from their belts like scalps. "Yeah. Yeah." The rest now agreed and smiled, showing me the white gummy mouth guards, preformed, over their front teeth. "Yeah. Yeah," swallowing their words.

❹

After the heats and the feature, workmen start taking apart the indoor oval, shoveling the dirt off the raked planks in the curves, and pitching the hay bales on the wagons. The scoreboard, hanging over the collapsing track, winks out and gathers into a solid black cloud suspended in the haze of dust and exhaust. I hold my scarf up to my mouth, filtering my breath through the wool scented with unburned gasoline. In my head, I conjugate the winners with the races as I trot beside my father through the corridor to the ramp, descend, detouring through the exhibition hall downstairs, makeshift pits, where the midgets are being loaded on the trailers. Some are being pushed up ramps; others are running up on their own power. The trailers are hooked up to pickups with their engines running, blending together in an anxious idle. Someone touches a butterfly and then lets go as we turn. He still wears a sooty balaclava and metallic fire suit. One-third the size of the old front-engine Offys, the midgets pack up like grips, a roll bar no bigger than a handle, the decals on the cowling like those old travel stamps on steamer trunks—Champion, Monroe, STP, Goodyear, Hurst, Fram, Borg-Warner, Bell. Chains ratchet through axles. Tailgates slam, and lights come on. A truck guns and stalls and starts again. They will drive all night tonight and race tomorrow in Kokomo. We head for the doors.

Outside in the dark parking lot, the air is cold and empty. father revs up the car and goes on and on about the way they turned into the skid, coaxes the car into gear and slips into the nearest street. As we slow for the first light, a pickup with a trailer coasts by. It enters the intersection as the light turns red, hits the bump at the crest of the cross street, and gives a little flip, like a fluke, as it eases down the grade on the far side and is gone in the night. Once more, because we are not moving, things begin to thicken, and the car closes in. Everything that usually escapes invisibly draws together in steam and smoke, finally heaves into a body, takes another breath, and disappears.

POWER

In the trunk of my father's car there was a Polaroid camera with packets of black-and-white film, striped with bands of gray to distinguish them from color packages. There was chalk in boxes marked like crayon boxes but pale and faded. The chalk dust powdered everything, messed in with the grease of the folded tar and feathered jacks. There were tape measures as big as plates, with foldaway handles, purple snap lines in tear-shaped canisters, rolls of masking tape, black tarry electrician's tape on spools, and white medical tape in unopened tubes. On the first-aid kit was a green cross, and Father used an identical but empty kit for his toolbox, which he also kept in the trunk with jumper cables and two spare tires. A bright-red cartridge fire extinguisher for A, B, and C fires, and flares in red paper, rolled orange warning flags and reflectors. And a twenty-five pound bag of lime. "For the weight," he said, "in winter."

Once, when I was little, we went to a Hall's drive-in, and I used the ledge above the backseat as a table. I spilled my drink, and it drained into the trunk through the rear radio speaker. The speaker shorted; the voice gargled out beneath the paper napkins and foil I was using to blot up the mess. Father was already outside, the trunk lid up and the car rocking up and down gently as he slid the things around with a hiss that was transmitted by the metal of the car. I watched him through the crack left between the body and the open lid. He wiped up the drink as it dripped down and mixed with the chalk dust, smearing the floor. He checked his equipment and then rearranged it. Satisfied, he slammed the trunk lid back down, and it caught on the first time for once and did not spring back up again as it usually did. He even hesitated, expecting it to pop up again. He tapped the trunk once and looked up at me in the rear window, surprised by his own strength. The car still rocked gently up and down. The pigeons circled and settled back to the ground.

Father worked as the director of safety for the phone company and used the camera and the tape measures to investigate traffic accidents involving the company's trucks. He spent part of every week taking pictures of wrecks, visiting accident scenes, and reconstructing what had happened. At night on the dinner table, he would unroll his schematic drawings of street grids. Colored rectangles stood for cars and trucks. Sometimes he would use tokens from board games. He penciled in vectors and numbers, all done on pale-blue veined graph paper. "I know that corner," I would say. He frowned as I put a glass of milk down on a parking lot. I told him, as I chewed my sandwich, of this great crash on Spring Street or how the coral color of Jim Musbaum's Chevy at Baerfield Raceway matched the color of that car there. I pointed and smudged the picture. Father frowned again, answered that this man overdrove his headlights. Staring off, he recalled conversion tables, following distances, and reaction time. This man couldn't see and forgot about a blind spot. "He didn't honk his horn at the alley opening." Those types of things. "Don't spill," he warned.

The rest of his job concerned prevention and education. He distributed drivers' education films that always culminated in a fatality, gave tests, put warnings on windows of trucks. He modified mirrors to magnify, came up with catchy slogans such as "Look alive in '75." He also kept a black briefcase in the trunk of his car, up by the seat. Every now and then he would simulate accidents to test first-aid skills and response times of police and fire units. He used the briefcase then.

I went along one time and watched him. He had arranged for a smashed-up car to be left in a certain ditch by our house. After putting on special blood-smeared and torn clothes that he kept in his kit, he added splashes of fake blood for fresh wounds and lacerations. He put on a medical-warning bracelet that said he was allergic to sulfa drugs. To see if they would check. He then threaded a rubber tube up his sleeve and taped it to his arm. At the other end of the tube was a rubber bulb like a perfume atomizer. He held the bulb close to his chest and with his free hand pumped more blood from a plastic bag he wore suspended from his neck. The blood went through the tube and out the other end, where it spurted like a severed artery at his wrist. In his kit, he had plastic casts he could strap on a leg or arm which approximated simple, compound, or complex fractures. He had ACE bandages that had been treated to look like burns, first to third degree.

He wedged himself through the broken windshield of the car, careful not to cut himself on the exposed sheet metal, and tucked his legs under the collapsed dash. Appearing to be pinned, he affected the shallow breathing for shock. His hand out the window, he tried a test beat or two from his wound and it squirted, a trick plastic flower on a lapel.

"How do I look?" he asked.

"Pretty bad," I answered truthfully.

"Good, good. Go call those numbers."

I left him there and went to a phone booth to call the police and the company's own emergency squad. By the time I returned, I could hear the sirens coming up the bypass. I stood a little way off and looked at my father slouched and unconscious. A red trickle bled down the car door. The shadow his hair cast darkened his forehead. A rear tire had sprung a leak, and the car was settling slowly. His finger twitched.

Passing cars slowed down. Some stopped, pulled off to the side. Passengers got out and ran up to the car. There were sirens now. Someone was directing traffic. The police and the ambulance pulled up. I went closer and saw some police clearing the area, explaining to those who tried to help. The police thanked them, but there was nothing anyone could do. The emergency crews cut away the door with a gasoline-powered tool that shook the car and sounded like a chain saw. My father's head rolled back and forth in the seat. Someone bent over and yelled in his ear. Someone else held the bleeding wrist. On the other side of the car, they broke out the window, trying to free him that way. There were more sirens now, summoned by passing motorists, and a television crew that must have been in the area, listening to the police band. Father was on the ground, and they could not stop the bleeding. They were bringing blankets. A man's hand was streaked red between the fingers. There was a scratch on my father's earlobe just flushed with blood. A piece of glass must have caught him when they broke the window. I could see him stretched out on the ground through the legs of people standing around. A wrecker pulled up. Its brakes coming on and a radio playing. Another man stood up from where he had been crouching over my father. There was no more blood. Someone pronounced him dead and laughed shortly, pulling back the blankets and wiping his hands on my father's shirt.

EXHAUST

When we passed the sign near Penalton which warns against picking up hitchhikers because the penitentiary is so close, the motor home slowed and pulled over. The Erhmans led everyone out the two doors, and we lined up along the drainage ditch and faced in the direction of the prison. The prison water tower was silhouetted now and then by sweeping searchlights. Low to the ground and this far away, not much else could be seen. The men started to shout.

"Come on out, Russian," and "Now's your chance." Between each chorus, they would pause to listen, then huddle, deciding what to say next. Lining up again, my father would pace them, "one, two, three," directing with his hands.

"We're waiting."

A Funk Seed Hybrid sign was on the fence by the road. The cornfield was empty. There was not even an echo.

"He's not coming," someone said, and we got back in.

Starting up the road again my father said that it was a shame I had to see trials in a year when turbine cars were entered. "I miss the sound," he said. He waved his head as if following an imaginary vehicle from left to right and pursed his lips together to imply a sound, because that was what the new engines did. Imply a sound.

We stopped once more that night. A few miles from home we pulled off into a closed weigh station. I got out and climbed the ladder to the roof of the motor home. The siding was cold as I sat down under the TV antenna cocked like a cafe umbrella. Across the highway was an identical station. It was Closed, too. Beyond that was a barn. Visible in the circle of the mercury light was the name of the place, Belle Acres, painted below a smiling image of the Good Sam Club that spotted the dark barn, a hex sign. Good Sam smiled broadly, eyes bugging, his halo tilted back out of the way.

My father and his friends were running races up and down the driveway. They ran heats, two or three men at a time. Someone sat at the finish line with a folding TV table and campstool keeping score. As they ran, their shadows spiraled around their feet, scooting between the pools of light.

Father ran easily, won his heat, slowed down way beyond the finish line, and then turned and limped back up the apron. I applauded alone until I was interrupted by a car honking its horn as it went by on the interstate. I turned to wave. A new race started. Father, passing on his way back to the starting line, looked up at me and jerked his head from left to right performing the first half of a double take, pretending to hum along as the silent racer paused before his eyes. He hobbled back up the drive toward the hut, where his friends were jumping up and down on the scale. He bent over now and then to catch his breath.

They ran a few more heats until the man at the TV table fell asleep and put his head on his hands. The Erhmans led a walking tour north, toward home, examining shoulder material. As they began to sing, they disappeared into the night.

Father and I went back inside the motor home and started up the engine, waiting for them to return. More and more trucks appeared on the highway. The sky paralleled the black field, leaving a space in between. He listened to a horn blasting down the road and to the engine beneath our feet. "Something's missing," he said, swiveling in the captain's chair. He talked until the engine died, out of gas, fitting word into word until I finished sentences he had started. I could no longer tell where we were by the sound the night was making. But by then it didn't matter; we had been carried on, by the dead center, to where it already was the next day.

The Deaths of Modern Philosophers

I.

One philosopher, while eating a piece of bread, steps into a street in Paris and is run over by a bread truck. It is said he looked both ways. He had torn a bite-sized piece of bread from a baguette, placed it in his mouth, and begun to chew. He stepped into the street. He stepped into the street either with his left foot or his right foot, and it is always a street, not an avenue or boulevard. There, he was run over by a milk truck. Or he was run over by a bread truck. It depends upon which version of the story one hears. That it was a truck seems to be important, and that it is some kind of truck is important also. For a long time, it seemed to be a "milk" truck, but now it seems to be some other kind of truck, "milk" trucks being rarely, if ever, seen on the streets of Paris and, thus, an inaccurate detail. So it became a "wine" truck instead for a while and then a "bread" truck when it was remembered the philosopher was eating bread when he was run over by a truck in a street in Paris. It was at this moment, when the moment was remembered fully, that the truck that ran over the philosopher became a "bread" truck.

2.

Another philosopher was killed while smoking on a veranda. It was after the war. Or it is thought the philosopher thought it was after the war. Or that the war, recently not over, was now over and the precautions one takes during a war, such as staying out of sight and not calling attention to your position by the glowing ash tip of your cigarette, were, now that the war was over, not as pressing as they had been only days before. I should mention that this philosopher was not a combatant, not a soldier, but an ordinary civilian albeit a modern philosopher of some notoriety. And it was night. And the war was over. It was a pleasant night, warm, not humid, comfortable. An air of sadness attaches instantly to this incident's gesture of joy. The act of smoking in the open after the war is over! Lighting up under the stars after years of smoking in blacked-out interiors. I imagine, as he was shot on a veranda, that the philosopher emerged onto said veranda by means of large French doors, the glass of their mullions miraculous survivors of the same said war. The opaque curtains billow in the doorway as the philosopher strikes a match, drawing the attention of a nearby nearly invisible partisan sniper. However, we can never be sure. Some would argue the recklessness of the act, that though the philosopher knew the war was over he would surely also know that not everyone would know the war was over. There was still a risk at showing oneself. And there is this final mystery: One survives by one's wits for so long and then survives only to the moment of one's not surviving any longer.

3.

In the movie we will be making about the deaths of modern philosophers not all the deaths we hoped would be of the nature above. Not all deaths of modern philosophers can be the results of freak accident or chance, can they? Not all can be hit by milk trucks while crossing the street or be shot while smoking on verandas a few days after a war is over. Some must die of natural causes or, at least, diseases that, in a way, are natural and, in a way, are not natural. In our research we have asked living philosophers how dead philosophers have died. Invariably the living philosophers tell only the stories of the deaths of the dead philosophers that dramatize these ironies or paradoxes. These anecdotes are certainly visual, which is a necessary ingredient as we are making a movie, but we would like to have uncovered a death of a different sort to give relief to the pattern of deaths that was emerging. There was the report, mentioned by several philosophers, of the philosopher who was preserved and stuffed after he died, and kept in a closet at a college. But this, strictly speaking, wasn't so much the actual death of a philosopher but the way death, for this particular philosopher, was being spent. There was a question also as to this philosopher, while he was living, living outside the range of what we meant as "modern," though his body, in death, has definitely survived into the period we are now calling "modern." We did see the potential in the possible scene. The camera panning around the perfectly still philosopher. He has been posed seated and affixed to a wheeled chair. The antique quality of his clothing is, perhaps, a shade more bizarre than his own taxidermy. Perhaps, too, we could, during this moment of contemplation, add to the film another level of contemplation, i.e., the filming of the filming of the dead philosopher, the two cameras using the same track circling the body and in the final shot, the one shown to an audience, employing footage from both cameras. There would always be a camera in the frame with the stuffed body. We haven't ruled this out yet.

4.

A third philosopher thinks he dies on the operating table. An arthroscopic instrument has been inserted into his body. He has been lightly sedated for the procedure so that he might watch the progress of the camera through his gastrointestinal tract, which he now contemplates as a single hole coring his body. A television monitor floats overhead. His doctor has encouraged him to watch. The drug administered to the philosopher is categorized as an amnesic. The immediate discomfort of the operation will never register in his memory. The doctor tells the philosopher what he, the doctor, is doing, what he, the doctor, is seeing on the monitor. The philosopher, though he is there for those moments, forgets them instantly as the drug scrubs away the arriving memories. This philosopher, the one who will think he has died, finds himself, at first, thinking of another philosopher, a colleague, who did actually die while he, the philosopher now forgetting what he has seen of his slick colon, watched the philosopher, his friend, die of pancreatitis there in a hospital bed. That philosopher's diseased pancreas secreted its enzymatic fluids indiscriminately. His body was digesting itself. That is what he said. "My body is digesting itself." All of this was happening on the insides of the philosophers who looked, on the outside to all the world, as if they were lightly sleeping. This is death, the philosophers think, or this is what death is like. One philosopher wants to remember the way it feels. But then he dies. The other wants to remember the way it feels. But then he forgets.

Four Susans

Lazy Susan

Susan took him home to meet her parents. Her parents had kept her bedroom exactly the way it had been when she was in high school. He was lying on the four-poster bed looking through her yearbooks, The Cauldron. He turned to the back of one from her senior year. The freshman pictures were minuscule, cells in a hive. The pictures enlarged as he paged through the classes, sophomores and juniors. The seniors, finally, stamp-sized and autographed. Susan's portrait, an embarrassment of hair, a string of studio pearls at her neck. He could see in it the Susan he knew, though shadowed by age and an airbrush long ago.

"Susan," he said to her, "a lot of Susans."

"Tell me about it," she said. "Just as many Michaels."

She was standing at the foot of the bed watching Michael as he flipped through the pages. On every page three or four Susans at least. Susan, Susan, Susan.

Her parents had turned on the television in the family room. They had all eaten dinner together in the breakfast nook. The table was a round maple thing with heavy turned legs. The whole house was Colonial with milk-glass lamps topped by frilly shades, hardwood chairs with spoke backs and curving arms, talon feet and and pinecone finials. In the corner, a Franklin stove boiled over with philodendra. The television was shuttered in a cabinet originally carpentered by Jefferson.

On the table was an ancient lazy Susan. Her father had made the same old joke about it and his daughter's name. It rotated slowly on its own as they removed and replaced the dishes and plates, condiments and seasonings. It was a function of gravity and balance, the frictionless slide of ball bearings, but it appeared motorized like a display at a grocery store or museum. After dinner, they did the dishes at the sink while her parents rocked in the glider on the porch. Susan spun the lazy Susan like a wheel of fortune, a spinner from a board game. It twirled and twirled.

Susan stood at the foot of her bed watching him skim through her high school yearbooks. They had been lovers for years now, though they were maintaining the illusion that they were not for her parents' sake. During the visit, he would sleep in her brother's room. Her brother was an actuary in Milwaukee. She looked around her old room at its clutter of souvenirs, every innocuous object emitting its own secret life. She pressed herself against one of the bedposts, the one she had used as a child. The post had been lathed, swelling and contracting, cut with channels, knobs, and grooves. The wood was stained and distressed on its corners, the cherry color worn away. It wasn't until she moved out of this room that she started to touch herself. This was always better, but she had thought, back then, that her rubbing right here, again and again, had worn off the paint, had smoothed it finer than the finish on the rest of the frame, its polish another kind of stain.

It had been years since she had done this, and this still fit, the knurl scored in the wood, the abrading layers in her clothes, her skin beneath, the prickliness of her hair, how it felt again as she imagined again how it had been before, how always before she believed she felt even the grain of the quartersawn oak. Coming this way, she never made a sound. No one should hear. It was as if Susan was somewhere else, and this Susan, who was coming, was here but not conscious of pressing against the smooth wood, that turned, rippling whorl. With her hands on the post, she steadied herself, forgot she was there. She hardly moved, only pressed deeper into the infinitely complicated template of the wood, subtly molding each organic edge, fitting into the scooped-out shell of her past.

BLACK-EYED SUSAN

Susan, naked but for her glasses. She keeps them on. Sometimes wears an adjustable black elastic athletic band attached to each earpiece to keep them in place. She lets me slide the rubber loops onto the curving plastic, cinch them tight with the tiny slides. She puts on her glasses like goggles, reaches behind her head and snugs the buckle tight. Her glasses. The frames. Black plastic frames for the top halves of the lenses, silver wire rims below. Silver rivets at each top corner and at the temples. The delicate clear plastic pads resting on each side of her nose. Men's glasses. The glasses of the Johnson administration. NASA glasses. Vince Lombardi glasses. Colonel Sanders glasses. Malcolm X glasses. "I want to see," Susan says. I like looking at her naked, naked but for those glasses. She lives in one city, and I live in another. We don't see enough of each other. And when we do see each other we are more than likely. We like to meet in hotel rooms, motel rooms either here or there. The smaller the room the better. More mirrors then, designed for the illusion of space. She sits on the sink counter, her back against a mirror, looking over my shoulder as I stand in front of her between her legs. She is looking into the mirror on the closet door behind me. I look into the mirror her back presses against, see my back, my ass flexing. See Susan, her chin on my shoulder, looking into the depth of the mirrors reflecting back and forth. Susan, Susan, Susan, Susan. I sit on a chair. She sits on me. She tells me what she sees in the wall mirror since I can't see. I take the elastic strap between my teeth. I pull it tight. I gnaw on it. On her hands and knees she angles a hand mirror between her legs. She watches me go in and out behind her, above her. On her back with me on her, she hovers the hand mirror above us. The silver of the mirror pools between her legs. As I lick her, I see the mirror fog and clear. Fog and clear. She catches sight of us, shadows reflected in the blank screen of the television. We are unfocused ghosts from another channel bleeding through. I watch her watch herself on the screen. I watch her as she comes. She doesn't close her eyes. I see myself focused on the surfaces of the lenses of her glasses as she comes. I see through those transparent images, my refracted face, its contrasts of planes and angles. I see through the lenses to the other smaller versions of me, motes, floating on each glossy pupil's black concave dilation.

SUE BEE

Susan, you call. Your husband is out of town, your kids in bed. I walk over. All your neighbors have cut their lawns. The evening steams. There is that chorus of locusts, a hatch this year, the sibilant sawn to fricative and back, the z's spent to s's. The s, s, s, s. You are sitting on the front steps, drinking from a cold bottle of beer. You touch my arm with it and lead me inside where it is cooler. The dinner dishes are still stacked on the counter, with the spice tins, the pepper mill, the spent mix boxes, the flour jar open, the pans and skillet in the sink, a very slow drip from the faucet. "The place's a mess," you lisp, "and I'm a little drunk." You don't want to go upstairs. The kids are restless in the heat. You want to fuck in the kitchen, half-clothed on the table, the chairs. On a whim you grab the almost empty plastic bear of honey, pull the cap free with your teeth, the nozzle sweet between your lips, and turn it on its head. Kissing me, you wait forever, for the honey to run down, coating the inside. You squeeze its belly, run a bead of honey along my cock, smearing it with your fingers, then spreading it with your tongue so that it coats the whole length. It takes hours to work my cock inside you. A drop of water collects on the lip of the faucet. A dew of honey clings to your hair. You rub your clit, tease your hair stiff, then lick your fingers and smell the resin of the rosemary, the tupelo, the tulip poplar, the alfalfa, the clover the honey was made from. We can hardly move, my cock caught fast deep inside you, our mouths stuck to each other, sucking the honey coming to our lips. We are still there. Why move? The children never wake up. The dishes are never done. Your husband never returns. The grass never grows again. The trees are studded with hundreds of cicada shells. All the bees are fossilized in amber. That drop of water trembles on the lip of the faucet always about to fall.

SUSIE Q

"Susan?" I hear him whispering in the corridor. I have a roomette on the Lake Shore Limited from New York to Chicago. He is riding coach on the Boston section. In Albany, the two trains hook up, the electric power blinking on and off as the cars are shunted back and forth in the yard. The old Pullmans creak as they are eased into each other, a shudder ripples through the cars as they couple, then again when the new engines pull the slack out of the train and accelerate into a curve sweeping out onto the bridge over the Hudson.

He is looking for me. We arranged this meeting. We haven't been lovers for years, though we stay in touch by phone, postcard, e-mail. This is for old times' sake.

"Susan?" he says. "Susan? Susan? Susan?" he whispers as the train reaches speed outside of Schenectady. Now it is dark outside, and the tracks are running through a cut, the high banks a sheet of black smeared here and there by a smattering of luminous trash reflecting the moonlight. I have the shade all the way up. I've turned out all the lights except the dull blue night-light near the floor. The little fan whirs above the door. I love the old pre-war cars with their stainless and gunmetal painted steel, the coarse orange brown fabrics smelling like old theaters. The nickel-plated hardware of the vents, switches, and fixtures gleams in subtle shadows. And I love the ingenious efficiency of the space, the way the sink folds into the wall, the pocket doors and the cubbyholes for glasses and jewelry, the racks for luggage, the disappearing closet, the secret compartment for my shoes that has another access door in the corridor for the attendant who will shine them overnight and return them polished in the morning.

"Susan?"

"In here," I breathe. I have already unfolded the bed, collapsing the chair with its complaining springs and hauling the mattress, bedding, and pillows from the hidden drawer behind the once upright seat. I've done this already naked as it is almost impossible to undress once the bed is in place. So I undressed while the train rocked by West Point, folded my clothes away. I put in my diaphragm while balanced precariously with one foot resting flat on the clever scissored armrest of the lounge chair and my butt, cold, propped against the mirror affixed to the inside of the sliding door. I tried not to think how I looked as I eased the diaphragm inside me, past the ingenious folds of my vagina. It expanded into place, foreshadowing the contraction and expansion of the roomette I then set about to transact.

He finds me at last. I am stretched out on the bed beneath its covers and blankets in the dark, punctuated only by the flashes of light sweeping by the window. He immediately begins to undress in the tiny space left between the bed and the door, which he has locked, manipulating the many moving parts of the metal handle and latch. My eyes adjust to the dark. In the shadows I can see him contort, wrestle with his clothes as if he is shedding skin too soon, as if he is making love to somebody else. He drapes his clothes over the recessed hooks, balls them in the corner. His penis springs up as he shimmies out of his shorts. It is at my eye-level and, in the dull blue light, I watch it expand and arch upward, another ingenious design. Above me, his head catches in the collar of his shirt he is too rushed to unbutton. His taut cock inches from my face transmits the rhythm of the train's movement, quivers and twitches as the steel wheels stutter over the joints of the rail beneath us. I fight my way out from under the covers as he strips off his socks and toys with the clasp of his watch. I work my way up onto my hands and knees. We say excuse me to each other as we bump and lurch into each other and with the train. At last, I am facing the window, my knees on the edge of the bed, my feet flat against the door on either side of his knees. He stands with his back against the door. He fumbles looking for the spot. I reach back through, making a few jerking attempts to grab his flexing cock as it recoils against my thigh, my cheeks, and then I guide him in.

I wanted to do this, this pushing against the picture window, pushing back against him. The train is running along a wide flat river, the water level route, an advertisement of a smooth ride, no heavy hauling over hills, over mountains. The compartment leaves so little room that behind me he can only grind against me, pushing against me and then pulling my hips, pulling me hard against where he is pinned. Outside, out in the country illuminated by the natural light of the moon, the layers of distance emerge—the streaking pattern of things close by and the slow creep of outlined details in the distance. I follow the lazy meander of farmyard light as it falls away, a blazing billboard on a distant hill as it burns out. There are sudden bursts of red at the crossings, the Doppler of sound, streaking across the window like rain. "Susan," he says. I feel him come. I can't always feel it inside—the sloughing of the spasms, each less intense than the last—through the skin, but this time I do.

And later, after a series of intricate maneuvers, we have bent and twisted our bodies into this position of rest. He's turned on the reading light over his head by flipping a toggle by my big toe. Instantly, we appear, reflected in the window, tumbled together, entwined with each other, the bed, the roomette. He consults the national timetable, noting that we will gain an hour as we head west. He reads to me the names of the towns we will go through, through the night, passes time relating the nicknames of rail lines: The C&NW, the Cheap and Nothing Wasted; the Rock Island Line; and the New York, Susquehanna & Western, the Susie Q. He turns off the light and toggles my right nipple with his left hand. In the dark, I feel around for my vibrator I've stored above the folding sink, an old Sunbeam with the heft and graceful lines of a Lionel gauge toy train car. I connect it up to the AC socket by the reading light.

At the head of the train are three massive diesel engines powering generators creating current for the electric motors turning the driving wheels pulling us along at eighty miles an hour. I plug into a tiny fraction of that power, some spilled amperage. The vibrator hums like a toy train's transformer. The thrum of those real engines gets communicated through the metal of the cars, carried across the couplings where the gaskets kiss. I feel his hand wrap around mine on the machine. The steel wheels squeal on a radical curve that brings us back to that river. We can feel the inertia of all the weight as the train coasts down a grade. The timetable says we have hours and hours, and the trains are never on time. The hum of the vibrator harmonizes with the pitch of the engines throttling up, four cars forward. We can see the engines, their strobing lights as they wrap around another curve ahead. The current streams back through the train as the sound of the horn peals off like skin. I nudge the vibrator's nob along the water level route, tracing the contours of the terrain. We are in no hurry. We are taking the train. He whispers, a decibel or two above the purring running though our fingers, through our arms, into our shoulders, through our bones. I listen to the names of the stations we'll be passing through, our possible destinations: Sioux Center; Sioux Falls; Sault Ste. Marie; Soo Junction; Sooner, OK; Susie, Iowa; Susanville; Susanna, someplace; Susan, Susan in Montana.

"It's a quarter to three…"
—Harold Arlen and Johnny Mercer

Four Dead in Ohio

It doesn't help that the girl is not a student, had run away and found herself on May 4th kneeling next to one of the bodies. The .30-06 round from the Ohio National Guard troop's M1 Garand rifle found him there. It doesn't help either that he too found himself at this shared space and time, the bullet entering his mouth, on his way to, let's say, a literature class that would consider a contemporary poem self-consciously meditating on the efficacy of poetry to accomplish anything of real importance in the real world. The bullet strikes him through his mouth, enters his brain, killing him instantly. Meanwhile, the physics of the recent fusillade, the thermodynamics of the energy released in the reaction shaped within the brass precinct of the crimped cartridge, the military science of massed and sustained and suppressing fire is expressed irrefutably in the outcome and recorded in the phototropic mechanics of the chemical emulsion of contrast, heightened by the technique of burn and dodge, captured in the famous photograph. At the same time 342 miles southeast, a soldier, a member of the Third Infantry Regiment (The Old Guard) attached to the Sentinel unit, stands post at the Tomb of the Unknowns at Arlington National Cemetery. The soldiers of the Old Guard are the only troops in the United States Army that can parade with bayonets fixed, a privilege that commemorates an action taken at the Battle of Cerro Gordo in the War with Mexico. And the Sentinel on this day has his bayonet fixed. He glides along at ninety strides per minute marching the twenty-one steps on the mat in front of the tomb, pausing twenty-one seconds before turning and repositioning his M1 Garand rifle with bayonet fixed to the shoulder opposite the tomb, pausing another twenty-one seconds, and then walking another twenty-one steps back past the sarcophagus where the original Unknown Soldier is entombed and the slabs of marble on the plaza floor entombing the Unknowns from the Second World War and the Korean Conflict. What isn't known now is if there will be a fourth Unknown from the war being fought in Vietnam. No one knows how it will resolve. The war in Southeast Asia has only now expanded into other theaters of operation, into Cambodia and Laos. The knowledge of this has sparked protests around the country. At Kent State University, in Ohio, four are being killed at this moment by the massed, sustained, and suppressing fire of the Ohio National Guard. The Sentinel standing post wears no rank insignia to assure that he will not outrank the unknown rank of the Unknowns he guards. What is not known at this moment is that the current war in Southeast Asia will present a problem of knowing and not knowing. The kind of fighting being conducted there, the advances in forensic sciences, especially in the fields of mitochondrial DNA, will make it impossible to not know from now on. There will be, in the future, those who are still missing. The Lost will be lost during the conflict in Southeast Asia, but there will no longer be the question of identity. Any remains found—a crumb of bone or sliver of sinew, tuft of hair, piece of tooth, sample of skin—provide a sufficient key. The crypt of the Unknown for the Vietnam War will remain empty, will be, at some future date, rededicated, no longer the resting place of that kind of uncertainty, and will be transformed to another uncertainty, to the empty bed of those who simply disappeared, who have left no trace. The girl kneeling next to the body of the student in Ohio—I feel as if I should know her. I feel I should know the body. I should know everything. They are missing. They are missed. There is something missing. Everything is missing.

La Honda, California

On the living room floor, Neil Young sits tinkering with an O gauge Lionel engine, a Nickel Plate Berkshire, as big as a loaf of bread, black, detailed down to the handholds on the running boards and the pilot. The bell swings on its gimbal, each coal in the tender etched, given depth. He unscrews the sandbox cowling. There is a wired portal inside the guts of the toy. He seeks to bug the engine with a silicon chip. Imprinted in its circuitry is the music of the real locomotive. He recorded it, a run-by in Lima, Ohio, a static display brought back to steam. He stood in a crowd of men with directional microphones aimed, reel-to-reel Wollensaks running, amplifying dishes focused as the engine spun its wheels, caught and coughed, huffed to life with that thump thump thump as the exhaust expelled. He got it down, wired, this riff. That pant and this hiss, remembered in the fused sand, coded in the cinders of ones and nils. A miniature speaker is hidden in the rig, buried behind the grill of the smokestack. If it works, he thinks, the sound of the bellowing smoke will bellow out like smoke. He sets the engine on the rails, pets it like a pet. Its running lights dim, merely sopping up the leaking amperage before he turns the juice on full, twisting the knob on the transformer. The toy train starts, begins to move, jerks, all electric and steamless. Then the sound streams from the tympanic boiler, vibrating a diaphragm no bigger than a pencil's eraser. The sound sounds real, he thinks, sounds as if you were there, reduced by scale, a diminished chord, but, still, polished by the memory, the memory the sound has evoked, and he waits, listens closely, knows, there, there will be a long sustained sad slow whistle at the crossing, a kind of warning, and, even in miniature and over this great distance and lost time, a lament.

He was eighteen months old when his father (a student here protesting the continuing harassment on Lynch Street that then bisected the campus and gave egress to the white outsiders who threatened the students emerging from Stewart Hall) was shot dead in front of Alexander Hall. This was a few days after the killings in Ohio. Two killed in Mississippi, twelve more wounded. The police used Browning pump-action shotguns, and later the FBI estimated over four hundred rounds struck Alexander Hall, where the police line had swept the protest from Lynch Street—named for a black elected official and not, ironically, some grim historical designation of purpose. This was made clear years later when the man's initials, J.R., were affixed to the signs, changing the word from an act to actor. After the shooting, as the wounded were carried to the hospital, the police (according to testimony) deliberately picked over the ground, retrieving the spent shells. The pictures of the aftermath reveal and witnesses report that the building was "riddled" by gunfire. The windowpanes of the five-story dorm were all shattered, and the blue decorative panels were shredded by overlapping patterns of shot. His father died of wounds from two double-O gauge pellets in his brain, another piercing his right eye, a fourth buried under his left arm. He returns to the word "riddled," its inadequacy to describe the ferocity of the damage meted out that night. He sees the building every day. There is now a grassed-over plaza where Lynch Street once was, a monument for his father and Green, some solid slabs of marble. In his grandmother's garden he used a riddle to sift the dirt fine from stone and other debris. The screens in the dorm room window were ripped and torn. He shook the dirt back and forth, sieved it through the riddle, and the pebbles, double-O gauge and larger calibers, collected in the concave mesh with, sometimes, a piece of glass, a bottle cap, a bone.

What happened happened. He panned out the dust. What was left was leavings, a cairn of small stones, evidence only that something was over, done. And all the meager residue can be, in retrospect, made-up, manufactured, faked. His life, this life then is a fiction, a made thing. His father's death a fact. A fact, yes, the fictions, the residue of his death all around him. He likes to read the building, left standing, stopping on his way back to his own dorm, placing his fingers in the still visible and accessible (what shall he call them?) bullet holes, in the brick façade, a kind of Braille, a blind riddle, a kind of real.

It was true. He made nothing much from his invention—the famous gas-operated, semiautomatic rifle that he developed as a government employee at the Springfield Army Arsenal. The rifle, everyone agrees, was an essential part of the American success on the battlefields of the Second World War. John Garand surrendered any right to compensation, signing over his patents, the licenses to manufacture, to the government, his employer. He never drew more than his civil service grade. His name, the name that named the rifle, was a kind of compensation. At his funeral, the honor detail of three—a sailor, a marine, and a soldier—snapped off seven volleys, live rounds, saluting the creator of the weapon they were using to salute. The .30-caliber slugs, twenty-one of them, now following their own logic, arched over Springfield, Massachusetts, propelled by the expanding gas of the ignited powder, that expansion of gas the phenomenon that Garand insightfully captured and returned to the gun's receiver to eject the spent shell and automatically chamber the next round in his rifle, which was then ready to be fired by the next twitch of the trigger. The ceremony left one bullet each in the magazines of the three rifles. The M1 clip holds eight bullets. The spent magazine was the one design flaw. The automatic ejection of the clip made a distinctive clicking sound and often warned an attentive enemy of the rifleman's momentary vulnerability as he reloaded. And this was exactly what the soldier, a private first class from Lima, of the Ohio National Guard deployed on the campus of Kent State University, was thinking as his exhausted clip ejected after he finished firing a salvo into the mob of students in front of him. The metal clip made a flat, pinging counterpunctuation to the sharp crack of the eight previous quarter notes—the bullets' staccato ignitions. The distinctive report of the Garand M1 rifle. As he rammed home the fresh clip, squeezing it into the guts of the Garand with his thumb leveraged against the polished wood and steel, he was reminded of the anecdote, probably apocryphal, of the standard ration of ammunition issued to firing squads, how one weapon is secretly loaded with blanks, which allows all the members of the squad to cede responsibility, to believe that someone's actions might have no consequence, or, more exactly, one's action might not contain the lethal ingredient, so rendering that action a reenactment only, a kind of theater, a play, a ritual that is both real and not real, where something happens and where something only appears to happen. The blank is a placebo, more potent in the mind than the body. Later he will see his picture in *Life* magazine, captured as he reloads the magazine of his Garand M1 semiautomatic rifle, just before he shoulders the weapon and fires again into the smear of the crowd of out-of-focus students off in the distance now on his left flank, a bank of fog in that depleted background.

The Four Sides of a Triangle: Proof

A TO B

Yesterday
I took your picture once while you were in the bathtub having tea. You held the cup to your lips, the saucer beneath the cup to catch any drips. Your hair was wet, combed back on your head. Your breasts floated on the surface of the water. I had a slide made, and, yesterday, with you gone and me alone in this rented apartment, I taped it up in the middle of a big picture window above my desk, a chip of stained glass. I look out that window, out through you looking up at me in the steam taking your picture. Each night, with the lights out in my apartment, I watched through her window, a woman in the building across the street step from her shower and reach first for a towel to wrap around her wet hair.

B to A

Not That Long Before

You took my picture as the baby crowned, his hair matted and
matte black, a shade darker than my own. His head pulsed out
when I pushed, slid back in after. It was months later you developed that unfinished roll and I found those pictures with the
other pictures. There was the picture of me, of the dark dome
of my baby's head in the oval frame of my stretched labia. It
had been the next-to-last one that came back in a pack which
contained the series of silhouettes of me a few nights before the
night my water broke. I wanted some evidence of how I looked,
how dark my nipples had become, how rich and thick my hair.
With a wet finger I made myself hard. I teased out a strand of
my hair. I pointed to that dark line which had developed, dis-
secting my belly, running from between my breasts around and
down, dark against my skin as if someone had drawn it with
a crayon or lipstick and that disappeared almost immediately,
along with everything else, after.

A to C

About the Same Time

I take your picture as you make yourself come, the blank print snapping from the camera. You take it from me as you roll over. As I slide into you, you hold still, meeting me with a little grunt I force out of you. All the time you are watching the print develop. It begins with the small black speck of your hair, your hand growing from it, your arm spreading up your body between your breasts and leading to your taut neck and sharp chin, the wet sheen of your parted lips, your open and unfocused eyes.

A to B

Years Before

We all had our picture taken that weekend, the four of us, using a one-hundred-year-old camera. We dressed up in antique clothes—hats with feathers, high collars with floppy bow ties, lots of buttons. The single lens on the camera had been replaced by one with four apertures, and, afterward, we watched as the plate of tin was snipped into four smaller squares. The etched image on each was the same, the four of us in disguise, posed and stiff, holding our breaths, trying not to blink, not moving for a minute, but each was also minutely different because of the slight distance between each lens that focused this one long exposure. Later, in our room, we listened to them in theirs make love, the thin motel walls separating the headboard of our bed from the headboard of theirs. I had brought magazines with pictures because I thought it would help, but hearing them that way had the opposite effect of what I had hoped. You got dressed, embarrassed, covering your flushed skin. You disappeared into the bathroom to pull your hair back into place. I looked at our two metal squares. I looked at her, and I looked at her. Back and forth, back and forth, trying to catch the slight shift in the angle of sight, the four lines of vision looking back at the camera then and, now, at me seeing this seeing.

FAQs

FLIGHT LEADER

So, yesterday I am on the phone with a group of students from Mary Washington College who are asking me questions about writing, an interview for a new magazine they are starting called *Pendulum*, and there is trouble with the connection they are trying to use—they are trying to use Skype for the first time—and each time they connect they sound like the sound of ripping cloth or more exactly muffled ripping cloth, and then a recorded voice with a British accent comes on and says this phone call is being recorded and then the call is cut off, and then they call me back several times until they connect, and then they ask me the first question which is a question I get often when I do interviews which is how do you find the time to write?—or maybe something like, do you need time to write?—and I am getting ready to answer my frequently answered answer when this ripping sound comes tearing into the house as if the ripping sound in the phone has leaked out and been amplified on steroids, and I look up and see the silhouette of a jet aircraft cut through the quadrant of mullions of the window I am sitting across from, streaking through the graphed paper of the tree branches, overwhelming the static of the phone connection, and I ask them, did you hear that?, and they all—it is a conference call, and I think there are four of them, but I can't be sure—answer, yes, and I tell them the Blue

Angels are in town, and that was a Blue Angel practicing for the air show that will take place tomorrow over at the airfield right across the river from my house.

Outside now, a second jet, dark blue and close enough to the ground I can see the gold trim and the gold number 2 in Helvetica painted on the outside port surface of the port vertical stabilizer, and the jet is so close to the ground (I have gone outside now, and I don't think the voices on the phone know I have, but they can't help but hear the screaming of the jets as they vector back and forth over the neighborhood doing a maneuver they call an opposing knife's edge) that I can see the rudder flexing, and the control surface that is the whole horizontal stabilizer digs into the air, ricocheting the jet up up up, and then the afterburners kick on and through that roar I hear the second question which is what is the difference between fact and fiction?, and I am preparing to answer that one with my frequently answered answer about how a fact is a thing done and a fiction is a thing made so that even the most real thing, after it is done, has no reality, and how even the most made-up thing, when it is made up, has a reality—the reality of a book, say, of words on paper, a transcript you can hold, manipulate—when the two jets meeting at the apex of the loop they have both been pulling begin to emit a dark blue smoke that I will learn later is a paraffin-based solid vaporized by the flame in the engines, and the punctuation of the smoke, a kind of cursive wave, is already drifting to the north as the planes (one tucked under the wing of the other) disappear over the horizon toward Mississippi.

FAT ALBERT

The sound, too, of the two jets is drifting away, though it seems (when you do hear anything) the sound is always trailing way behind the jet that is actually making the sound, or, even stranger, the echoes from some other run-by are running ahead of the jet, reverberating, coming to meet the jet as it dives toward the ground, and the sound is bouncing off the ground up to meet it, a kind of stutter or shriek, and the students on the phone ask me if I think teaching has affected my writing, and they can actually hear through the phone the sound of the jets bouncing off the sky and the ground and the trees and the river and the houses, and I give them an answer about how writing isn't like the other subjects of the university, how it is more like a gift that runs through us all, both students and teachers, that what is received must be given away, that art is erotic property, property that stays in motion when, suddenly, a huge blue C-130 cargo airplane, the one the Blue Angels named Fat Albert, rises up behind my house, as if it were a big balloon floating up, almost nicking the top of the longleaf pines in my neighbor's backyard, its four turboprops digging into the humid air as it lumbers so slowly; it is so slow, especially after the blinking speed of the jets, that it doesn't seem to have enough oomph to remain aloft, always already about to fall, as it is more like a blimp, a zeppelin, wallowing now right overhead as it rolls port, showing me its belly like a whale sounding and stalling, sliding backward, it seems, but then splashing forward, a graceful awkwardness out of the water, over the golf course, its overstuffed rounded and rounding organic shadow casting on the organic cutouts of the greens and bunkers and ponds, and the plane shakes, straining to find an inch of lift, and hunkering down to gain momentum, and then seeming to levitate, wagging its tail and launching, like a navy-blue cetaceous cumulus cloud, shading, now blotting out the bloated sun.

SLOT

The jets are back as the intermission clown car of the cargo plane settles down for a landing on the other side of the river, and the jets—there are four of them now—in their famous formation of four, emerge from behind a cloud, diamond-shaped, the fourth airplane in the slot beneath and behind the lead plane that's wingtip-to-wingtip with his two wingmen's wingtips, but that is hard to see, hard to say, because what is behind or below or above changes instantly effortlessly constantly, it seems, as the planes move through the delta-v of this calculus, rearranging themselves in each dimension—x, y, z, and time—and from this distance, it looks as if there is just one plane instead of four, so precise is the handling as the "they" that is really an "it" roll and pitch and yaw as one, and the students have all been talking to me on the other end of the phone, asking their last question, saying this question coming now at me at the speed of sound, at the speed of light, is their last question, and it is this: would I consider publishing something online, as their magazine *Pendulum* is published online, and would I send them something to publish?, and with the four blue jets up in the blue-going-to-white sky, their manufactured blue smoke spilling from them, another signature, with serifs and accents and underlines, I tell the students that I am working on a book of fictions made up of things made up of fours—the four chambers of the heart, the four seasons, the four humors, the four winds, etc., etc., etc., etc., and I am working on something now I will try to finish and send to them to consider putting in the magazine, and I am watching the formation reposition itself into what I will learn later is called a Double Farvel, with two of the four planes inverted, creating a mirrored image of each other, before they break apart once again, corkscrewing through the air, vectoring to each corner of the sky, reining in their speeds, then raising their noses at an extreme angle to almost stall, and then extending their gear, banking, and heading for the airport over the river, and I tell the students that the Blue Angels seem to be finished for the day, and the pilots of the F/A 18s will now attempt what they call a "landing" on land but that they usually "land" at sea, on an aircraft carrier (they are Navy planes, after all, and the pilots are not pilots because in the Navy a pilot is someone who pilots a ship not an airship, so these pilots are naval aviators), and they are about to land on land and not on the deck of a ship with a tail hook and arresting cables, the ungainly and suddenly ungraceful difficult ending to what has been all effortless and elegant, the falling, gliding, silence, all taken back with a vengeance, in the final maneuver called, simply, a controlled crash, the only true answer without question...gravity.

Four Eyes

MOOSH

I see him goggled with his glasses, sitting in the sitting room, the space that is the split-level of the split-level, between the upstairs and downstairs, where he has come to live with my Aunt Mad and her family, blind by then. He shaves by feel and misses patches of whiskers on his cheek or leaves swaths of stubble on purpose. He grabs my hand to skin his skin. "Moosh," he says, and "Moosh" again, sands my hand. His eyes, magnified, run behind the useless lenses of his useless eyes. I see the scum of the cataracts, enlarged by the glasses' lenses, mica veneers, a cloudy wax beneath the waxy glass. The right eye blinded outright, a spring sprung from a couch long ago—a darkness penetrating, spiraling into the aperture of the iris—as he moved furniture at the Hotel Indiana where he was a custodian of cushions, a janitor of the terrazzo. The whites of his runny eyes are nougat. They, the eyes, weep as if they've forgotten that they are weeping, more a welling leak that tears and tears. "Moosh," he says and says again, those double Os scooping out the sight for the sound. At Grandma's wake, years before, no one saw him disappear. I found him later in the basement of the old house—the basement dug out for the dirt to be used in the backyard garden—lost in the dark, trapped in what had been the coal bin once and now was the root cellar seamed with sacks of seed potatoes gone bad, their eyes sprouting a pulpy fur of fingers.

MA

I see her see the saints, Anthony of Padua, the patron of lost things, lost people, and Jude, the patron of losing, of lost lost causes. She read with a glass, magnified, squinting, coaxing the print to grow. She mussed the Mass cards, spread them out on the kitchen table like tarot, like my baseball cards, the statistics, the details of the dead, the final prayers, recipe cards for funerals. I fielded my cards across the table—St. Mickey, St. Willie, St. Aparicio, St. Sandy, St. Ernie—my voice introducing them to the audience of her, a public address booming, echoing in the vast stadium of her kitchen, her echo doubling the litany of the canon. Later, when she decides to die and then dies, she will say that the saints have said it is so, so she does. That was after I lost my eyeteeth, pulled to make spaces for the spacers. The new bands smarted, wired my mouth closed, a declension—tender, tenderly, tenderness. I look angelic in the first communion portrait, a pseudosaint, orthodontic. She looked at me askance. Cornered me in the corner of her eye. She saw me as another icon, saw me suffer under a *mal occhio*. So, she made the *mal occhio* mirrored back at my *mal occhio* to combat it. At the kitchen table, she mumbled the mumble while drip-dropping the *olio* in the water, watching until, at last, it collected itself into the shiny slimy worry beads she worried, the sign I'd been seen, and then spat and pinned the amulets of twisted horn to pierce open the bad glance. I saw her see the saints in the light falling through her kitchen windows. They talked to her in pulses of light, plosives of color. I followed instructions, building the scale model of the Avenger, its parts spread out on the floor spread with morning papers, the words worming under my gaze. It was blue, the airplane, and its wings folded and the decals were stars. The furniture was wrapped in plastic she polished. I fogged the clear plastic of the toy canopy

234 michael martone

with the dissolving glue on my fingers. The pilot's head was the size of a pea. I fit tab A into slot B, lost a blue piece in the nap of the rug. I caught her looking as I looked.

I see her, eyes closed, in the bed she is going to die in. I have just arrived, taking the red-eye overnight to make it in time. Everyone will say she waited for me to arrive, and when I did arrive we didn't wait long to witness the last laboring breaths, her eyelids fluttering. Everyone says she had been dying a long time, sitting up in her chair, staring out through the picture window, awake through the day, through the night, seeing shadows in the shadows, dust in the clouds of dust blown up from the ball diamonds in the park across the street. Everyone said it was the cable, the witnessing all the Eyewitness News that put her over this edge, the flickering loop of muggings and murders in the Loop, daily box scores of death. I'm not so sure. I watched her watch out all my life. Stare. Always there, she was never there. She wore trifocals, their optics fragmenting her eyes, fracturing the light, bluing there, going to indigo, then violet, her unblinking eyes a puzzle beneath the broken-up stains. The television was black-and-white, even after color had been invented, and the screen was haloed by a lighted frame advertised by Zenith to soften contrast. Her chair was angled so she could catch the oblique pictures bouncing from the TV and the ones glancing in through the picture window. She watched me for her daughter, my mother, who worked as I was growing up. I watched her fall asleep sitting up, her eyes not closing. Playing in the front yard so that she could keep an eye on me, I made faces and waved my arms to startle her pictured inside the window. She didn't start but didn't take her eyes from me, the optical illusions of flat portraits where the look follows you back and forth, and I went back and forth, her mirage of me, the only movement her eyes panning as I moved. No one knew where she went when she went behind her eyes, but everyone agreed that as she failed she went there more and more, her eyes turned inward. We wondered what she was imagining, what she saw when she wasn't seeing. We all asked her all the time what she was thinking when she was thinking and what did she dream when she dreamed and, "Oh, nothing," was what she always answered when she answered at all.

I see blue, yellow, but I am deficient in the reds and greens, see them only through crossed wires in my mind. Knowing grass is green, I see the gray of the gray I see as grass, a grass green when I think about it. It has always been hard to explain, how the brain's circuitry saturates the absence with this solid mass of missing information. It's in the genes. He was truly color-blind, and I could half-understand the gradient of grays his brain fudged with, niggling the nervous mechanism of misfiring. Imagine this pale world one big paint-by-number pattern and the pallet, this spectrum of grays, deflected only by intensity, by darkness and light, by value but not by hue, all drawn out within the outline until the brain supplied a pigment's alias. The brain is always fooling itself. He was an electrician, a member of the Brotherhood, whose union buttons pictured a fist squeezing a bundle of jittery lightning. Each year's button screened a different pastel shade. He wore the current year on his beige porkpie hat. A green, I think. He wired together every school science fair projectfor me. Each year, I displayed the schematics of circuits, series and parallel, illuminating big Christmas tree bulbs—in primary yellow blue red orange green—screwed into the porcelain sockets. See, I would say about the series, when one bulb burns out the circuit's broken. Without the light, the colors left, blacked to black. He stripped the copper wire of its plastic insulation, crimping the coating, each with its own tinted sheath, wrenching it from the wire underneath, and then threaded the white copper wire into the screw connections connecting. The wires came in all colors, of course, the scraps of insulation exhausted confetti. I saw what he saw. Saw it in the way he saw it. Not knowing what is missing, a transmission of this lackluster lack. We watched the television skewed to black, to white, even as it announced its living color. Spies were everywhere, always hesitating over the spilled-gut circuitry of some explosive device, attempting to ascertain which wire to clip to defuse the bomb, sorting through the nest of leads, a gray coiling spume of the same. We watched the beaked pliers peck and tease, all shading and shadow, one wire now balanced on the whitest edge of the scissor. No, not that one, he said into the depths of the invisible scanning light, light drained of its knowing.

Mount Rushmore

WASHINGTON

Freud fucked us up, this Father business. The Mother business as well. He, Sigmund, is the inventor of the modern novel, is *the* novelist of the twentieth century, the founder of the form. He is the Father, that again, of the notion of Character and even more importantly the notion of the character of Character, this business of depth, this business of three dimensions, this business of complex. The forefather of the epiphany of The Epiphany and the transformation of transformation of Character that follows. He, Freud, elicits in me a kind of envy, yes, Envy, that I have not, in all my years, invented or, in all my years to come, will never invent, any Character as real as Ego, as real as Id. There! There are fictions for you. So contagious as to jump the page, reformulate the brain chemistry so completely as to deny the efficacy and accuracy of Brain Chemistry to explain the brain. His invention of the Subconscious and the Unconscious naturalizes inside us (Inside Us!) the idea of the Subconscious, the Unconscious (See!) as if these fictions are not fictions. I like the bib of slag spilling down the General's chest, a graphic demonstration that the head of the Head of State was always in state there inside the mountain. See the limestone-wigged helmet of the figurehead on the brow of the cliff ship! The lithic waste is the cascading, foaming bow wake. George is a kind of Venus in drag and Penis in person, the titanic member being the progenitor of his Country, sure, but also Love, I guess, or at least that compelling drive of Sex, emerging from the sea of solid rock.

He was the writer. Well, Lincoln, too, wrote, signed on to write Jefferson's sequel. And Jefferson is the one whose back-story has legs. The heritage of his transmitted DNA decoded as avidly as the Declaration is parsed for intention. My favorite plot twist? The branch of Hemmings's children by Tom who passed into Ohio, refusing to cotton up to the analysis of their genes, preferring White-ness over Jefferson-ness. How odd our desire that this one have a life that is narrative, not simply anecdote. And irony too. Backstory and, there on the escarp-ment, he's got George's back. The inventor of political parties, the originator of difference. The Great Deconstructor has the least "face." No distinguishing marks save that distinction of no distinguishing marks. Okay, red hair, but this is a mono-chromatic mountain. Jefferson pulls duty, in two dimensions, flat visage on the screwy two-dollar bill. J is our K of presidents. Anonymous and somewhat known with the suggestion there are things one wants to know. And inside Jefferson is Madi-son, the symbiote inside the big brain, the watch in the pocket. Madison writes Jefferson; Jefferson writes *America*. *America* is the Great American Novel.

ROOSEVELT

Reading left to right: Roosevelt. The Modernist whose medium is stuff, stuff like mountains, like canals, like painting battleships white and sending them on a performance piece around the world. Probably his idea to create the thing itself, this wacky stunt in South Dakota. Or at least it was in the air he breathed, expelled. His is the spitting image of the contemporaneous Zeitgeist, the modesty of the placement of his visage tips off the self-consciousness of the facade. The least equal of these equal giants but nonetheless the Great Sculptor of the ideal of giants. The last of firsts but the first of lasts. There is real artistry in the rendering of the pince-nez. The glasses are there but not. A transparent reproduction of Transparency. Transparency the dominant ideology of the age, our age. The trick of Realism, its tricklessness. See, these busts bloomed on the mountaintop, a spontaneous generation like maggots appearing on rotting meat. WYSIWYG is what you see and what you get from this point on. No bull. The eye is drawn to those eyes magnified by the invisible glass. What are you looking at? The writing of novels, I think, is so beside the point, isn't it? One writes novels to write the author of the novel. The book itself does not last, is not carved on the side of a mountain, is not printed on money. Funny, the New Critical transparency was to focus on The Work and not The Author of The Work. But it is always *Marvel's* "To His Coy Mistress." Every work comes with that apostrophe of possession. The Author ain't dead. The Author ain't even ain't.

LINCOLN

The most dead one. How did Washington die? Jefferson? Roosevelt? Lincoln's death was the one dramatized, in a theater no less, by an actor acting and acting. History is scripted. The show goes on. Literally, the show goes on. *Our American Cousin* performed daily like clockwork. The clocks all set for ten after ten. What ever happened to pageants? The great theatrical recreations of historical events by ordinary citizens, descendants of the participants in the original events, on the sites where the original events first transpired? Sure, the Mormons perform each summer, on another mountain in New York, the visitation of the angel to the Prophet Joseph Smith. Now there's a novel! But the art form of the pageant, the Pre-Postmodern art form, seems to have waned. Perhaps. Perhaps pageantry continues but is only now disguised as Real Life, Story and History the same. The recent War in Iraq was staged. It was held in theater. How did the President watch the performance? Not that much differently than I did, I bet. Like a King in Shakespeare watching a play on stage upon the stage. Like the Subjects of a King watching the pageantry of royalty, of war. My favorite part was the soldier, wounded in the hand, waiting for the evacuation by helicopter, who had the word HAND written on his forehead, talking to his mother, half a world away by satellite phone, talking to his mother in real time (Real Time!) while I watched. That was my favorite part. Lincoln's forehead was a stage. In the movie, *North by Northwest.* All of the presidents look on when the actor Cary Grant playing the role of Roger Thornhill playing the role of Mr. Kaplan performs a staged performance of his (Cary Grant playing Roger Thornhill playing Mr. Kaplan) death all witnessed by the back-projected image of the mountain, there, through the window by the barbershop quartet of stone. At the moment of the assassination The Real World approaches harmony with the Fiction of the World. *Sic Semper Tyrannis!*

Four Fourths

That summer I read all of Chandler, Hammett, Cain, one pa-
perback book after the next in an old eight-story apartment
building on St. Paul Street called the St. Paul. On the fourth
floor, I had one room and a bathroom that served as the kitch-
en, the hot plate on the toilet tank. My apartment had been a
bedroom in a bigger apartment next door, cannibalized into
its own space generating rent, ninety-five bucks the first of
the month. I had filled it up with used office furniture, dinged
gray-metal bookcases, and a store-cut foam mattress on rough
pallets on the floor. Out the one window, I could see over
Lovegrove Alley to North Charles Street and the park beyond
with the statues of Confederate generals and Edgar Allan Poe,
who looked in stone a lot like John Wilkes Booth. It would be
easy here to say it was hot that summer, but it wasn't. For some
reason it wasn't hot and not even cool, but cold. The room's
one doorway had two doors—a solid oak one that could be left
open for ventilation and still be screened by the second one,
a painted pine plantation shutter that let in some air and the
echoing sounds from the hallway. There was another door in
the room leaning up against a wall next to the bookcase stacked
with the detective novels I was reading. I had found the door
in the basement. I liked to look around the old building, see
how it had been renovated over the years, how everything fit
together. There in the basement with the storage lockers, the

coin laundry, and the old coal bunkers was a room made out of warped studs and unfinished drywall. The door was open. A janitor's room once, I guessed. There was a bed frame, a broken chair. I looked behind the door, closing it, and discovered the inside side covered with bits of paper glued or thumbtacked or stapled to the wood—gum wrappers and cigarette packs, ticket stubs and matchbooks, a ferry schedule, racing forms, magazine advertisements, paper watch-faces, fortune cookie fortunes, and Mass cards. A private's sleeve chevron stripe, oyster shells, dominoes, a child's block (the letter M), several kinds of keys and coins, a comb with some teeth missing where the brad went through. And everywhere between the paper appliqué and the odds and ends were dozens of every kind of screw and nail holding nothing, it seemed, but screwed or pounded into the inside of the door at different depths for their own sakes. I unhinged the whole door one night and took it back upstairs to my room. I'd read in bed. I read the door and my books. It was cold that summer. I'd turn the page and look up, get distracted by the door. Something new, I'd find it there. Stamps. Baseball card. Time card. Bottle cap. Betting slip. Evidence. The fireworks that Fourth of July were being launched from Memorial Stadium on 33rd Street not that far away. I had found the way up to the roof. I bought a folding beach chair, aluminum tubes with webbing, and took it, a blanket, and a book with me to the roof. I unfolded the chair on the wooden boardwalk that seemed to float above the gravel roof, sat down, and waited. It was cold. I said that. I wrapped up in the blanket, read. I was the only person on the roof, though I could hear the crowds of people down below making their way up St. Paul and 33rd Streets to the stadium. It took a long time to get dark, and I read *The Big Sleep* until I fell asleep. I woke up finally in the silence after the loud cracking booms of the firework finale stopped, the smoke of all the explosions, black on the black night sky, drifting south toward the Inner Harbor.

July 4ᵀᴴ, 1980, Ames, Iowa

That summer I moved to town a month early before the job started and rented an apartment on the ground floor of an old brick house near the power plant downtown. At night, I walked to Main Street through Band Shell Park that did have an old band shell used, I found out, for concerts once a week by the city's band, wearing uniforms left over from the high school production of *Music Man*, playing Sousa marches and *Sound of Music* songs at dirge tempo. In the branches of the oaks beyond the band shell, a cow, a Jersey, perched, or so it seemed, content and grazing. Boyd's Dairy's life-sized sign swayed above the ice cream stand, suspended by invisible wires from old flagpoles. Boyd's served four flavors—chocolate, vanilla, strawberry, and a daily special that was usually bubblegum. I got a scoop of chocolate in a cup, walked down Main Street to the deserted train station, and sat on the platform under the eaves, my back against the wide clapboards, and looked out over the double-track right-of-way. I waited for the next train going through, east or west, forty or fifty a day, grain trains mainly, made up of closed hopper cars or gondolas painted in ice cream pastel colors hauled by the green and yellow engines of the Chicago and Northwestern, the Cheap and Nothing Wasted, blowing the horns through every crossing all through town and punctuated on the end with a caboose in a blindingly bright shade of safety yellow whose brakeman or conductor in the bay window usually took the time to wave at me as I waved back with my pink plastic spoon. When I first moved to town, I walked through the park and past Boyd's Dairy and up Main Street to the Hotel Muhm to have my hair cut by the barber whose shop was in the lobby. That summer I was reading westerns, starting with *The Last of the Mohicans*, *Shane*, and *Little Big Man*. I had *The Virginian* when I went inside, and began to read it after I sat down to wait my turn. Then the barber finished with the customer, and the customer paid while the barber dusted the seat of the chair with a towel. I dog-eared the page in my book and sat down in the empty seat, waiting for the barber to drape the sheet around my neck. "I don't cut long hair," he said. "OK," I said to the barber standing behind me. "I said," he said, "I don't cut long hair." My hair was long, I thought, that was why I came in for a haircut, but not that long. Before I could say anything more, the barber said, "I don't cut your hair." And I got up and left. When I opened the door to the flat, I saw the door I found in Baltimore leaning against the far wall of the big empty living room that had been converted into my bedroom by the convertible couch converted into an unmade bed. I still had to finish the unfinished white pine wood bookcases, staining them later to look like dark oak. Soon after that, my tooth began to ache, one in back on the left, the lower jaw, from the cold daily ice cream, and I had to find a dentist. I didn't have a car then, so I walked into the first office I could walk to. The dentist was able to have a look right then, no waiting, and I sat in the chair with my finger still in my place in *The Virginian*. My wisdom teeth were impacted, all of them, and the dentist recommended they come out as soon as possible and recommended the long holiday weekend. I had been told that there was a neighborhood parade on my block—bicycles and red wagons tricked out with crepe paper and streamers, kazoo bands, batons, hula hoops, and everyone with little flags. Recovering after the procedure, I could take my lawn chair and sit by the curb, see the kids ignite snakes on the sidewalk and light sparklers in the daylight, watch the riding lawn mowers trailing bunting and the dogs and cats dressed up like minutemen. I never made it to the parade, only imagined it in my stupor brought on by the pain pills I was given, the leftover effects of the amnesia drugs that kept me awake for the removal of teeth numbered 1, 16, 17, 32 but left me remembering nothing, nothing of it until I woke up on the train platform, my ear to the ground, the steel wheels stuttering over a rail joint, waiting for this train, convinced that a wave from the brakeman or the conductor was all I needed to get better, the cool mint colors of the cars already gone, forgotten, a balm.

JULY 4ᵀᴴ, 1983, BRANFORD, CONNECTICUT

That summer I rented a house in Branford, a shoreline village
outside New Haven. The house, an old foursquare with a big
screened-in porch, was built above a pebble beach overlooking a very calm Long Island Sound. Long Island itself was in
the distance, a thickening of the pencil-line horizon off to the
south. I read, in a hammock strung up on the porch, all of Patrick O'Brian's books set on sailing ships during the Napoleonic
Wars, which always mention the hammocks strung up between
the beams of the lower decks of the frigates, the men-of-war,
the ships-of-the-lines. I would look up from the book to see the
Sound off in the distance—through the screen, the branches of
trees, and over the roofs—suddenly filled with sails of all types
reaching across the cove and then turning and tacking back
down east. Speedboats darted across the wakes, the only wave
in the water, going up on step and slapping back down to make
a sound that would reach me many seconds after it happened.
When I wasn't reading, I walked through the neighborhoods,
the houses mostly year-round places whose inhabitants lived all
the time at the beach so that the novelty of the ocean had worn
off. They vacationed elsewhere. On the cross-country drive to
get there, I went through Amish settlements in Indiana, Ohio,
Pennsylvania, and stopped once in one of the stores and bought
a big, black, broad-brimmed flat straw hat I wore as I walked
through Branford and down to the beach with my folding
chair and flag-striped towel to watch the boats wheel, the
fang-shaped sails stirring in the smooth water with the bright
sunlight amplifying what little chop there was, a sprinkle of
sparkle. I rolled up my long pants to the knees and waded out
into the shallow water. The breeze that pushed the boats blew
further out. The shade from my hat cast a black shadow like
a hole into which I could step, fall completely through. I had
driven out to Branford in a '67 Dodge Dart I inherited from

an aunt. The temperature gauge had never worked until it did one night, instantly jumping from C to H as I drove through fields in Iowa, fireflies sparking off the corn all around me. The radiator blew, blowing fluid through the hood onto the windshield. Ever after, mechanics, who loved working on the ancient engine, the old slant-six, clucked when they saw the blood-red that rust had painted the engine and its compartment. From Branford, I drove the Dart into New Haven, stood in line for a seat in one of the pizza places there, something the guidebooks said I should do. By the end of the summer, I ended up liking Sally's more than Pepe's, not so much for the pizza as for the many pictures of Sinatra on the wall there. I waited by myself in the lines outside and often sat with strangers inside, taking up the odd seat, and only mentioned I was spending the summer in Branford if anyone asked. I read about old sea battles and walked to the beach and through the town and then back up to try to write something myself—a story or a poem—as I rocked slowly back and forth in the hammock on the porch. Or, as a change of pace, I hiked up the road toward the interstate, to the Trolley Museum and rode an old street car—the PCC salvaged from Philadelphia, the bright red open-sided convertible car from Brooklyn, or the drab trolley from the St. Charles line in New Orleans with the destination placard scrolled to Desire. The cars trundled through the salt marshes and scrub forest, sparks spilling from the overhead wire on the turns. At Short Beach, where the track ended, the motorman got out to lower the trailing trolley and then forked up the leading trolley to contact the wire. He got back inside, flipped the backs of the seats over rattan benches to face the front, and powered up the car to go back in the other direction. I turned the lights out in the house the night of the Fourth. The neighborhood around me was dark, the houses emptied out. The local families going into New Haven to celebrate, a vacation from the permanent vacation the village seemed to live. There was no moon but plenty of stars drifting south and west. Far away on the north shore of Long Island the fireworks there began, launched to bloom silently just above a seam in the dark. The explosions were so small that I couldn't tell the patterns or be sure of the color, only the intensity of light. The porch screen blurred the little smudges further, framed them in the pricked openings of the wire mesh. It is all perspective, the miniature bombardment that breathed out and then smeared, falling back into the sea. Up and down the length of the island, the static scatter of sparks, as if they were signaling each other, a couple dozen patches flaring up, tendrils of one or two high altitude rockets arching back over the lit-up pulse of smoke. Fleck of rust. Burning mold. A random pantomime that seemed to communicate, in some subdued but desperate code, that something urgent was happening somewhere else.

That summer I went back home to sell my parents' house, living there, sleeping in my old room, getting the place ready to put on the market. I had to cull through everything, decide what I would put in the garage sale, what I would give away, what I would cart off to the dump. My father collected souvenir golf balls he kept in pressed-paper egg crates. Each ball was printed with a different stencil or decal commemorating some event, a company or tournament logo, sports team mascot, fortune cookie saying, motivational motto. My mother framed pictures using the same frames over and over, stripping out the picture and mat, replacing it with a new mat and photo, then storing the old one behind the new one sealed up inside the brown paper backing. Opening up the paper backing of a picture was like opening a Christmas present, with the gift being the layers and layers of past pictures, of annual Christmas photos, say, July Fourth picnics in the backyard, stashed there. The Christmas shots were department store studio pictures of the three of us and then just the two of them through the years. The wallet-sized copies had been sent out in the Christmas cards. I read science fiction at night, books about the future after a day of grubbing through the past. I read brittle paperbacks, foxing pocketbook editions I read first when I lived there—Dick and Clarke and Asimov and Bradbury's *Martian Chronicles*—on the same couch I had read them years before. I worked on curb appeal, cutting the lawn in a checkerboard pattern like my father had. I shaped the hedges, cleaned the gutters, painted the shutters, changed the seasonal wind sock from Easter's green and purple to the striped and starred bunting of Memorial Day that would do for the Fourth of July. The backyard butted up against the boundary of an office park with its cluster of brick and glass box buildings sloping away gently down the contour of a hill to a pond where a gaggle of Canada geese milled. In the parking lot of the nearest building, an endoscopy office, my parents used to watch the fireworks fired from the top deck of the parking garage on the college campus on the other side of the bypass. It was easy to drag some chairs and a cooler to a spot there and watch the lot fill up with pickup trucks and vans of families arriving to hold vigils of the night coming on, the sun falling toward the campus. In the dusk, legal bottle rockets lifted off of truck beds. Firecrackers sputtered on the ground next to the gathering vehicles as they crept along looking for a parking spot. Cherry bombs spooked the geese that spat. In the black windows of the next building over, I could see the glinting rows of computers, their screen savers, I imagined, flickering and rolling. A contract company of the post office that remotely examined badly addressed mail and routed it remotely to where it was supposed to go. The screen savers saving the screen, the flashes there reflected in the glass of the windows as if each window pictured its own tiny fireworks display. I thought about the workers who would be back soon enough at those consoles after the holiday, scanning the lost and diverted mail scrolling on the screens, attempting to read the blots and smudges splattered on the envelopes, the fractals and fragments of the stuttering hands of correspondents from somewhere. They would try to put a spine in some smear, make fragments mean something once again, the parts more than the whole or at least something whole enough to mean. Like that "i" there in that cloud of inky sky. I imagine the dark dot dotting that "i" as a concentrated black hole, an absence collapsing into the zenith of a rocket's launch, exploding over the straight streak of its exhaust. For that instant, a lit mass of a million billion pieces flaring then nothing. More than nothing. And nothing more.

Chili 4-Way

When you were in college, at Butler, you would drive out
Michigan Pike to eat at the Steak 'n Shake there. It looked like
a Steak 'n Shake, but it wasn't quite right. It looked the same
as other Steak 'n Shakes—black-and-white with the chromium
fixtures and the enameled tiled walls and ceramic tile floor. The
staff wore the paper hats and the check pants, the white aprons,
and the red bow ties. But often you were the only customer.
You sat at a table, not the counter, and scanned the menu as as
many as a dozen waiters and waitresses waited for you to order.
This was a training restaurant for the restaurant chain, self-
conscious of its self-consciousness, a hamburger university.
There were waiters and waitresses in training watching how
your waiter would take your order, and there were waiter and
waitress trainers who were being followed by other waiters and
waitresses in training watching the waiter and the waiters and
waitresses watching the waiter taking your order after bringing several glasses of welcoming water. They crowded around
the table in their spotless uniforms like hospital interns around
your bed, waiting, taking notes on their checkered clipboards.
There were television cameras everywhere and television monitors everywhere displaying what the television cameras where
recording. There, the grill cook and the dozen or so trainee
grill cooks pressed with the fork and spatula the meat pucks into
perfect steak burgers. There, one after the other flipped each

patty once, crossed the instruments at right angles and pressed down again forming the perfect circles of meat, the evidence of this broadcast on snowy monitors next to those displaying the scoops of ice cream falling perfectly and endlessly into a parade of mixing shake mixing cans. There was even a monitor that showed the bank of monitors and one that showed the monitor showing that monitor, and in it the endless regression of televisions within televisions, the black-and-white clad waiters and waitresses and the grill cooks and prep chefs moving like a chorus line, constructing your two doubles that you had ordered an acceptable duration of time ago. And the caterpillar of service snaked with your plates of perfectly plated food held by the waiter at the head-end trailed by a conga line of identical servers back to your perfect table where the television cameras panned to focus on you eating your two doubles and showing you eating your two doubles in the monitor that showed the monitor of the double you eating. And everyone in the place made sure you had everything you needed and said they'd be back to check and then came back to check and asked you if you wouldn't mind filling out the survey about the service and food and a survey about the survey and the survey about the survey's survey. The sandwiches were perfect. And the milk shake. The French fries were all exactly the same length and arranged in a pleasing random jumble. The real stainless steel cutlery gleamed, and the real dishes and the glass glasses gleamed. As you left, at every empty table, an employee wiped and polished the Formica tabletop, watched over by two or three others, nodding unconsciously in what you took to be approval.

She would meet him when he was in town, when he was going through town, at the Steak 'n Shake right off I-69 on 96th Street. They both remembered when this part of the city had not been part of the city, had been nothing but farmland, nothing but woods. She grew up in the city. He grew up in another part of the state. They met later after both their lives were settled. Now 96th Street was all strip malls and box stores and freestanding drive-ins. Sometimes, after they would meet at the Steak 'n Shake, they would decide to drive separately to one of the motels nearby and spend a few hours there before she would go back to work, her family, her home and he would get back on the road to drive back to his home, his family. Or he would stay the night, call his wife to say he was too tired to keep driving, would get an early start the next day. On the nights he stayed over, he drove back to the Steak 'n Shake and had dinner, trying to get the table they had shared hours before. In the parking lots outside, as the parking lots' lights came on, teenagers gathered in crowds of cars. Everyone out there milled about, switching rides, changing places, slamming the doors, flashing the car lights. Some of the kids would come inside to order shakes and fries, take the order back out between the pools of light to pass around the drinks and the bags of fries to their friends in the shadows. He watched through the plate glass with its camouflage of advertisement the purposeful loitering in the lots outside. Earlier that day at the same table, they had talked about how things had changed and how they wanted them to stay the same. She always ordered a Coke but Steak 'n Shake had its own brand of pop. King Cola. It tasted the same, she always said, but it was different. He always ordered chili, and as they talked he crushed each oyster cracker separately in the plastic bag, one at a time, turning the crackers into finer and finer crumbs, a dust of crumbs, before he would tear open the bag and pour the cracker crumbs into the bowl of chili. That day when she ordered the King Cola she was told that Steak 'n Shake now served regular Coca-Cola. The waitress waited while she considered. There was a Diet Coke now too, and that's what she ordered after she thought about it. When the waitress came back with the drink, she dropped off the bags of crackers, and without thinking, he began to pinch and pop the crackers inside the bag. He asked her how the new cola tasted. She used a straw. The same, she said, and different.

Bob called. I had been out of town. I had just walked in. I was hungry after the trip. The phone rang. It was Bob.

"If anybody asks where you were Saturday night, you were with me," he said.

"Okay," I said. "Where were we?"

Bob thought for a second. "We were at the old Steak 'n Shake on Keystone."

"What did I eat?" I said.

"What? What did you have to eat?"

"At the Steak 'n Shake. If someone asks."

Bob thought again.

"You had Chili 4-Way."

"Okay."

He hung up, and I went back out to find something to eat in earnest. The car was still warm. I drove over to the Steak 'n Shake on Emerson Avenue. I looked at the menu. There was Chili, there was Chili Mac, there was Chili 3-Way, and there was Chili 5-Way. I had remembered incorrectly.

NORMAL

We visited Normal to eat at the original Steak 'n Shake. The chain was founded in Normal in 1934, and the first restaurant was still standing after all these years. We liked to eat at the Steak 'n Shakes in Indianapolis, where we are from, that are all modern and new but retain, by design, what we believed was the look and feel of the original. We especially liked the trademarked logo of the disk with wings and the slogan that graced the actual restaurant china: "In Sight It Must Be Right." The company history online has pictures of the original Steak 'n Shake in Normal that looks even more retro than the retro restaurants they are building now. We could see how they were trying to retain, in the present, a suggestion of the past. Then, there were carhops, too, and marquee lighting with signs that swooped and curved into streamlined decorations on the roof. It was all very modern for its time and, now, in the pictures looked like the past's idea of the future. And here we were in that future looking back to a past that, for us, never was. Turns out that "In Sight It Must Be Right" meant something specific back then. We could see, if we were customers then, the cooks grind the steaks into ground meat right before our eyes. The fine cuts of meat being turned into the ropey cables of meat as the cooks in immaculate white aprons turned the old-fashioned cranks of the machines. We guess, back then, people didn't trust what went into things like that, that eating out, then, was more of an adventure. So we wanted to see for ourselves, the past, go back in time, we thought, to see the real past in Normal instead of what was left of the past today in Indianapolis. Turns out we were too late. By the time we got there—driving through the farmlands of Indiana, Illinois, the fields dotted with cattle gazing on the green grass of the gently rolling pastures passing by—the original Steak 'n Shake had been demolished, or was in the process of being demolished, the yellow bulldozers still moving the ruins around into neat piles of rubble. We parked the car and watched them tidy up. We mixed into the crowd of onlookers watching. The setting sun, shining through the arch of water being sprayed on the debris to keep the dust in check, created a miniature diminished rainbow over what we had come looking for.

Four Signs

There is an economy of form found in nature. Look at the horn, a helix, the same pitch as Watson's DNA contemplated in Bloomington, Indiana. Is there a message here to be transmitted? Perhaps a flagpole. No, only a name. SCOTT'S. Now that jogs some ancient racial memory of thrift tacked onto all this abundance.

And, Watson, what genetics. What genie's been engineering the produce? The green fuselage of cucumber, the warhead carrots, the blimp tomato. Nothing in the world expresses these exact colors. Lemon yellow, orange orange. The pineapple, shaped like a stomach, turns into an eggplant when you look at it from the other side. The pair of pears, the green pepper and the red pepper. What is that? An onion? Garlic? Radish? A sprig of cherries, the same color red as the tomatoes and red peppers, and something unnameable out in front. It is the shape of a fruit, the dusty color of a vegetable. Which reminds me of the old saw about tomatoes—fruit or vegetable?

It is a stock boy's nightmare. His pyramids spilling from the grassy green counters of produce. His legs, a blur, a cartoon. The ripe fruit rolling, splitting open as it was meant to do. The seeds are dispersed everywhere. Vines, then, beginning to grow from behind the canned goods, a jungle there in aisle four.

It is like an explosion, with all the tricks of photography— time lapse, slow motion, cropped, retouched.

It is a vending machine that cannot stop vending. Lucy is our Eve, the housewife, with a bandana done up in horns. She reaches, plucks, eats endlessly.

It is that old television game show. Contestants sweep through the aisles, dumping food into cart after cart.

It is the terror in the eyes of the child posed next to the pumpkin bigger than he is.

Scott's big horn screws itself into the clouds. At night I can hear the worms in my garden. They cast long shadows with their casting, twine, untwine, leaving empty holes in the black earth the next morning.

PERFECTION

The loaf of bread is as big as a boxcar. Derailed from the sign, it scissors upward, its end sheared away and crumbled as if it were too much to ask to simply open it. Perhaps the whole loaf is to be used at once, and no one thinks to save the bag. The apparent carelessness of packaging, like the clear window of a written style, is transparent, ignorable. Not technique at all, but content. A one-pound loaf. You have held it in your hand. At this distance, it seems no bigger. Art has fooled you again as you reach out to squeeze it.

But it is yellow. As yellow as her hair. As yellow as the coat of butter (not waxy, not melted) spread evenly to the crust of the single slice she will always be eating. It is like the kiss Keats talks about on the ancient preserve jar. The red of her lips just meets the yellow of the butter. And the curve of her mouth Us into the parabolic arch of that slice. And her blue eyes are looking up away from the bread and butter as if, at any second, those blue eyes will roll all the way up beneath her creamy lids at the first instant she realizes just what it is she has tasted and finds it impossible to stop tasting and to stop saying Mmmm and impossible (all reflex now) to stop herself from closing her eyes as she will find it impossible to stop from closing her eyes when, later, she will kiss that boy at the picnic, their lips slick from the buttered bread they have eaten, the golden buzzing of bees in their ears, and the yellow light of the sun pressing on their closed lids.

But it is white bread. Where is the heel? You are in the middle of things. The slices keep falling, full face, the landing profile. The stack of bread on the plate never rises to shut off this stumbling. It is a steady state. It is another illusion you live by. It is the plenty that is never quite enough, like the bottomless cup of coffee. It is *almost* perfect. Each slice a slice closer to the whole truth. Each slice a slice closer to the end of this story and even beyond the end to the last blank pages, whiter without printing, at the end of the book. A book that was a story. A story that was like your life.

But wait, there is more.

POWER

My dad was a janitor all his life over at the GE. We lived on
Brandruff Street by the Wabash tracks. From our backyard,
where we kept a garden of trellised tomatoes, pole beans, and
grape arbors, we could see the top floors of the factory beyond
the rails and warehouses. I staked the plants. Strips of white
cloth trained the stems up the poles and wires. GE's got fac-
tories everywhere, making all kinds of things electrical. The
Broadway GE made the lightbulbs. My dad worked third trick.
He changed lightbulbs with new lightbulbs off the line. Union
rules, that old joke. Yes, it took three guys, two to turn the
ladder while he held the bulb. On the roof was the GE sign.
GENERAL ELECTRIC spelled out in thousands of bulbs.
The old intertwined initials blazing in a circle of script above
it. G and the E laced together. Each night, my dad woke up
and, ready for work, sat with me in the garden. We listened to
the plants grow. Fireflies sparked upward off the tips of the lush
leaves. The trains shunted back and forth in the yard. With
binoculars, he focused on the burning sign, floating above the
roof. Later, I watched him, a blurred shadow, crawl across the
light, making his way along the brilliant scaffolding, to the single extinguished bulb. I had to look away. Only the brightest
stars were in the sky, the rest washed out by all the light of the
city. My father kept his eyes closed as much as he could even
behind the polarized window of the welder's mask he wore.
He'd look away, he told me, to where he thought our dark
house would be, where I would be in the vast darkness below.

PALETTE

At night after closing, the crazed blacktop of the parking lot is sealed, the thick tar swept along the split seams, slapped about cursively with sopping mops that splatter and spray antimatter milky ways, black stars on black backdrops, the constellations unreadable in this light, a kind of Palmer primer of crippled capitals, detached legs and leaking ovoid gestures gone awry, creases on a palm incised, scored, toothy selvage. Over all these alphabets and glyphs, a slurry film is broadcast by machine, all pneumatic nozzled steamed sheeting, plowing back and forth, lapping the air-brushed edge over the edge, masking (a mat of matte black hermetic iced devil's food cake, empty black void, a desert dessert) the edge edged with another edge. And after that, while this new nothing dries, the night crew tees up some comped cones à la mode taken from the soda jerk on overtime at the take-out window. These little lamps of lactose lit-up, winnowed with each flickering lick. They're a kind of optical illusion, floating on the air, that their operators (doused in shadow camo leotards of silky asphalt splashes) make disappear.

In the dark, they watch the painter in spotless overalls overhaul the scaffolded sign out front of the Shoppe. It's an artist's palette with eight moons of vibrant neon colors jewelling its rim and a rendering of three sable hair brushes thrust through the illusion of the thumbhole. The script *A* of the store name drips toward the hummock of the ending *z*'s ascender, loopless, the italic flourish of its blobby tail, the abdomen of some oversized insect, the splat of the apostrophe, all mimicking the French curve of the big ol' kidney shaped sign, all hip that then goes all square, intersected by the rectangular sign within the sign, all business and no art, the special message board of misplaced applications—M B3EF NO ODLES, TH TUR KEY, F BBQRIBS.

They watch (as the earth's crust cools, sculpting their triple dips of neon-colored ice cream into a concrete demonstration of Zeno's paradox of time and space) the painter paint the pictures of paint, mixing paint on his own homemade palette (a slab of scrap wood) dabbing red paint on the red "paint" of the red paint of the sign-sized palette.

The painter arcs his way through the whole rainbow of color, each one a substitution for flavor, a gigantic graphic synesthesia, of ice creams already melting into metaphors, comparisons, these synaptic associations made in the palette-shaped brain, wedged into our cone-shaped skulls. This is like this and this is like this and this is like this. It is harder now to tell the painter from the paint. More licking. More liking. More this-ing. The stars overhead look like stars in the sky. The blacktop looks like blacktop. The ice cream tastes like ice cream. The sign looks like Sign. The artist painting the sign, who looks like an artist painting a sign, signs the sign with something that looks like, when you look at it closely, even in this unfathomable and defining blackness (a color that is both all the colors and none of them), another sign.

Thought Balloons

1.

On a long reach, the leading airships in the breakaway pod jockey for position as they drift into the third turn near South Bend during the 17th running of the Tour d'Indiana. Dirigibles, blimps, balloons—all manner of lighter-than-air craft—vie for the coveted Otis R. Bowen Cup in a thrilling race, often taking months to complete, covering the four corners of the state.

2.

In the distinctive barn-red livery of International Harvester, a tractor blimp plows the anvil top of a fertile cumulonimbus, kicking up a trail of cirrus clouds in its wake above the parched summer fields near Monon, Indiana. Following close behind, a John Deere zeppelin prepares to sow the newly turned furrows with seeds of silver iodide in the hope of sparking needed precipitation, a practice invented by noted atmospheric scientist Bernard Vonnegut, brother of Hoosier novelist Kurt.

3.

A rapt crowd of Hoosiers observes as the Oolitic Fire Department douses the smoldering wreckage of the Derek Jeter balloon on Christmas Eve 2002 after it slipped its tethers during the Macy's Thanksgiving Day Parade in New York City. The three-story balloon, depicting the Yankee slugger sliding head-first into second, eluded detection during its month-long free flight over the heartland until its fiery reentry in the limestone country of south central Indiana.

4.

Casper Kastellnick, of nearby Port Royal, Kentucky, expertly rides the buoyant atmosphere produced by the world-famous helium springs outside Vevay, Indiana. The lighter-than-air air geysers erupt inertly on a predictable schedule and are of such duration and magnitude as to allow local aficionados time to master their spectacular levitational displays.

Four Places

A Room

First, there's the sun (which is eclipsed by the moon {the moon itself obscured by wisps of clouds} haloed by the luminous corona) which is a ball of gas (which is a state of matter characterized by the lowest density and viscosity). All this, in the corner of the stamp (the whorls of raised ink {exactly like the oily residue of thumbprints left by your correspondent} of printing, expanding like a gas {expanding until evenly distributed within its container} to its edge) near the selvage. Now (wait {a second}) where am I?

A Town

Pictured: the recently discovered and described "predicate." Here, the verb of being has just come into being. An "am" can't even simply sit since "sit" hasn't been invented yet. The local population is, however, intrigued. They've begun to "be." They have been naming things for decades, are on the verge of naming, "have been naming," a verb. Some "nouns," like "name," are not just nouns but verbs also. Shown in the inset: Things they have "named." The "adz." The "hibachi." The "bustle." The "gyroscope." The "puck." The "quotation mark."

A VILLAGE

"Who dreamed us here?" the inhabitants of this village ask in their dreams. They try, upon waking, to renegotiate the covenants inherited from their ancestors—the dazzling hue of their houses, the shifting distribution of their neighborhoods. Their undreamed dreams accumulate, cloud the black, black night with sparks of color. They forget to ask. They ask. They forget they've asked. They ask. Who smudged out the road that was never there? Who erased the sense of a sense of direction? They dream: "Who dreamed us here?" "Did you?" they ask. "Did you?"

A RESORT

Spring finds hundreds gathered here to stand for something else. The participants remember to observe, and the observers remember to participate! Everyone remembers to remember! A lock of hair becomes a copse of trees; a fingernail turns into a placid lake. At the cocktail parties, you are encouraged to sample canapés of your own fingers but forget, until you remember, you have no way of picking up your own finger! And later, they unfold the map! Its scale is 1:1! It corresponds exactly and fits like skin! It is your skin!

Four Calling Birds

"Calling birds" refers to colly, or collie, birds.
"Colly" or "collie" means "black." It comes from an older
English word for coal. "Colly bird" is the European blackbird.
Common in parks and cities in Europe, it looks like a dusky
version of its cousin, the American robin.
Both belong to the thrush family.

VEERY

The next time they talked on the phone, she told him she
had just started to come when she heard her daughter return
home downstairs and call out to her. Falling from the bed, she
ran across the room to close the door. As she ran, the orgasm
caught up with her, the blood rushing from her head, her legs
turning spongy, compressing beneath her. When she came, he
knew, she often expelled a multi-syllabic, "Fuck," and he could
hear, though it was distant and hollow with echo (in her haste
she hadn't had time to disconnect), the first fricative transmute
to a plosive burst of greeting, a schwa-y "Whah," closer to the
first notes of her daughter's name. The next time they talked,
she would tell him how intense it was to be moving through the
spasm, all inertia, entropic, irresistible, spilling as she spilled
toward the door, her momentum carrying herself and the door
forward to a slamming slam he could hear clearly. She said
it was like a cartoon, the motion so suddenly staunched, her
writhing, her worming. Her back turned to the door, she slid

slowly to the floor with the squeak of naked skin on enamel paint, one hand fumbling behind her head for the lock's knob while the other, between her melting legs, tugged at herself, plucked out the minor key tufts of sensation as she settled bare-assed, panting. In fact, the next time they were on the phone, the retelling of this last time was enough to take her over the edge again, the conjuring up of the sprint across the room, the throbbing pulses racing through her racing legs, turning the ground beneath her viscous. "Fuck," she said distinctly in his ear. What he did not tell her about that previous time (the time she left the phone connected on the bed to rush to the door, coming while she ran) was that he continued to listen over the distance, hearing the padding feet and the grunting climax and the call and the slamming door and the puckered squeak of her skin on the door. She had been using a vibrator, one that plugged in, and it continued to hum, the sound dampened by the bedclothes. It nested near the phone, creating a humid occluded silence, overdubbing the static hiss sparking off the wire. He too had been about to come when he heard her hear her daughter's voice and start her stumble for the door. Had he come, he wouldn't have uttered a sound, intent, instead, on listening to hear the "Fuck" slip out of her and positioning his release beneath hers, emitting a kind of melted sigh for her hard consonance to ride on. Now that she was gone, he slowed his stroking and continued to listen closely. There was a window open. It was late spring there, and he swore he could hear the percolating silence of the warming air as it infiltrated the mesh of wire screen near her bed. He lived miles to the south where the spring had long ago turned torrid, his room closed up and dark. He rolled onto his side, insulating his ear away from his other ear, encasing it with the pillow that filtered the bass line purr of the whole-house AC cycling outside. He heard her then miles away talking with her daughter through the door, the door acting as a kind of resonator, transmitting the mundane news that she'd been napping, asking for a moment to get dressed. The vibrator went dead. She unplugged it and pulled it to her, a clatter hitting the floor, the scrape of it as she coiled the cord, the vibrator's hard plastic case stuttering across the sisal rug. He heard drawers of various timbres slide in and out, the little rattle of the swivel pulls against the plates. The jittery knickknacks disturbed in the haste. He heard her, he swears, dressing, her jeans on first, standing, the flat stomps as she skipped twice to balance, the stereo tramp of both feet finding the floor as she pulled up the pants. He listened for the zipper and heard it. Then the soft whisper as she rolled a T-shirt onto her arms followed by that stopped–up submerged sound as her hair, silk, slid through the abraded collar. She walked flat-footed to the door, brushing out her hair as she shuffled, the pitch changing as she stopped, then the sweep of all that hair over the top to brush from behind and below, currying the muffled mass of it back up over her bent bobbing head. And then he heard her leave: the volume of her diminished in his ear, the distant depleted report of her, calling her daughter's name, descending as she descended the stairs. The silence settled out heavier than air. He pressed the phone closer to his ear as if to inject his own hushed self into the recently disturbed acoustic there, to detect any sonic smidgeon left in the mix. Her swallowing. A footfall. Those eyes blinking. He boosted the gain of his signal, attempting to catch her shallow breath breathing. Instead, all he heard in the stillness, spilling in from the open window, was a birdsong, a slurred series of downward inflected quarter notes. Each note tripped progressively lower in pitch, spiraled, cascading down a scale. It began again with a simple, non-inflected cheep, ended with a rolling trill. It was one of the thrushes. The hermit or the robin. He had told her at the beginning of the call that all the flocking robins in his neck of the woods had disappeared a few days before. I am sending them your way, he had told her as they began. A kind of foreplay, he had thought, releasing songbirds north to her along with the heat, the seasons turning, his own sprightly combination of suggestion. There it was again, a long lowering run, arranging itself into a fragment, a phrase, an adjectival clause that modifies a person, place, or thing, an intensifier that amplifies. Very. That sounds like *very*. *Very*. Very like *very*.

Their answering machines matched, and they started leaving messages for each other. Beige plastic boxes with a keyboard of buttons—play, fast-forward, erase, rewind. The tape spooled in a transparent cassette stored in a compartment inside. You could see the sprockets turning in the cassette as you listened to it play through a clear plastic window in the lid. Nested in the buttons, a red LED lit up a number indicting the number of calls. Depressing *play* released the message into the room through the low fidelity speaker wired in such a way as to make everything sound melancholy. They tried to keep each other's tape filled with the magnetic imitations of each other's voice. He would come home to find the machine's number glowing, 21, say, or 25, 22 messages only to find each one of the messages another piece of one long call from her, the machine starting, then cutting her off after a proscribed interval. Each new message contained another message about the message left just before, the procedures she endured to redial and connect, the transitional phrases of "where was I" and "Oh, yes" linking all the calls together in the end, a long self-conscious apology for taking up all the tape with the series of calls and indicating that this was a very long and convoluted way to say something she should be able to say simply—that she loved him. She loved him. He was fond of leaving one long message on her machine. Each machine had a setting that allowed for varying the duration of the machine's patience. He expected that he would have to leave a long message, and so he spoke extemporaneously though sometimes from notes and at length about his day, and at every transition point, he linked his mundane and ordinary activities with the phrase, "and I thought of you when…" or "that made me think of you…" or "I told myself to remember to tell her." And then he would tell her, tell her the structure of his thinking as he thought, of his remembering as he remembered it. Both machines, doling out their seconds, initiated and terminated the time with a nasal beep, flattened bleat, the sound of which programmed itself, a concussion, into each of them. They dreamed of the beep, found that in the messages they would sometimes beep themselves, a charm to ward off the inevitable, rapidly approaching real beep. The sounding of it, the anticipatory silence before it, and the sound itself, and the other silent silence after, its punctuation. They started and stopped on the cue. On cue they entered the noisy space of their connection, and on cue they became again disembodied, distant, silent. They liked the old machines for the mechanical magic they conjured; playing the message, each other's voice filled the room, evoked the other in three wraithlike dimensions that made the voices seem almost corporeal, an actual body solidifying around the skeleton of vibrating air. Each could be in each other's next room, calling down the hallway around the corner. As time passed, the messages began to be more complicated, as each of them attempted to pack the other's tape with more and more information. It started when one of them played a song in the background. A news report on the radio followed, a commercial on television picked up inadvertently. The sound from the street below, the dishwasher turning on, washed over the string of words strung on the spooling, the unspooling tape. Soon, it occurred to both of them that they could play back to each other each other's messages to the other. There, on the answering machine, was the new message and underneath it, in the background, the previous recorded message of the now listener's voice leaving a message. The machine recorded the message of the improvised duet of person and the person in the machine speaking in waffled mono that mimicked a stereo track, leaving a message and at the same time responding to a message that had been left. Those layers now recorded were then played when the next call was made. And the next message added another layer of past messages to the mix. More and more silent spaces on the tape filled with words, words turning to syllables turning to diphthongs and ligatures turning finally into a deep layered mist, bits of alphabets, static murmuring, incomprehensible mass, but strangely intimate, ancient, prehistoric, preverbal. The acoustic of amniotic fluid. Warbles, squeaks, smeared thumps. It was a repertoire of sounds they stole from each other and then gave back as baroque, rococo, atonal fugues. All of the noise became a foil to the final track they applied, recording each other's orgasms over and over again, the wall of auditory stimulus building up from a triggering beep, each other's name burbled up as a downbeat, beating, the gulped hiccupping of breath backbeating, all percussion, cussing counter punctually, attempting to fill in every iota of silence with any un-silent utterance, collapsing all the space between them into the compact sonic puck of the solid absence that mocks and mocks and mocks and mocks them both. The sound then turned liquid, sizzled, finally, like rain, like a tidal rush, a sound your own blood makes in your own ear when you hear it, when you hear it when you listen for it.

RED-WINGED BLACKBIRD

His room in the Amway Grand Plaza Hotel overlooks the Grand River at the point at which it is interrupted by an artificial rapid, a concrete stair-step that spans the river, symmetrical tiers tearing up the glassy flow, an organized baffle. Beyond the river, he looks down on the pie-wedge slice of the Gerald Ford Museum, its acute angle, a cursor, arrowing back to him in his cockeyed corner room. He teaches geometry and finite math to 9th graders in an Indiana junior high and sells Amway on the side, but soon, he thinks, it will be the other way around. Everyone knows the money is not so much in selling the product—detergents and soaps and perfumes and vitamin supplements—but in selling people on selling the product and then selling them the product they would sell. He likes the geometric progression of the profits, the curving curve of results, the logarithmic rhythm of getting rich quick as his network of distribution compounds and compounds and compounds and compounds. As a numbers person he understands this better than most, loves to diagram, for a prospective distributor, the trellised architecture of the scheme—names within boxes, networks of radiating beams of connecting emanations, doubling down the gridded yellow legal pad. He looks the part. The white poly short-sleeve shirt, the dark waffle knit tie at his throat, the heavy glasses of glossy black plastic with the bitten end of the right temple earpiece. "It's not rocket science," he tells the prospective distributor, but his looks suggest it is. He's an analyst from Rand, a grammarian of overflowing flowcharts.

A woman in the lobby of the Amway Grand Plaza Hotel—not one of the conventioneers of Amway distributors checking in nor a member of the native elect Dutch Reform who people the environs of the Grand River Valley of southwestern Michigan, but a buyer of office furniture from Philadelphia, touring the nearby Hermann Miller factory—sees him and thinks without thinking that there's a man who needs to get laid.

Instead of getting laid he, the sober conventioneer, returns to his room to order dinner in, prop himself up in the king-sized bed blanketed with the scalloped sheets of notes from today's sessions sorted into piles, his nest feathered. Along the river outside, he sees the copses of rushes in the eddies, rafts in the backwaters along the banks. Perching blackbirds bow over the cattails. The birds launch themselves, dozens of them, intersecting and crisscrossing, squawking, he imagines, to settle once more, jostling on different roosts. From this distance they are dots, fluid punctuation, floating decimal points. He knows the hotel around him is full, its hundreds of rooms occupied with men and women unmoored, at loose ends, and most are here to make connections, construct a honey-combed armature of enterprise—one big hive, the whole ball of wax. The company anoints itself with the moral disinfectants of god and country, and the scrupulous cleanliness marketed in Grand Rapids comes backed by pious guarantees of godliness. But he knows that that filth, that ugliness is as human as apple pie, that he and the company count on it. Hygiene may be the main business model, after all, but the company includes a line of euphemistically disguised lubricants, pheromonal colognes, and atomized herbal propellants in its catalog, samples of which he now deploys upon his own body as he begins to masturbate, listening as he does so for the sounds of other humans all around him, all the rooms filled with humans, making love—the beat of the headboard, a howl from a hissing shower, the giggle that picks the locked connecting door, the spillage of dead weight onto the ceiling that's also a floor. He comes into the sink, reaches beneath to the fascia board of the vanity for a tissue only to discover the built-in dispenser is empty. He pops off the chrome cover to get to the empty cardboard box behind it. The room is stocked with a replacement along with all the other amenities, all Amway brands, of course. He finds hidden behind the empty box a Polaroid picture, the first of many he will find, of a couple having sex, or at least he thinks it is a couple because the pictures are all cropped down to cunts and cocks, lips and tongues, mouths and nipples, hair and hair. The first stowed behind the box spills out onto the faux marble floor. It takes a moment for him to sort out the abstract angles and lines, the trapezoids and rhombi, and when he does, he stares at the fleshy flesh before him, stares it back to the strange plane of the start—solid slabs of his first impression—so he can experience again the sensation of the optical illusion, fading out and back into focus. Now he senses that these surround him, little treasures that are themselves a kind of treasure map. He finds more and more of them. One behind the notice tucked into the plastic sleeve tacked to the door. Inside the zippered upholstery of the armchair cushion. Beneath the desk blotter. Behind the pictures of the lake dunes. On top of the television wardrobe. Inside the dry cleaner's bag. There are three in the Bible. And each time he finds another he starts to search for more. Within the folder of stationery. Under the automatic coffee pot. There is a growing pile on the bed mixed in with his notes of projections and testimonials. He begins to put animated sequences together— four frames of a cock first disappearing inside a cunt then further in and then completely inside only to emerge, in the fourth picture, glistening, the sheen on the skin like the sheen on the still undeveloped print of an instant photograph, the emulsion beginning its wet work, evaporating into the schematic of solid geometry all pyramids, cones, cylinders, and spheres. Bounded space and its infinite absence. He shuffles the prints once more, deals them again onto the cluttered bed, a four-handed game. It is all chance, permutation, game theory that results. How long it must have taken them, he thinks, to create the fragmentation, so many moments of passion—sets and subsets, intersections of oblong fields of Venn diagrams, x's and y's. Each reading of the cards promises a prediction of some future from the residue of a past. He thinks, then, of Christmas and the last day before dismissal. He has his classes listen to a scratchy record of "The Twelve Days of Christmas" and poses for them an algebraic puzzle to pass the time. How many presents in total does the true love receive? The one partridge and one pear tree multiply through the course of the round to twelve each. The two turtle doves covey up to twenty-two. There would be thirty French hens, and thirty-six calling birds, etcetera. Etcetera, etcetera, etcetera, through the whole progression of obsessed love. Outside now, the red-winged blackbirds have left their perches along the river, launching from the cattails that then rebound, bristling. The birds levitate into a cloud around a much larger black bird, a crow or a raven in full flight fleeing the dive-bombing, tag-teaming attacks over the overly neat rapid rippling below. Another and another bird peels out of the cloud to intercept the distressed bird attempting to maintain a little altitude. It all takes place in silence, a harried sketch of vectors plotting velocity, gravity, and drag. Even to his trained eye it is impossible to count them all. The red-winged blackbirds can't stop, continue to create this silent racket, persistent pantomime, suspended in the lowering sky.

BLUE JAY

Each married to someone else, they were conscientious enough to call their spouses when they were away together with each other, taking turns to dial home or receive a call while the other busied him- or herself in the bathroom of the hotel room, reading the local attractions magazine. But the room, big as it was, was not big enough to damp the half-heard half conversation going on nearby, making both the participant and the eavesdropper self-conscious, so that the latter got dressed and left the room to take a walk around the property, to loiter in the lobby, or even to have a drink in the bar, half-watching the sports spill from the television floating overhead, finally to call back to the room from a house phone in the elevator lobby and hear the operator report, more often than not, that the line was in use, asking if you wished to leave a message. Leaving the room meant the one leaving had to get dressed since most time in the room was spent undressed—fucking or relaxing after fucking, recovering from fucking, eating and drinking naked in the room. Room service is ordered after fucking and received by one of them, wrapped only in a robe or draped with a long nightshirt that will be stripped off before getting back into bed to feed each other and to talk about what each of them does when they are not together fucking, their lives apart from each other with their own other, who—soon after they have finished their salmon and salad, the warm white wine, after they have both come again—they will call and tell, the person on the other end of the line, what he or she had for dinner and how from the tower of this hotel you can see an endless parade of airliners drifting across the window on approach to the nearby airport, so slow as to seem they would almost stall, fall out of the sky altogether, one after the other, in the dusk, their lights strobing and the exhaust of their engines muffled, to be sure, but still registering a noticeable sound, a muted bellow that rattles, at the right pitch and harmony, the safety glass in the aluminum frames of the hotel's windows. After many nights like this, over many different occasions, in many different airport hotels, no one gets dressed or strays very far from the bed when the other one phones home; instead the one not talking on the telephone fits him or herself into the negative template of the body next to him or her, watches the muted television using the remote to scan the channels in silence as the conversation continues, and the jets outside slide down the glide path, yawing, pitching, rolling, making that yawning roar, turning, as the time passes, into diffuse shade then into simple pixels of a constellation, of pulsing lights that outline the now absent bulk of the darkened backlit shadow of the falling fuselage. A hand rests on a stomach, a leg is thrown over the other's leg as the call continues, half-heard queries concerning that day's mail, the children's school, an appointment rescheduled, the changing weather. The halfhearted embrace proceeds in the midst of the phone call—the mumble at the ear; the other hand, scanning with the remote the blinking television, has evolved from the past's position of polite neutrality, the mutual drifting separation, to this, this cozy almost domestic new intimacy with the lover who hasn't, until now, shared this part of his or her life and the lover who hasn't, until now, wanted any hint of that life overheard, now settling in with this new order of cobbled-together proximity, shrinking distances over distance. The free hand finds a trail of drying come along the belly or on the inside of the thigh, and a finger begins to pick at the crust of it, flaking it with a nail, and as the lover's conversation with home burbles above, the archeology of the skin begun in starts and stops—almost as if this patch here was sterile field divorced from the rest of the resting body—starts to turn more serious, the touching now turning into a shallow massage disguised as absentminded petting, as the voice on the phone that has been so even and controlled spikes a slight fever, a heightened pitch.

They glare when they look at each other, hinting at the hint of anger, both about the interruption of the phone call and the phone call's interruption, that gives way to the furthering of the sexual steps they have been perfecting in the hotel room, the one on the line now barely putting together a string of non-committal head-nodding affirmations to whatever question has just come through, the conflicted look torn in two between the here and there and the now and now, attempting to sort out the unimportant stimuli from the immediate noise and, at the same time, focus the full attention on the faraway, the evening of the evening on the other end of the wire. His cradled half-hard cock rolls in her hand. She holds his hand, his fingers inside her, hard against her to keep them from moving. He shields his nipple, directs her kisses to the rib below. She blocks her ear opposite the handset from his breath. All completed in stifled silence. This end of the conversation kept up. Fucking again, now, through the phone calls, silent, suppressed, turned inward, listening hard to the rasping in the ear, the receiver pressed hard against the head as if each of them, when it is their turn, hangs on to some handle of sanity, anchoring their consciousness while the body below is being dismembered piece by piece. It is a kind of sex toy, the telephone, vibrant but inert, innocuous, a chunk of putty-colored plastic molded to the ear, enzymatic magic, the fulcrum around which they turn, and turning, they both now want to say something, to speak, talk, change the subject, bend it over something, move the conversation from the ear to the mouth, feeling the coming words come, emit the innocent protestations of longing, of feeling the distance and the night closing in, of missing you so much, of letting loose the shared formula of words developed over all these years of partnered arrangement to propel the change of the subject, to signal the desire for desire, speaking the cracked-open code to the loved one on the other end of the wire—"Let's come. Right now. I am almost there already. I'll wait. It's late"—all the excuses of coaxing as the coaxing continues, the lubrication of the imagination, and when she comes, when he comes, the others over there, they come with a long report carried through the lines by means of jostled charged electrons, and the lovers, embedded, ears glued to the phone, listen together, in love now with listening, connected and connected. And after the after, together, in the hotel bathroom, they brush their teeth together, heads down, avoiding the mirror, rinsing and spitting at the same time, getting ready for bed, for sleep. The hotel provides a box that plays a provided CD of ambient sounds taken from nature—the seashore with a running tide, a rapid waterfall scouring a rock ledge, wind in a stand of pine—all designed to cancel out the cascading turbulence of the landing jets, the climbing jets that, as they turn to their outbound headings, tear open the sky, ripping ripped cloth. This shouldn't work, they both think on the edge of sleep, in the dark, their heads filled with a catalog of auditory interference, this should not work, this empty glen, the oak forest in the background, the swish of wiregrass, the drill of a bird's call. This should not work, the rough edge of a blue jay's squawk filing down the aggregate of air oscillating at random and without end, all around them.

Author's Notes

1. Michael Martone was born in Fort Wayne, Indiana. He is a largely airborne vapor prone to gather over deforested landmasses and to accrue at times in ice pack at high altitudes. It is believed that he originated as a weather assault planned by inland aboriginal peoples upon their coastal colonial oppressors, though records are vague as to how his instigators lost control of him. If Martone currently has a political bent to the wetnesses he perpetrates, such inclinations are unknown. For a time, he was the proven accomplice of a herd of bison that assembled from the aggregate oatmeals of various air caves. He roamed with these creatures, providing a necessary buoyancy for their frequent rituals of cloud mimesis. Martone also served as general counsel for a society of basil plants that sought to expand its collective bargaining potential during the Herb Riots of the previous century. He converted himself into a kind of olfactory grid, transmitting coded scents at supersonic speeds and thus greatly accelerating the conclusion of that conflict. In perhaps his most legendary pursuit, Martone became intimately involved in translating the languages of several quartzes, salts, and bituminous coal veins on the high plateaus of a few interconnected deserts. During his sessions with these substances, he would acquire a luminescence frequently misconstrued as the hallmark of a divinity. It was only when he snowed upon the chiefs of these tribes—a sign of mutual vulnerability nearly forgotten among the consolidation of ceremonies from one

generation to the next—that they accepted him as a benevolent force, a fog of kindness. Once the confusion was resolved, Martone quickly developed the crystalline mnemonics necessary for cataloging various tenses and cases within an octadecimal index easily replicated by most research institutions on islands and peninsulas alike. In more recent eras, Martone has preferred to disseminate himself among the vernacular rains of infatuated corks and other highly permeable substances. He says he enjoys the sensation of thinness he feels at such moments. He says he enjoys being all around us.

2. Michael Martone was born in Fort Wayne, Indiana. He is regarded as one of the most dominant athletes and arguably the most gregarious personality in sports history. He wrote an autobiography (*Martone Talks Back*), preserves an online presence for his fan base, produced a number of albums (*Biological Didn't Bother*, *Martone-Fu: Da Return*, etc.), and starred in select movies (*Steel* [1997], *Kazaam* [1996], *Blue Chips* [1994]). He has played for four NBA teams: the Orlando Magic, the Los Angeles Lakers, the Miami Heat, and currently the Phoenix Suns. Martone graduated from Louisiana State University and is the only current NBA player with an MBA (Master of Business Administration). Martone is also one of the few NBA players in history to reach the NBA Finals with three different teams. His charisma on and off the court helped create his worldwide reputation as "Godfather of the NBA." As a result of his father's influence and military background, Martone has made public service a priority in his life, ranging from donating to charities and organizations across the country to working as a reserve police officer in Los Angeles, Miami, and Phoenix. He intends to pursue a career in politics and/or sports ownership upon retiring from the NBA. Martone has many famous quotes, and his wisdom has earned him the nickname "The Big Aristotle." However, his most famous quote may be in response

to an inquiry as to whether or not he had visited the Parthenon during his trip to Greece. Martone replied, simply, "I can't really remember the names of the clubs that we went to."[1]

3. Michael Martone was born in Fort Wayne, Indiana, and was a two-sport athlete at North Side High School. While the majority of Martone's athletic success came as a football player— he gained fan-favorite status as the goal-line fullback in the Power I jumbo-package, the pro-Redskin crowd drawing out the O in his last name whenever he made a particularly effective block—he had always had a love for basketball, like most Indiana schoolchildren upon learning the fabled story of the 1954 Milan High School basketball team, the smallest school ever to win a single-class state basketball title in Indiana. Furthermore, Martone's obsession with the number "4" caused him great stress while playing football, as it was difficult to score four points individually—the great pride that Martone would feel when crossing the goal line for a touchdown would often be marred by the disheartening feeling that he had scored six points and scoring four points that evening would be unattainable, unless, of course, Martone would have a career day and score seven touchdowns and one two-point conversion, bringing the amount of points scored to forty-four. Therefore, Martone would feel a sense of relief when football season came to a close and basketball season began, as the scoring rules of basketball were better suited to even numbers. Martone lobbied the coaching staff to play power-forward (otherwise known as "the 4") despite having the body type of a guard. During Martone's senior year, the Indiana High School Athletic Association adopted the three-point field goal in men's basketball—a curious move not only in Martone's eyes but those of the Indiana basketball purists who associated the three-point line with

---

1 From Internet Movie Database, www.imdb.com.

the flashiness of the American Basketball Association and Indiana's own Indiana Pacers, who exuded a more up-tempo and high-scoring style of play. Martone, an excellent shooter from long-range, suddenly had a new moniker, one he believed to be a pejorative: a three-point specialist. Martone would release the basketball at its highest point, and the Redskins faithful would again shout his name, extending the O to almost agonizing lengths as the ball inevitably would find the bottom of the net, sending the crowd into a frenzy and Martone sulking back down the court to play defense. Once, a defender from nearby R. Nelson Snider High School crashed into Martone as he was shooting a three-point basket. As Martone stumbled into the Panther bench, the ball found its way through the basket and Martone was awarded a free throw and a chance to complete a four-point play. Martone, overwhelmed by the chanting crowd and his excitement in finding some sort of loophole within the game of basketball, missed the free throw badly to the left, where it was rebounded by a member of the visiting team. From that point forward, Martone would stay after practice shooting three-point baskets while Happy Walters, the son of one of his mother's friends, would shove Martone while Michael Kern, another son of one of his mother's friends, would kneel behind Martone, causing Martone to learn how to make a three-point shot while falling over in hopes of increasing his chances to complete a four-point play. This technique of kneeling behind a person while an accomplice shoved the aforementioned victim, causing them to topple over, began to be known as "Martoning" or "getting Martoned," and thus Martone became synonymous with bullying techniques in school yards across Indiana, whereas the four-point play would become associated with five-time NBA All-Star Indiana Pacer Reggie Miller, with whom Martone has had little interaction.

4. Michael Martone was born in Fort Wayne, Indiana, on August 22, 1955, and he often wonders what date will be the date of his death. Is this the day? Or this one? Or this? Martone wonders if there is a zodiac for the dying, a dead astrology, like the one that casts its influence over the newly minted. Martone likes the idea that one's course of life is plotted by the arrangement of the heavenly bodies at the time of birth. Or is it the time of conception? The notion that a particular concoction of electromagnetic forces monkeys with one's subatomic genetic grouting in order to predestine the randomness of one's life intrigues Martone. The physics of the universe act in concert or in conflict to narrate an interesting, eventful, illustrative, entertaining life that most often masquerades as a series of random accidents, happenstance, bad breaks, and stupid moves. Death, being for some a mere transition in the ongoing incremental perturbation of life post-life, rearranges the dénouement into another, a mirroring rising action on the other side. There—is some kind of dark matter at work, a negative mechanical deus ex machina, nudging this new plot of plot points there in the grave plot? He wonders. So, to be safe, Martone celebrates each day as his last, the end of his story, his death-day, on which he lights the candles on the cake and never blows them out, swallowing his breath, telling everyone the wish he didn't make.

Acknowledgments

I thank the editors of the following magazines for including a take or two or four in their albums:

Third Bed, Post Road, Other Voices, Puerto del Sol, Chicago Review, Fugue, Brooklyn Rail, Hotmetal Bridge, failbetter, Northwest Review, Cutthroat, Short Fiction, Indiana Review, Seems, The Antioch Review, Talking River Review, The Bellingham Review, Parakeet, Bomb, Western Humanities Review, Croonbergh's Fly, Tusculum Review, McSweeney's, Stone Canoe, New Orleans Review, American Voice, Southeast Review, mud luscious, Second Run, Nebraska Review, Rio Grande Review, Chicago Review, Keyhole, Salt Hill, The Johns Hopkins Review, Mississippi Valley Review, Nerve, Smut, Cavalier, Mid-American Review, Pendulum, symploke, Hunger Mountain, American Letters and Commentary, Sentence, Windless Orchard, Southern Indiana Review, The Prose Poem, Key Satch (el), 100 Words, American Short Fiction.

"A Perimenopausal Jacqueline Kennedy, Two Years After the Assassination, Aboard the M/Y *Christina*, off Eubeoa, Bound for the Island of Alonnisos, Devastated by a Recent Earthquake, Drinks Her Fourth Bloody Mary with Mrs. Franklin Delano Roosevelt, Jr." first appeared in *Field Guide to Writing Flash Fiction*, edited by Tara L. Masih and published by Rose Metal Press.

Thanks too to the College of Arts & Sciences at the University of Alabama for providing the funds to make the completion of this book possible.

Smile! Team FC2: Lance Olson, R.M. Berry, Brenda Mills, Dan Waterman. Jeffery DiLeo, Carmen Edington, Tom Williams, Charles Alcorn. Lou Robinson, Lou Robinson, Lou Robinson, Lou Robinson designed the cover and interior pages. Mindy Wilson proofed, edited, queried, corrected. Cheese! Team Team: Susan Neville, Mike Wilkerson, Michael Rosen, Jay Brandon. Look up, Team Alabama! Sandy Huss, Robin Behn, Joel Brouwer, Wendy Rawlings! Peter Streckfus, Kellie Wells, Dave Madden, John Crowley! Hold still! Lex Williford, Joyelle McSweeney, Kate Bernheimer, Bruce Smith! Paul Maliszewski, Melanie Rae Thon, Nancy Esposito, Chris Leland & Osvaldo Sabino, you all didn't blink. This started with the photo booth in the Woolworth's of Central Square, Cambridge, Massachusetts, and my former students who submitted their finals finally! Thank you! Carl Peterson, Kate Lorenz, Brian Oliu voguing! Yes! Team Y: David, Robert, Arty, Sam! Fierce! Marian Young! Hold it, Jim Harpole! Jo, unretouched! Don't blink! Sam & Nick, Mom & Dad! Now, just one more, Theresa! Everyone, everyone watch the birdie!